Paul Micou is the author of three previous novels,
The Music Programme, *The Cover Artist*, and *The
Death of David Debrizzi*, all of which are published
by Black Swan. His new novel, *The Last Word*,
has just been published in Bantam Press
hardcover. After graduating from Harvard in
1981, he lived in Paris for three years; he now
lives in London.

Also by Paul Micou

THE MUSIC PROGRAMME
THE COVER ARTIST
THE DEATH OF DAVID DEBRIZZI

and published by Black Swan

Rotten Times

Paul Micou

BLACK SWAN

ROTTEN TIMES
A BLACK SWAN BOOK 0 552 99501 0

Originally published in Great Britain by Bantam Press,
a division of Transworld Publishers Ltd

PRINTING HISTORY
Bantam Press edition published 1992
Black Swan edition published 1993

Set in Linotype Bembo

Black Swan Books are published by Transworld Publishers Ltd,
61–63 Uxbridge Road, Ealing, London W5 5SA, in Australia by
Transworld Publishers (Australia) Pty Ltd, 15–25 Helles
Avenue, Moorebank, NSW 2170, and in New Zealand by
Transworld Publishers (NZ) Ltd, 3 William Pickering
Drive, Albany, Auckland.

Printed and bound in Great Britain by
Cox & Wyman Ltd, Reading, Berks

For Anna U

CHAPTER ONE

'These are rotten times,' said Lloyd. 'News from every quarter grows blacker by the day.'

The outbreak of war had found Lloyd James in high spirits, atop an Italian Alp. A mug of hot chocolate in his hand, his face tilted towards the sun, his body humming with good health, he thought he might never have been so contented.

'Ghastly,' Owen agreed, holding his beer glass up to the sun, then taking a lingering sip.

A group of their compatriots at a nearby table listened to the war on a shortwave radio, as if it were a football match. One of them, in the certainty of being out of the enemy's earshot, said that it was about time someone bloodied Johnny Arab's nose.

'We have to try to remember everything, Owen,' said Lloyd. 'We have to be able to tell our grandchildren what it was like during the war.'

'I'm concentrating as hard as I can. I'll jot down a few notes later. I'll tell them the beer was cold and the women were delicious. Or vice versa.'

'I'm going to tell them about the hoarding of tinned goods and sugar. How we sent our servants to the country. Especially how brave you were, Owen. How you kept up our spirits with anecdote and song.'

The war clattered away on the radio. The table of Britons cheered for their side.

'It's good to know that one can count on the patriotism of the lower orders,' said Owen, a member of the lower orders himself. 'It's you toffs I worry about.'

Lloyd and Owen had met at university. There Lloyd had cultivated an aimlessness that had pointed at more artistic and unremunerative pursuits, while Owen had been aggressively directed; it was surprising, therefore, that Owen had struggled since then to find his niche, while Lloyd had rather annoyingly ridden a magic carpet of personal and family connections into the world of material wealth. Only the death of his father – under circumstances Lloyd preferred never to think about – had given him the incentive to follow the wise advice of a friend who predicted that the London property market looked primed for explosion. With great reluctance Lloyd had entered this field. He was slightly less hesitant to repeat an initial investment that had doubled its value in eighteen months. For five years he repeated this procedure, arguing that he did so only for the welfare of his semi-orphaned little sister, until the same wise friend told him that a sane individual might think about cashing in his chips. It had always appeared to outsiders – and especially to Owen – that Lloyd had made his money without lifting a finger, that important funds had fallen into his lap during a time of boom. He had ridden what he called the 'property escalator' with such aplomb – and such impeccable timing – that his accumulation of modest wealth looked positively immoral in its ease of acquisition.

As for Owen, life had thrown a number of obstacles in his path that only the most uncharitable observer – and Lloyd –

would have claimed were of his own making. An early, ill-considered marriage deflected him from his newspaper work. A weakness for embroidering the truth, and a tendency to panic under duress, marked him as unsuitable for journalism. Despite these traits, he managed to build up an utterly unfounded reputation for himself as Owen, the action man; Owen, the veteran of countless bloody skirmishes in wretched lands; Owen, famous for dispatches scrawled in his own blood and sent by personal carrier pigeon; Owen, who posted home a piece of Soviet shrapnel supposedly plucked from his own shoulder – with his own knife – to be used as a paperweight on the desk of his despised and cowardly editor.

In fact, Owen had rarely left London, and then only for relatively safer climes. His first foray into broadcast journalism had found him gibbering, live, into a telephone in Paris, reporting that street battles between demonstrators and police had left 'five killed, some seriously.'

Years went by, as they were wont to do. Owen found himself in every way unlike Lloyd: he was crippled by mortgage, unemployed, and unable to think clearly any longer about avenues to salvation. It was Lloyd who had come to his friend's rescue, when he hired Owen to act as Sales Director of a new business he had almost unwittingly initiated.

'Aphrodisiacs?' Owen had asked. 'Do they *work*?'

'First lesson,' Lloyd had replied. 'Never answer that question.'

In fact, Lloyd's aphrodisiac was a mild and harmless astringent. It was available in lotion, spray and salve. For more than two years now, Lloyd and Owen had travelled the world, taking orders for the aphrodisiac and subjecting themselves to the late and sordid hours their clients tended to prefer. As the war babbled away on the radio, they realized that nearly half of their market had just gone up in smoke. It would mean more trips to Japan. Lloyd was tired of Japan, tired of aphrodisiacs, tired of people who said, 'Do they *work*?'

'Buy me out, Owen,' said Lloyd, on the Alp. 'I can't go on.'

'Now, don't talk that way. You owe your customers product in a time of crisis.'

'The market will collapse. War is the ultimate aphrodisiac. There is great potency out there at the moment.'

'But people will get depressed in the recession, or recessed in the depression, and need a bit of firing up.'

'Untrue, Owen. Even the Japanese will tighten their belts, so to speak. The only reason anyone bought our product is that it is so expensive. They might as well have bought gold and rubbed it on themselves.'

'I thought they did that, too.'

'I'm out, Owen.'

'What about Little Vic?'

Little Vic was Lloyd's sister, so nicknamed because she was ten years his junior. Whenever anyone had accused Lloyd of destructive capitalism during his property develop-ing days, he had pointed to his responsibility for Little Vic, and likewise more recently when they accused him of chicanery. With their mother bitterly remarried, strange and estranged, Lloyd's arguments were more than an easy excuse for self-enrichment. He had put Little Vic through univer-sity. He had bought her a small mews house in London. He had paid her bills for two years while she tried to think of something worthwhile to do in what remained of the British economy. In fact, Lloyd had been quite a self-conscious model of fraternal support. He thought Little Vic had turned out splendidly, and this was a source of pride that almost mitigated the embarrassment he felt each time he divulged to someone the nature of his new business.

'Little Vic will be fine,' said Lloyd. 'Don't you worry about her. Nina and I got her a job at Caesar.'

'Caesar' was the accepted pronunciation of the acronym

CYSR, which stood for the Committee on the Year of the Special Relationship. The idea behind CYSR was that as Britain backed clumsily into Europe, her self-preservation demanded a 'concretization', as the jointly drafted inaugural press release had put it, of the vague political, linguistic and even spiritual bonds that were believed by some to exist between the United Kingdom and the United States. The Committee itself was composed of six hale and enthusiastic Americans and six exhausted and reluctant Britons. The Americans envisioned multi-media events staged in both countries, encompassing political debates, theatrical productions, literary tête-à-têtes, economic and industrial handshaking, battle recreations (careful not to mention the common enemy by name), pop-music festivals, talks, speeches, lectures, hands-on information transfers, symposia, conferences, conventions, building-site openings, cornerstone layings, ribbon-cutting ceremonies, dedications, joint this, joint that, the Queen giving great big hugs to not quite so stupendously rich American dignitaries, a great mutual Special Relationship in living colour with all the pomp and glory a superpower can lay on. The British contingent envisioned headaches, foul weather, paralysed funds and even worse weather.

Nina Corrant was an old friend of Lloyd's family, whose name often came up in Owen's conversation when he decided to say that Lloyd ought to get married. Lloyd had pointed Nina in the direction of CYSR, and used a coincidental family connection to influence her hiring. Nina had taken on her job for the Committee in the belief that she would spend a great deal of time travelling in the United States. In fact, only months into the schedule, it had been decided that Britain would host all of CYSR's varied spectacles, owing to, as a CYSR communiqué had put it, 'perceived negative trends in home-site US interest quotient'. In other words, those few Americans who had heard of the Special Relationship had thought it worthy of support only in so far as their corporate logos would appear on US television screens; a quick survey of television news organizations indicated that – with luck – CYSR would command two and a half minutes of network air-time on the day of its closing ceremonies, when the Princess of Wales was supposed to travel to the White House and utter eight or ten words pertaining to the *special* feelings of closeness she felt towards the American People, as personified by the First Lady. If everything went perfectly, one of her boys would gambol on the White House lawn with a young American commoner picked at random through corporately sponsored lotteries. No air-time, said the ostensible sponsors, then no deal. CYSR returned to Britain to stay. Lloyd thought the whole idea was idiotic and doomed.

'Good for Little Vic,' said Owen, who was the only other person in the world who was allowed to use Lloyd's sister's nickname. 'Lunatic organization, though working with Nina ought to be a pleasure. You should marry her, you know.'

Lloyd reflexively brushed away this suggestion without a word. It was easy for Owen to say, since he had taken public vows never to marry again. Owen threatened every now and then to have himself sterilized, just to reduce the chances of anyone's taking undue interest in the prospect. Owen had become, in the way that irresponsible, unsteady, unpredictable men sometimes do, a rather accomplished ladies' man. Certainly his new line of work had proved an effective ice-breaker. His pleasant looks and athletic build came alive when he spoke to women. Being tall, he tended to stoop winningly, like a victim of a particularly heroic war wound. He talked quickly and passionately about nothing at all, his body undulated with enthusiasm, his bright eyes exuded sympathy, his dark eyebrows worked themselves into charming arches of understanding. Most importantly, Owen was relentless. The odd thing was, as Lloyd knew better than anyone else, Owen was absolutely sincere. He told women he thought they had lovely eyes, and they simply had to believe him. He would never dream of joking at a woman's expense, of boasting excessively about his conquests, of saying anything that he wouldn't say to his girlfriends' faces. He was terrifically useful company on a skiing holiday, and his magnetism helped to balance his friendship with Lloyd, who was simply good-looking and rich.

The two men finished their drinks after a toast to the last run of the season. It was time to go home to London. Lloyd skied with grace and calm; Owen skied like a hooligan. Lloyd paused frequently on the slopes to memorize the views, the light and the sensation of smallness; he needed the mountains, back in London. Owen never stopped – perhaps he was still unable to do so, even after twenty years of skiing – and made it to their favourite village bar in eight minutes.

In the evening of the same day, Lloyd and Owen sat next to each other as their aeroplane took its place in a stack over London. The winter night was strikingly clear. London's sprawl reached to all horizons. Orange and white streetlights drew a familiar map below. In his window seat, Lloyd inspected the city as if it were a spider's web. He picked out his own square, and Little Vic's mews, and Nina's street, as the jet banked heavily through the air. The captain's voice came on the overhead speakers to say that they would probably not land for thirty minutes. Lloyd decided to shave, for he always insisted on arriving in London looking fresh and relaxed. Granted permission by a passing stewardess, he squeezed past a half-dozing Owen into the aisle.

The aircraft's cabin, thick with residual smoke and boozy sleepers' breath, hummed beneath Lloyd's unlaced shoes. The lavatory door unlatched itself as he arrived, and a bleary passenger with wet hair and a badly stained shirt stumbled out into the cabin.

'Excuse me, pardon me,' they said to each other.

Lloyd locked himself in, and sighed. It was good to be

alone. On the other hand, he suspected modern airlines of bugging and filming their lavatories in an effort to combat terrorism. He smiled at the mirror and said, 'I know you're taping me and I don't care. Now watch me shave.'

He washed his face with soap and tepid water. He appraised his wind-burned complexion, and the raccoon eyes left by his dark glasses. He ran wet fingers through his thick hair, and sucked in his cheeks. Yes, the Alps had been good to him this time. He took out his electric razor – a fat, ergonomically designed hand-grenade-shaped machine called The Whisker – turned it on, and proffered his right jawbone. The razor produced a momentary buzz, then whined down to nothing. The Whisker's battery had died. As an experienced and well-prepared traveller, Lloyd was able to pluck the razor's cord from its black plastic box. On the wall to the left of the mirror was an outlet marked 'SHAVERS ONLY'.

'That's me,' said Lloyd. As if in reply, a speaker overhead brought word from the captain that landing at Heathrow was now just twenty minutes away. The captain also advised passengers to remain seated.

'In a minute,' said Lloyd. He plugged in his razor, turned it on, and felt it hum to life. He began to shave his chin just as the aircraft banked steeply to starboard.

Lloyd shaved happily for two or three minutes, bouncing around in his closet and thinking, as he often did aloft, that Leonardo da Vinci would have given both his arms to experience air travel just once; Lloyd flew tens of thousands of miles every year, and it bored him.

He shaved his upper lip, moved over to his left jaw, clicked out the sideburns clipper, kept at it. He liked returning to London clean and composed, and had been known to change suits and socks in mid-flight. The captain came on again, just as Lloyd had addressed his prickly neck, to announce that beastly weather awaited them. Lloyd's electric razor snagged on a neck hair and began to groan. He clicked open its top and tapped a fine powder of shaved whiskers into the stainless-steel sink. He closed the razor again, and turned it on. He finished shaving after a series of quite sudden bankings and plunges. A seasoned traveller and one-time student pilot himself, Lloyd was not affected by this in the least. He rather enjoyed rattling around in his private booth in the tail of a gigantic aluminium tube, high over England. He reached out with still-damp fingers to unplug his razor, grasped the plug, and saw a blue flash.

Lloyd found himself on the floor, his head wedged in the corner, his feet up against the door, in darkness.

'I'm alive,' he said, in case he really was being monitored by the crew. 'I'm OK. I'm getting up.'

He struggled to his feet in the darkness, opened the door so that he could see, and groped about for his shaving equipment. Calmly, but tingling all over, he assembled the razor and cord. He stepped out into the cabin. Faintly dizzy, and somewhat embarrassed, he regained his seat only seconds before the landing gear was deployed. Only then did Lloyd realize that he must have been unconscious for several minutes.

Owen remarked on his friend's long absence.

'I gave myself a manicure,' said Lloyd, who had noticed a burn mark on the nail and fleshy tip of his left forefinger. 'Actually, I blew a fuse in the loo and knocked myself out. Electrocuted myself. I feel very strange indeed.'

'You'll live. I feel a bit queasy myself. All this banking and turning, bumping and plunging.'

'Pitch, yaw, slew,' said Lloyd, surprising himself with this choice of words. 'The inner ear can't handle all three at once.'

'Quite,' said Owen. 'You don't look at all well. Your hands are shaking. You— oh, here we are.'

Their jet touched down on the windswept runway. Lloyd looked out over the wing at the airport terminal. 'Heathrow,' he said aloud. 'This is the two hundred and seventy-ninth time I have landed at this airport.'

'What did you say?'

'Sorry, nothing. I had a nasty fright back there.'

'It certainly would have been a silly way to go,' said Owen. 'Burnt to a crisp in a jet's loo. You would have been famous. One of a kind. I'd have written the headline myself, of course: "*Shock Horror!*"'

'All right, Owen. I feel awfully strange.'

'Don't we all, here in war-torn England? Oh, it's horrible to be back. Everyone will want to talk about the war, instead of our heroics on the *pistes* and the debauchery of our *après-ski*.'

'To think', said Lloyd, 'we were in the war zone just ten months ago. All gone now.'

'They'll be using the aphro for antiseptic, I should think, poor bastards.'

'All gone now,' Lloyd said again. He felt very strange indeed. 'I remember it so vividly. All our friends. What a fate.'

'No weeping, chum. They're around the corner in Knightsbridge, I expect. Somewhat chastened, is my guess. No matter what you say, my view is they'll need product.'

'You sound like a drug dealer, Owen.'

'I *am* a drug dealer.' They considered this verdict in silence for several minutes, until Owen said, 'Come along now, the door is open.'

Lloyd and Owen sped through passport control and retrieved their skis and luggage. An unusual number of soldiers and police occupied the arrivals hall. A tank squatted near the taxi rank. Lloyd felt unsteady on his feet. Owen noticed, and relieved him of his skis.

'You'll be all right,' said Owen. 'We'll just get you home.'

Lloyd reclined in the taxi. Owen turned on the heater. Warm air blew up Lloyd's trousers as he rubbed his eyes and stretched. The driver immediately launched into his opinion that Johnny Arab was getting what he deserved, and asked if his passengers knew what he meant.

'We'd heard,' said Owen, sliding the partition closed.

' "A curse shall light upon the limbs of men," ' said Lloȳd, for no apparent reason. Then, '*Bellum omnium in omnes.*'

Lloyd could scarcely believe he had spoken these words. Shakespeare was one thing, but he *never* remembered his Latin.

'What's that?' asked Owen.

'Nothing. Sorry. Very odd. I must be exhausted.'

Lloyd still felt a tingling down his left arm, and a slight ringing in his ears. He looked out of the window at dark and wind-blasted England, and said, in a monotone, ' "Regions Caesar never knew thy posterity shall sway where his eagle never flew none invincible as they . . ." '

'Now this is scary,' said Owen. 'What's come over you?'

'Jet lag,' said Lloyd. 'It has to be jet lag. Haven't you noticed a more pronounced feeling of *déjà vu* when you've—'

'You don't get jet lag flying home from the Continent. You've gone insane, that's what it is. Snow madness, or something. It's that German girl you were with. I warned you.'

'Maybe.'

Lloyd closed his eyes and leaned his head against the side of the cab, and that is when it happened: his memory opened up for him like an infinite filing cabinet. He was able to select a file at will, extract it from the mass of other files, open it, and read to himself its detailed contents. It was quite nauseating, at first. He riffled through categories of knowledge without the slightest effort. Here was his Latin, all of it, shining and pure. Here was quite a lot of Plato; over there an ingredients and vitamins list he must have read on the back of a breakfast-cereal box; and over there – good God, over there was every word of *Ulysses*, which he had made the mistake of reading in its entirety, on a dare, more than fifteen years ago. He opened his eyes and rubbed them, but still the pockets of information burst like fireworks in his brain. He

17

saw his tax returns dating back ten years; he shut out this unpleasant image and focused on an article he must once have read on the Malaysian palm-oil industry. Bored, he called up the Bible, and realized with some regret that he must have read less than one tenth of the work. All of this mental activity happened in seconds. The sensation overwhelmed him to the point that he was almost afraid to test the limit of his newfound power. He suspected that he might be dreaming, or that one of those Japanese drinks or meals consumed on recent business travel might have been spiked with a time-release psychotropic drug.

The muffled taxi radio described massive air bombardment of a land that Lloyd involuntarily remembered had been released from British mandate in 1932. He discovered that his memory was less like a storeroom than like a database, that he could trigger detailed recollections instantaneously, merely by the suggestion of a subject. 'The White House says,' said the radio, and Lloyd thought, 'Grover Cleveland was married in the Blue Room.' Lloyd had visited the White House as a child. For a moment Lloyd thought it might be a great deal of fun to remember everything; then he fell asleep.

'We're home,' Owen said, shaking Lloyd's shoulder.

Lloyd awakened not remembering, as it were, that he remembered. He told Owen he felt fine, just needed a little rest, and said that he could manage his skis and bags. He instructed Owen to put the taxi fare on expenses, said thanks and goodbye, and ascended the steps of his building. It was not until he reached into the coat cupboard to turn off the alarm – and saw the fuse box – that he remembered the blue flash in the aeroplane's lavatory. Could that, he asked himself, have had anything to do with his strange sparks of recollection in the taxi?

With mail sorted and tea brewing, Lloyd confronted the warehouse of his mind. It was astonishing. He hoped it wouldn't go away. He would never lack for entertainment.

18

He would be the envy of his friends. He had become the proverbial walking encyclopaedia. Now, *there* was a thought. What if – what *if* – he could simply begin to memorize a library full of the works he had regrettably ignored during his lengthy and ill-spent education? He could know everything. He could know it all.

He rushed to his bookshelves. He selected a fat volume of an antique encyclopaedia he had inherited from his father, and opened it at random. He read a full column, then closed the book. It was no good. He could remember one or two of the entries, but it would have been beyond him to repeat the information he had read with any depth or accuracy. Strange, really, when he could recite by heart every one of the entries he had glanced at during the past ten years. It seemed, as far as Lloyd could make out, that whatever he had known up to the point of his electrical experience aloft was now his to regurgitate. Nothing new, it appeared, could be imprinted upon his brain with the same perfection and clarity.

Still, thought Lloyd, not bad. He was disappointed not so much that this quasi-magical effect would not extend to future learning, but that he had read so relatively little during the thirty-five years prior to the event. He might not know it all, but he certainly knew a great deal; he had perfect hindsight.

Now it struck Lloyd that there might conceivably be financial gain to be made of his condition. This could mean the end of his aphrodisiac enterprise. He had never meant to go into aphrodisiacs. It was one of those opportunities that had come along during the period when he was self-consciously responsible for the welfare of Little Vic, and it had worked. He had always promised himself that he would get out of aphrodisiacs, out of world travel, into something riveting and productive, just as soon as Little Vic was on her feet. Little Vic had been very much on her feet for two or three years, and no alternative had presented itself to Lloyd – until now.

Lloyd strode around his flat reciting poetry, classifying biological organisms, pretending to rebut military experts with precise dates and casualty figures, imagining himself at an Oxford high table fending off daft opinion with solid fact. 'I'm sure you must mean Beninonatmavitch,' he said. 'And not possibly in 1764, owing to the poor chap's death in November of the previous year.' God, this was going to be fun. Lloyd would abandon aphrodisiacs, and become an intellectual.

Little Vic would love this, too. One of the most insurmountable obstacles Lloyd had always seen between himself and everlasting good relations with his sister was her evident intellectual superiority. She remembered a great deal, and continued to learn. She was well informed on a number of topics, and had even had occasion to publish her knowledge and opinions in one of the country's smarter newspapers. Lloyd had defended himself against this by saying that, as she was *ten years younger* than he, she would soon learn the relative triviality of factual knowledge. He had stressed his street-smarts, and kept his mouth shut. All of that would now change. He would introduce an interesting titbit here, an arcanity there, until Little Vic noticed that he knew an enormous amount. He would pretend he had always known an enormous amount, but had considered it vulgar not to wear his considerable learning lightly. 'Perhaps you are right, Vic,' he would say, 'but if I'm not entirely mistaken, the physician's name was Cerimon.'

Lloyd could see that he had to be very careful not to come across as an arsehole. Subtlety was the watchword here. Easy on the Latin. Very easy on the Russian Literature – on which, it appeared, and thanks mainly to a Russophile girlfriend at university, he thought he might now be the world's greatest expert. With the proper balance, Little Vic would be amazed. Lloyd drank cup after cup of tea, reclined in an inherited swivelling armchair, and leafed through the vast catalogue of his mind.

★

Lloyd awoke the following morning with a clearer-than-usual head, and his perfect memory intact. Always prudent about his health, and as ignorant as the next man of the human brain's workings and resources, he rang a doctor friend named Porris to seek advice. Lloyd had employed Porris's services three years before to ensure that his aphrodisiac was harmless, even when abused. Porris was the only person known to Lloyd who could accurately be described as a polymath. If Porris had been American, he would have been very rich.

Porris returned Lloyd's call when he had time to talk, and Lloyd related his remarkable experience aloft. When Porris asked for proof Lloyd simply dipped into his cavernous memory and recited a dry passage of scientific jargon that he had probably read at the age of eighteen. It said something about Lloyd's condition that he could recite it without at all comprehending its meaning.

'This is from memory?' asked Porris.

'Any requests?'

'Oh, let's see. A few bars of *Beowulf*?'

Out popped several lines concerning Grendel.

'All right,' said Porris. 'What can you tell me about the periodic table?'

Out came the elements, one by one.

'This is terrific, isn't it?' said Lloyd.

'It is,' Porris agreed. 'But by no means as uncommon as you might think.' Typically, Porris added that he had just been reading up on the subject. He said that there were dozens of documented cases of people who had survived electrical shocks – usually massive ones – who for some time afterwards possessed phenomenal powers of recall.

'Do you mean to tell me this won't last?' Lloyd asked.

Porris allowed that it probably would not, and suggested that Lloyd enjoy it while he could. He said the condition was known in Europe as Tourraine's Syndrome, after a French fireman who had been badly electrocuted in the wreckage of

21

a burnt-out hotel. He had regained consciousness reciting long stretches of dialogue from the comic books he had read as a child, as well as a great deal of fascist literature he had studied in the privacy of his home.

'So I have Tourraine's Syndrome?' asked Lloyd.

'Full blown,' said Porris. 'Strange, with such a small shock. Come and see me. I'll have you examined and tested.'

'What, brain scans, electroencephalograms? Snip my cerebral cortex? Run dye through my lobes? No, thank you, Porris. And keep this to yourself, will you? Owen saw how strangely I behaved, but suspects nothing.'

'Science needs you, Lloyd.'

'I don't need science. Tourraine's Syndrome, indeed.'

'Who knows what the other effects are? You have to be careful with these things.'

'I feel perfectly fine. I probably have just a bit of it. Practically no volts at all. It was a shaver outlet. If it went away with Monsieur Tourraine, it'll go away with me.'

'Actually, Tourraine—'

'I don't want to know about it. I'm going to relax and enjoy it, all right?'

'Suit yourself. Strictly your decision. I just ask that you watch for side-effects. I hope you won't mind if I check on you from time to time? It's only because you're a friend that I don't bundle you straight into hospital.'

'That's why I called you instead of a real doctor, Porris. Check on me if you like.'

Lloyd thanked Porris for the information, put down the phone, and almost immediately felt the first noticeable side-effect. Now, this was extremely peculiar. Very odd. He shook his head and blinked his eyes. It was strange, especially because there was no physical discomfort attached. It was entirely in his mind, and at first almost ineffable. Yes, there it was, an insistence, a nag – a part of Lloyd's awareness asking for attention, demanding to be listened to, raising its hand . . .

It was a face. Lloyd had to sit down to see clearly whose face it was. It was Nina Corrant's face. Lloyd had to lie down to figure out why Nina's face had been projected on to the screen of his consciousness. This took some time, and the answer was at once annoying and irrefutable: Lloyd's newly rewired brain seemed to be telling him that he was in love with Nina.

Love was not normally a word that entered Lloyd's vocabulary, much less his stunted English emotions. The novelty of his present experience allowed him to analyse this newfound emotion – if emotion it was – to break it down into comprehensible segments. First, Lloyd decided, there was a certain amount of distress involved in looking at his mental picture of Nina, a distress that was only slightly less severe than the distress he felt if he forced himself *not* to look at her. Second, there was a not-altogether-manly tugging at the mental innards, a feeling akin to pity. Third, and not surprisingly, given the stunning new organization of Lloyd's mind, there was a colourful brochure of memories through which he could leaf at will, each page of which contained a happy episode in Nina's company, a memorable remark she had made, an attitude she had struck.

It had to be said that Nina was something of a beauty, especially by her family's standards. Her father was a squat little man who shattered all traditional expectations by looking, if anything, far worse in his officer's uniform than he did in mufti. After the war he had become a drastically failed spy. Nina's mother was a kind and energetic woman who had made the best of her family's peripatetic life by socializing frantically wherever she found herself, from Singapore to Düsseldorf, but who did not attempt to disguise or alter a premature frumpishness that had people offering her comfortable seats or an arm to climb a short flight of stairs. Nina's twin brothers were weedy youths who took after neither parent, and yet were still not what one would call good-looking boys.

Nina was different. She possessed a self-confidence that was either the product or the cause of physical attractiveness. Lloyd had known her all her life. His father had served under Nina's father, Colonel Corrant, and maintained their friendship when they returned to London after the war. There had been the occasional summer weekend with the Corrants, joint holidays abroad, and the unspoken decision by both sets of parents that Nina and Little Vic ought to become best friends. Lloyd had always been characteristically aloof – except once, a memory which even now he could not bring himself to address. Owen's repeated suggestions over the years that Lloyd ought to marry Nina gave further support to the messages that now crowded Lloyd's thoughts.

He could not ignore these messages. They emanated, after all, from his own subconscious. In a way, Lloyd thought, it ought to be every Englishman's dream to unlock hidden desires, and to have them thrust their propaganda to the fore. He was not, in other words, entirely against the idea of being forced to be in love with Nina.

Lloyd realized with a stab of anxiety that he was unable to control the emotion insinuating itself into the area behind his eyes that he considered to be the centre of his being. The more he told himself that it might not be a bad thing, the more he resented the idea that it had required an electric shock and Tourraine's Syndrome to force the conclusion to the surface. He should have known. He should have given in to subconscious instinct. He should have listened to Owen.

What if it was too late? He had seen Nina regularly enough, of course – they shared a large circle of friends – but a certain amount of vigilance might have been desirable. Lloyd worried more than he might have otherwise, because there appeared, at last, to be a substantial man in Nina's life. The mere thought enraged him, despite himself, as it would not have done a few minutes ago. A *man*. A terrible, terrible man. A man whose name Lloyd could hardly bring himself to remember, though of course he remembered everything.

Lloyd liked to think that he had nothing against Americans. Or at least, because he was so widely travelled, that he was more generously predisposed towards them than the average Englishman. But this man, Lloyd thought, sounded perfectly ghastly. Lloyd had been alerted to the American's existence – and to the possibility that Nina might be the object of his imperialistic designs – by Little Vic.

To start with, there was the American's name. Mentally, Lloyd choked on the word. The American's name, for heaven's sake, was *Chad*. The little Lloyd knew or guessed about Chad he based on information from Little Vic, and from the occasional newspaper article concerning Chad's grotesque, right-wing governor father. If Governor Peele was anything to go by, Chad ought to be a real piece of work.

Governor Peele was at the height of his fame, for all the wrong reasons. Two of his long-held beliefs had collided in recent months, so that what otherwise might have been a local newspaper story back home had spilled into print as far away as London. Governor Peele, like so many governors, was a firm believer in the sanctity of human life dating all the way back to conception. He held this view with honest and honourable zeal, and was supported in it by a narrow majority of the constituents his campaign organization chose to poll. The Governor believed that abortion was murder, as surely as the garrotting of a rival in love. There was simply no question in the Governor's mind. The Governor also believed that it was in the Constitution's power to provide for legislation outlawing murder, and that the outlawing of abortion was not a separate issue. The Governor was said to be uncommonly convincing on this subject. He dispensed with debating opponents with great ease, as is often the case when moral certainty confronts liberal hedging. His argument had the beauty of simplicity, and if everyone had agreed with him there would not have been a problem.

25

What irked the Governor most of all was that abortion was legal in the United States – an amazing fact, and personally troubling to one who therefore believed that murder occurred daily in his state, with the law's sanction. Like any champion of a worthy cause, the Governor did everything in his power to curb the slaughter until such time as the law was changed. He publicly supported the intimidation of women who tried to use the state's abortion clinics. He split legal hairs until he was able to make it all but impossible for anyone but well-off women to terminate their pregnancies in safety. He neatly parried criticism from women's groups, who argued that he might not be able to see the issue from their side of the biological fence, by saying that he didn't care if he had to prosecute male abortionists for complicity to prove his point that murder was murder, no matter the gender of the killer.

With the word 'murder' still ringing out from one of his triumphant speeches, another kind of murder occurred within the borders of his state that would sorely test the Governor's creed. A woman named Claudia Brown was convicted of three quite nasty and premeditated killings: one by beating, one by stabbing and the third – the one that led to her arrest – by handgun in the presence of eighteen witnesses. All three victims were former lovers. Her confession contained the word 'revenge', and the sentence 'I am perfectly sane.' She refused counsel, confessed again in court, reiterated her belief that she had acted rationally, and was sentenced to death by lethal injection.

Governor Peele, not surprisingly, was as fervent a believer in the death penalty as he was in the rights of fertilized ova. On this issue he was obliged to rely more heavily on biblical scripture than on science, but he was no less effective in his argument that life was a right – held to be unalienable, even, by the Declaration of Independence – and that all rights could be forfeited under certain circumstances. A citizen who took away another's right to life had forfeited his own. Or, in this case, *her* own. If people were made aware of this rule, he said, they would be less likely to kill. If they killed anyway, their execution would serve the dual purpose of ultimate retribution in the name of the citizenry and an example to those who might at any moment be contemplating the abrogation of someone else's perfectly obvious and unalienable right to life. Governor Peele believed in hanging, electrocution, lethal injection, firing squad, whatever you like. He believed that the relatives of victims ought to be present at and, if they wished, participants in the execution.

Several men had been executed in the Governor's state in recent years, but never a woman. The Governor swallowed his innate and misplaced sense of chivalry, and decreed that the execution would go ahead once all avenues of appeal had been exhausted. This took only four months, for the Governor had stressed that, in order for the deterrent effect of the death penalty to work its magic, punishment ought to follow expeditiously on the heels of conviction. It might have taken longer had Claudia Brown not insisted that she did not seek an appeal, that in fact she wished to be executed *tout de suite*. It frustrated the Governor that Claudia insisted on behaving so much like a psychopath bent on going out in a blaze of glory, but he was a man of principle. He vowed not to commute Claudia's sentence. He vowed never to bow to the inevitable calls from his state and elsewhere around the world for a reprieve in the name of pity.

All might have gone smoothly. Claudia could have been lethally injected in the presence of the families of her dead lovers. One right could have been removed from the swim of things in payment for the disproportionate denials of three other rights. The state would have acted in accordance with the law. Claudia would be dead, and good riddance. What an unsavoury person she was, and what a great deal of misery she had caused.

All might have gone smoothly, that is, if Claudia had not announced that she was pregnant. This was shocking.

Everyone wanted to know by whom she had become pregnant, having been incarcerated for more than eight months preceding her conviction, and three months since then. Claudia refused to say, but suspicion inevitably fell on the male employees of her prison, and the male guards who had accompanied her to and from the courthouse. There was said to be a certain tantalizing sexiness about Claudia.

Now, here was a nettlesome dilemma for Governor Peele. What choice did he have? To execute Claudia while she was pregnant would seem to rob an innocent human being of its sacrosanct right to life. His instinct was to wait for Claudia to give birth before killing her. Claudia had to die. Her unborn baby had to live.

The Governor wondered if it might not be technologically possible to kill Claudia *just* as she went into labour, or when her baby was considered viable, and to deliver the infant into the arms of a pre-arranged, non-murderer foster mother who would never divulge to the child its unusual entrance into the world. This seemed rather macabre. The baby had to be delivered in prison – the Governor thought he could see that. A quiet adoption, and Claudia could be lethally injected only slightly behind schedule. Both of Governor Peele's most deeply held beliefs would be adhered to, two kinds of justice would be served, an unfortunate and thankfully quite rare episode would be behind him.

Now Claudia decided she needed a lawyer. She demanded two things: to be executed on schedule, and to have an abortion beforehand. Her lawyer said she wished to 'split the difference' with the outspoken Governor, adding that both abortion and execution appeared to be legal at the moment, whereas forcing a woman to have an unwanted child was not.

The Governor retreated into his mansion to think. He consulted his wife and his religious mentor. He aged visibly. Everything had seemed so simple to him before this crisis. It would require a moral stand, an act of principled determination – a finagle. The Governor emerged from his mansion, and let his will be known. Much as it pained him, he had decided that under the laws of the land, given that Claudia was still in the first trimester of pregnancy, she ought to go to the injection room and be dispatched, along with the innocent being within her womb. It would be a less cruel form of pregnancy termination than was the norm in the state's clinics, said the Governor, and quite legal. It was just one of those things. Had she been free, Claudia would no doubt have added her unborn child to her list of victims anyway. One law, one form of rights, had superseded another. It was the most difficult decision he had ever made. Claudia, and her baby, had to die.

Lloyd realized, as he flicked through these recollections of American criminal justice at work, that his conscious distaste for Chad's father was indicative of love's evil twin – jealousy. He really was jealous. He did not like the idea of Chad, though he knew little enough about him; Little Vic had provided Lloyd with just enough first-hand information that he could build up a profile of Chad's personality to serve as the focus of his sudden rivalry.

Little Vic believed that Chad Peele was lucky to have a paying job, despite the overwhelming influence wielded by his father. The younger Peele had managed to fritter away five years of his post-graduate youth playing golf in pro-am tournaments in a neighbouring state, then three or four more drinking case upon case of beer on a Florida beach with similarly disposed men who drove open-top off-road vehicles with roll bars and enjoyed pouring beer down the bikini tops of vacationing coeds. He surfaced from what had been his late twenties with a monumental hangover, a nagging suspicion that he ought to settle down and get on with whatever his life was going to be, and no appreciable dent in his trust fund.

Little Vic reported that Chad wanted to be President of the

United States. After all, the son of the formidable Governor Peele couldn't very well open a catamaran dealership on the coast and drink beer for the rest of his life. There were only two plausible alternatives for a man in Chad's shoes: wildly corrupt property speculation in his home state; or the presidency. Being naturally averse to business of any kind, if not to corruption, Chad chose the latter course. That meant politics.

It was simply unbelievable that Chad had lost his first bid for Congress, at the age of thirty-one. His victorious opponent was equally young, but completely unknown. He was poor, even. How was this possible? Chad's was supposed to have been a safe district. What the Peeles hadn't counted on was that Chad's opponent would be black – although 'black' was a word seldom used around the Peele household – and that quite a number of black people had been convinced to exercise their votes. For the elder Peele it was a mystery that his son's opponent had survived the race. Still, he handled the humiliating defeat philosophically. Governor Peele always said there was no sense crying over spilt milk; you had to get on with life. It was only young Chad's first bash at politics, and what was eight million dollars, anyway? The boy needed some international experience, be made to look senatorial – even presidential. Congress, after all, was for poor folks.

With no worthwhile ambassadorships for sale, the Committee on the Year of the Special Relationship was it. Chad brushed up on his geography, located London, even hired a college professor to write down a list of Things Never to Say to an English Person – Little Vic had seen it. (First on the list, a point that still confused Chad, was never to assume someone over there was English. According to Chad it was as if someone from, say, Oregon wasn't proud to be called American, the way the Welshers and Scotlanders went on about it. The Irish thing – well, Chad said he had been advised to steer clear of that topic altogether and, if forced

30

into a statement on Irish issues, to employ the word 'complex'.)

Chad's towering ignorance was somewhat mitigated by what Little Vic worryingly described as an easy, outgoing charm and a marked instinct for flattery – and his golf game was said to be superb. These qualities were handy, as the Committee of twelve that nominally employed him was chock-a-block with egg-head academics and up-the-hardway businessmen – just the sort of people who would make Chad uneasy outside his home state, where he was too rich to care. His brief was to set up a headquarters, hire a small staff, and organize like hell.

Such, at any rate, was Lloyd James's analysis of the American trespasser, fuelled as it was by an unexpected, roiling jealousy.

Tourraine's Syndrome had caused this problem; Tourraine's Syndrome could solve it. Nina would be bowled over by Lloyd's intellect. She would wonder why she had never added broad knowledge and intelligence to the list of her old friend's qualities. What could *Chad* possibly have that Lloyd did not?

CHAPTER TWO

'**D**arlings,' the theatrical director said. 'People, that's enough. Quite enough. Everyone go away. Go home. Off you go.' He waved his clipboard dismissively in the air.

Nina Corrant watched from the darkness of the back seats as the actors filed offstage, slack-necked and dejected. She had come straight from lunch with Chad Peele to this meeting at the Varrenwold Theatre. Rehearsals were already under way for a production of an all-American *Julius Caesar* – an appropriate work, under the circumstances. Shakespeare's Roman tragedy was referred to in the CYSR literature as 'a really great English show by one of the really great English playwrights.'

The director, Hamish Frederick, waited for the cast to leave the stage before burying his head in his hands. Nina, who had come to speak to Mr Frederick, walked down the aisle and sat down next to him. She introduced herself once she was sure that Mr Frederick had not broken down in tears.

'Nina Corrant,' she said. 'From Caesar. We had an appointment?'

Mr Frederick looked up. 'Say that again,' he said.

'I beg your pardon?'

'Say that again.'

'Nina Corrant,' she said. 'From Caesar. We had an appointment?'

Hamish Frederick dropped his clipboard to the floor and flung his arms around Nina's neck.

'Dear girl, thank you. *Thank* you.'

'I don't know what you mean,' said Nina, instinctively returning what was quite a friendly hug.

'Your voice,' said Mr Frederick. 'Your beautiful English voice!'

'Are you about to offer to cast me in a film, Mr Frederick? I won't fall for that, you know.'

'No, no. No, it's these—' Mr Frederick looked furtively over his shoulder. 'These *bloody* Americans. "*Crah Havoc, and let slip the dawgs o' waw-ur!*" You can't imagine the torture. I bit through my lip yesterday afternoon. Yours is the first English accent I've heard since eight o'clock this morning, save for my own. Hold on, you're the girl from Caesar, aren't you?'

'That is what I said, yes.'

'Oh, my. You're responsible, then? You've made this terrible thing happen to me?' Mr Frederick pointed vaguely at the stage.

The director, sitting down, was an onion-shaped man of sixty or so, with a closely cropped yellowish beard and white hair so thin that stripes of pink scalp alternated with carefully combed strands. He was a veteran of thousands of nights of Shakespeare. While not exactly loving the plays themselves, he nevertheless found himself so attached to the rhythm and timbre of the English language that the all-American cast had given him migraines from the start.

'I don't know what you mean,' lied Nina, who had

33

eavesdropped on a previous rehearsal that had taken place during the time when the American cast had valiantly attempted to adopt English stage accents for the production. They had since abandoned any such ambitions, owing to what Mr Frederick had called 'a certain, oh, *unevenness*' in the authenticity of the accents that emerged. A meeting was held, a vote was taken, and a letter signed by the cast was issued to the CYSR authorities pointing out that in the spirit of the Special Relationship, and considering what a really great playwright Shakespeare was, the accents didn't matter one whit. Besides, they hastened to point out, there was something kind of avant-garde about a lot of drawling, seldom-employed American actors dressed in togas declaiming in Elizabethan blank verse.

'What do you want, then?' said a surly Mr Frederick, once he had made up his mind that Nina was the cause of his torment.

'Nothing, really. You're on my itinerary for today. I'm to ask you how everything is progressing. I have to report back. Do you understand?'

'My Christ, it's nice to hear your voice,' said Mr Frederick, softening again. 'You can report back that I have lost my temper only once every four or five minutes, that the actors are pathetic, that this will be the worst production of any Shakespeare play in the *history* of the London theatre, that the sheer *earnestness* of these hopeless Midwestern queers and housewives is driving me out of my mind, and that as far as I'm concerned there ought to be *legislation* about who is and who is not qualified by right of class and nationality to speak out loud the poetry of William Shakespeare. All right?'

'Thank you, Mr Frederick. And I'm so sorry. I'm afraid you aren't alone. Caesar has caused a surprising amount of resentment. Oddly, the Americans are oblivious.'

'Oblivious, did you say? *Oblivious?*' Mr Frederick dropped two of his several chins into the V-neck of his cashmere jumper. 'I've had to deal with these people for ten days now, and all I get in return is "Thank you, Mr Frederick, such an honour, Mr Frederick, great opportunity, Mr Frederick, isn't Shakespeare wonderful, Mr Frederick . . ." My God. That tall man who plays Antony, that useless wanker, just keeps *smiling* through his speeches as if he were being photographed for a toothpaste advertisement. I asked him please to stop smiling and do you know what he did? He *smiled*. "Yes, Mr Frederick, thank you, Mr Frederick, such an honour—" '

'Mr Frederick?' Nina said.

'Sorry, yes?'

'Would you like a quick drink, to soothe the frayed nerves?'

'Dear girl,' said Mr Frederick. 'You are marvellous. You are beautiful,' he said, shaking his chins in admiration, 'and you are *English*.'

Nina's quick drink with Mr Frederick lasted three hours, and she learned vastly more than she would have liked about his failing third marriage, his step-daughter's ill-advised acting career, his natural son's homosexual promiscuity, his mother's refusal to die, his fifty-year grudge against a grammar-school classmate named Bates, his inability to afford a piece of antique furniture he coveted – and the way in which his lower bowel acted up after even a single pint of bitter. Nina found Mr Frederick jolly enough despite these complaints, and acceded to his almost desperate request that she drop by the Varrenwold Theatre more often than required by her CYSR duties. She put him in a taxi, and began her long trek home alone.

Nina was a tall and athletic woman of twenty-five. At one time she had been ranked third-best female tennis player in Britain (not that this meant there had ever been a possibility of her making the international grade). She tried to lead a tidy life, and was considered by her friends to be an underachiever. Her strength lay in languages, owing less to innate ability than to the advantage of having spent most of her childhood and adolescence abroad. Only a cynical refusal to believe in diplomacy – based on her father's depressing experience in the related field of military intelligence – had kept her away from a career in simultaneous translation. Nina's only claim to fame, other than her lightning serve and cruel backhand, was that she had been propositioned for employment by one of her father's colleagues in a Covent Garden restaurant before she had properly graduated from university. She had declined this invitation to become a spy, but behaved patriotically by never discussing the encounter with her father; her friends loved the story.

Nina lived in a one-bedroom flat in Fulham that was unreachable by public transport, infested with ants, below ground, airless, damp, surrounded on all sides by unemployed nihilists, and affordable only because she had indirectly inherited its short lease and small mortgage from her mother's dead bachelor brother. After seeing Mr Frederick into his cab, it was necessary for Nina to take both tube and bus to the most convenient spot on London's grid, and to walk home from there on long, strong legs. She told herself that the exercise did her good. On this occasion the wind was so fierce that she had to pause in doorways to catch her breath.

Only rarely did it occur to Nina that there was something odd about a well-educated tennis-champion daughter of a nominally successful father having to live on apples and water in a basement flat one hour from low-paying work; she tended to look on the bright side. The other people in her building had no work at all, by choice or otherwise (many of them were freelance writers). She had decorated her flat to her own taste, and felt comfortable enough there. She spent almost every other weekend in the country with friends. Her main hobby was restaurant tête-à-têtes with men. She had no difficulty filling her calendar.

This evening, as usual, Nina found her telephone answering machine blinking with the promise of friendly contact. She took off her shoes, and listened to her messages while slicing a green apple and pouring a glass of bottled water. There was a message from her mother, who had called during the day for a chat; her mother still seemed unable to accept that Nina left the house every morning to go to work and did not return until evening. There was a message from Chad Peele, informing Nina that their trip planned for the following day had been confirmed. They were to appear at a tiny grove near Northampton, where a group of American veterans of the Second World War, who had married British girls and remained in the United Kingdom, had planted spruce trees in l947. By lucky coincidence, all seven of the Americans and their wives were still alive and living in the area, and likewise their trees. The plan was to publicize CYSR with some newspaper coverage of their poignant reunion. In one of his most impressive and prescient executive decisions, Chad had pushed up the date of their publicity stunt, having predicted that it would coincide with yet another war in which the Special Relationship played a prominent role.

The third message was from Lloyd James. Nina emerged from her kitchen to listen more carefully to what he had to say. His voice sounded very odd. When his rambling message finally trailed off, she rewound the tape to listen to it again. He said something about wanting to see her some time in the near future, which was normal enough, though they usually met only at someone else's behest. Then he said something she could not quite understand, but which rhymed, and might well have been a snatch of poetry. He stopped in the middle of this, apologized, and repeated his wish that they meet some time in the near future. He gave his telephone number, and, for no apparent reason, the telephone number of the house where he had been born. He apologized again after this, laughed, mentioned jet lag, and rang off.

What a puzzling message. Nina had never known Lloyd to be incoherent or confused, or anything but direct. His friends had always considered him a caricature of a man in control. He lived for purpose and order. Nina hoped it wasn't bad news that had prompted him to call. She played his message one more time, found that he had indeed quoted miscellaneous poetry, and wondered again how it was that such a cautious and stable man had come unhinged.

There was *one* possibility, however, which Nina was astute and experienced enough to fathom straight away. But, no, she discarded it as soon as it had occurred to her. There had always been an almost incestuous buzz of romance between them – which on only one cringe-making occasion had flared up into overtness – and Nina found it highly unlikely that Lloyd had decided, after all these years, that his intentions were more than friendly or fraternal. His remark about jet lag might actually explain it all, Nina concluded, or he had dialled the wrong number by mistake and left a message intended for someone else. Nina resolved not to jump to conclusions, to call Lloyd the following day, and to run herself a hot bath.

Lloyd stared at his silent telephone. It was half-past seven, and still Nina had not returned his call. A second side-effect of Tourraine's Syndrome had made itself evident: he talked aloud to himself. Not only did he recite Shakespeare and elementary French lessons, but he uttered aloud the progress of his thoughts.

'I am consumed by love,' he said, still staring at his telephone. Then, 'A watched pot never boils.'

He turned on the television and, standing slack-jawed in the centre of his drawing room, watched pictures of precision aerial bombing. After declaiming a patriotic address or two, he switched off the war and resumed his phone watch. He was impatient to impress Nina with his newfound intellect, and to confess his love. He felt awfully virile. He allowed his mind to wander lovingly over his memories of Nina. A baby in her mother's arms, a tiny girl trotting across a lawn, a ten-year-old whacking tennis balls past the lunging rackets of her most athletic opponents, an adolescent with a crush on any man who stayed the night as her parents' guest.

Lloyd felt a stabbing pain in his torso as he remembered the one, the only time their routine flirtation had boiled over. Oh, *God*, the memory. He tried, as he had always succeeded in doing in the past, to block out the image of this particular episode. Tourraine's Syndrome had made that feat impossible.

It was a summer bank-holiday weekend in Surrey, at the country house of a mutual friend's parents. They owned a tennis court, and enjoyed having Nina out to dispatch the aggressive friends of their aggressive son. Nina was just eighteen, near the height of her game. The boys were all in love with her – with the exception of Lloyd, who was no longer a boy, and who thought of Nina as Little Vic's friend. This did not prevent him from admiring her backhand, nor from joining the lads in an appreciative analysis of her looks and sexuality. Lloyd was twenty-eight, locked into his responsible-older-brother phase. It had never crossed his mind that Nina, of all the girls he knew, could possibly be an object of his desire.

Something happened on the Saturday evening. It was warm and still, and the only sounds to be heard were the clicks of crickets and the *thwok* of ball against racket strings. Lloyd sat alone on the sloping lawn, worshipping Nina's impeccable tennis game. She played in the spirit of good fun, never putting away an easy smash; on the other hand, she never lost a set. Lloyd felt the sweat of a doubles match drying on his thighs. He applauded valiant gets, laughed at misfortune, called out support to the unsuspecting merchant banker who credited his own game and could not quite believe that the pony-tailed slip of a girl across the net was

39

blasting forehands past him at will.

Little Vic gamely acted as ball girl. Lloyd remembered how warmly he had felt towards his sister as she scampered unselfishly about the court. Little Vic was still girlishly skinny and intense, unlike her slightly older and more fully developed friend Nina. She really was a good girl, a brave girl; Lloyd could tell that everything would work out for her. It amazed him that she had never lashed out at the world, never questioned its justice, and had merely wept sensibly every so often when reminded of their gentle, stalwart father.

It was almost too dark to see the ball when Nina stopped sandbagging and served out the set. There was laughter and handshaking, and a barely concealed look of humiliation on the demolished merchant banker's face. The three of them walked up the lawn towards where Lloyd sat. Little Vic ruffled his hair as she passed. The merchant banker grunted hello. Then Nina knelt down, put a warm, moist hand on Lloyd's bare thigh, and said, 'I need you as my partner. Coming inside?'

Lloyd managed to say something appropriate in reply; inwardly he had seized up. He had felt the heat of her hand and warmth of her breath. It felt as if a chemical osmosis had transpired through their mingling perspiration. Nina stood up, still close to Lloyd, so that he could see the minute blond hairs on her tanned kneecaps. She walked away and left him sitting there, his eyes unfocused, contemplating his unwonted surge of attraction.

It was unthinkable that a night of sordid corridor-creeping would ensue, or so Lloyd told himself over and over again. No, he would banish the impulse from mind and body. Coldly would he bathe, furiously would he masturbate. A vile suggestion had presented itself, and it had to be fought off. Lloyd lectured himself like a parole officer to a recidivist pervert. He told himself that this sudden summer-evening lust was at best one-sided – that only embarrassment and years of self-imposed exile in Tasmania would result from attempting to act upon such an outrageous urge. He would be the disgrace of his family, a criminal and deviant in Little Vic's eyes.

Dinner wasn't easy. Freshly bathed, pink from victory on the court, Nina was the centre of attention in this tennis-mad crowd. Lloyd tried to sulk, tried to talk politics to adults, finally left the table when he thought he had caught a disapproving look from Little Vic.

If he slept at all before dawn, it was to be awakened at once by his lascivious dreams. He was aware that Nina slept not two feet away, beyond a flimsy wall. He tried and failed to drive out impure thoughts. He saw himself slipping out of bed, pausing to brush his teeth in the bedroom basin, creaking to the door, softly opening it, peeking into the corridor, and discovering Nina engaged in a mirror version of his intrepid movements. They would laugh, then silence each other with fingers to the lips, and bundle themselves into one or other of their rooms for several hours of thoroughly guilty and therefore exceptionally enjoyable love-making.

Lloyd tensed and arched his back like a patient undergoing defibrillation. This was *Nina* he was thinking about. How would he have felt if he caught one of Little Vic's appalling boyfriends scampering down the corridor towards – or, worse, away from – his sister's room? This thought and others like it, combined with sustained self-abuse and a volume of soporific literature, saw Lloyd off to sleep just as the dawn began to illuminate his room.

It was an exhausted, even *bruised* Lloyd James, therefore, who took to the tennis court a few hours later. He greeted Nina without quite looking directly at her. In his shame and fatigue, he found that he was able to keep his lust at bay.

'You aren't limping, are you?' Nina asked him.

'Certainly not,' he said, although it was quite possible that he was. 'Ah, here are our victims.'

41

The morning's fodder, a husband and wife in their early thirties who had decided that it was not extremely embarrassing for them to carry three rackets each, to wear headbands, wristbands, and other paraphernalia of the professional tennis circuit, took their places opposite. A jovial knocking up out of the way, the game commenced. Lloyd had played doubles with Nina enough times to know his station. He simply stuck to the net, an intent look on his face, crouched down with his racket pointing forward, and watched the enemy scrambling back and forth to reach the surgical strikes of Nina's back-court game. Only peripherally could he see his partner. His only expenditure of energy came between points, when he changed sides of the court, and of course when he served. His adequate service in play, he could trot up to the net and resume his post while Nina took care of business.

After Nina won the fourth consecutive game, the enemy began to complain about Lloyd's tactics. Nina good-naturedly agreed with them, and advised Lloyd to contribute even if it meant losing a point or two now and then. Lloyd, whose lack of sleep and other handicaps had subdued any competitive instinct he might normally have felt, remained stubbornly at the net as Nina served the next game. On the second point, in the middle of a long rally during which he might have fallen asleep without the entertaining display of the ragged opponents' desperate charges to and fro, Lloyd felt a stinging pain in his right buttock. He had been struck by friendly fire. Nina apologized for hitting him. Lloyd apologized for getting in the way, and trudged to the other side of the court. During the next rally, Lloyd was struck on the left buttock, much to the amusement of the husband-and-wife pair.

'That', said Lloyd, turning to his partner, 'was not a coincidence.'

Nina jogged up to the net. 'Poor thing,' she said, and, smiling with unmistakable mischief, reached out and rubbed one of his buttocks with her free hand.

Lloyd felt his head jerk guiltily towards the husband and wife, then quickly back to Nina, then down at the ground. He could not see a way in which the stroking of one's bum by a young lady could not be construed as flirtatiousness, especially when it was accompanied by a wicked grin and suggestive eyebrow movement.

When the game resumed, Lloyd played each point with fury and abandon, chasing down every ball and often intercepting shots better left even to an inferior partner. Fifteen minutes later, drenched in sweat, he smashed a set-winner so hard the ball bounced not only over the high court-side fence, but past a storm-damaged oak beyond. He pumped a fist in adrenal triumph, only to come crashing down from this elation when he saw the slow head-shakes of his opponents.

'Er, sorry,' Lloyd whispered. It was amazingly quiet on the court – one could hear birdsong – whereas a moment ago Lloyd had felt himself deafened by the roar of a tournament crowd. 'Time for another?'

The husband and wife declined, collected their spare rackets and towels and water-bottles and tennis shoes, and shuffled off to tend to their baby.

'That ought to teach them a lesson,' said Nina, who was suddenly so pretty Lloyd dropped his racket. 'Singles?'

'God, no,' said Lloyd. 'Look at me. I'm sorry, I don't know what came over me. Didn't sleep well last night. Possibly the food.'

'Poor thing,' said Nina, for the second time, and reached out to give his forearm a quick massage.

Lloyd exhaled more noisily than he had intended, as if he had forgotten to breathe for a minute. He found himself taking a look over her shoulder, then behind him, then through the trees towards the house – then realized he was doing so because he had been overtaken by an impulse to lean down and kiss Nina. He found himself leaning, leaning,

43

and just in time leaned all the way down to pick up his racket. This done, he started to make several excuses at once, having to do with phone calls and visits to the loo and a possible groin injury, but in the end was saved by the arrival of Nina's next victim. Wishing them both luck, he limped away towards the house.

Once inside and safely in his bath, Lloyd began to think he ought to flee. There was a girlfriend in London of some months' standing who could quite easily take his mind off his untoward new obsession. The bath is not the best place to try to take one's mind off lust, however, and after a while Lloyd found himself thinking, Hang on a minute, I'm behaving like a fool. I have a perfect right to emotions and desires. If I were, just to take one example, *Italian*, I would already have told all the other guests of my designs, and thrown Nina down on the court, tearing at her little white skirt.

Or would he? He could not be sure how much of Nina's now quite obvious flirtation was specifically aimed in his direction, and how much was merely a crush-of-the-day. He could not possibly ask his sister's advice on the matter, because to do so would be to open himself to ridicule if she replied that he had misinterpreted Nina's behaviour. He decided to soldier on, and not to lose touch with whatever Italian-style compulsions might come over him during the remainder of the weekend.

Open house was the norm on Sunday; drinks, lunch, tea and further drinks were to be had on a self-catering basis. Lloyd stayed out of Nina's path by barricading himself in his bedroom with nothing more than a few books and a pornographic imagination for company. When at last he emerged, exhausted and starving, he crept about listening for voices before entering a room. He managed to lay his hands on the ingredients of a ham sandwich, and as he ate this, standing in the kitchen, he was surprised by Little Vic.

'Where have you been all day?' she said. 'There was a crisis. One of the children – Peter – cut the ball of his foot on a twig or a rock. Horrible, bloody little single footprints from behind the court, up the flagstone path, across the floor, on the carpet, up the stairs, down the corridor, on the tile in the—'

'All right, yes,' said Lloyd. 'I can visualize it.' Little Vic was notoriously verbal. She told a good story, but every now and then her embellishments or attention to superfluous detail could be wearing.

'Peter's mother panicked and vomited all over their suitcases before fainting in the loo and nearly cracking her skull on the basin. His father tried to take charge but turned green too and was embarrassed that he was endangering his child's life by merely *pretending* to know what to do. Nina to the rescue! Bound the foot, popped a plastic sack over it to save any part of the house that hadn't already been thoroughly daubed in—'

'I understand, Vic.'

'I went along to the hospital with the green father driving and saying "Holy Christ, holy Christ . . .", and Peter started to realize that he was probably going to die—'

'He didn't die, did he?'

'Twelve stitches, but they wouldn't let me watch. There was a drunk woman in the ward with runny yellow sores on her shins and a purple bump on her—'

'OK, Vic. I'm eating.'

'Sorry. Nina said you played well together this morning, if a bit aggressively on your part. Isn't she super? *God* I love the way she trounces those men with their testosterone rackets and the horrible sweaty chests and their—'

'She is marvellous. What a talent.'

'You fancy her, don't you. You really do, I can see that you—'

'Don't be silly,' he said, as a piece of ham fell inconveniently from his poised sandwich and made a mustard splash on the kitchen floor. 'Whatever makes you say that?'

'Everybody seems to, that's all. Just because she has those, you know, all rounded, I suppose, and isn't it interesting that—'

'Vic, she's your friend. What if she spoke about you that way?'

Little Vic frowned. 'Now you think I'm envious when I'm not the slightest bit envious and I—'

'Of course not. No reason to be.' Lloyd found a sponge in the kitchen sink and wiped the ham and mustard off the floor.

Little Vic cheered up. 'Guess who I fancy, at the moment? No, you couldn't guess, you won't guess, but I'll give you a hint, he's not in this house at the moment and last time you saw him with me you said—'

'Not *Owen*, surely to God.'

'Technically, yes. But only because I have to have someone to tell Nina about and we both want to train ourselves for the time being to be keen on older men. It makes everything particularly good when you think that he's been married, he's a *divorcé*, and so charming to everyone and a *foreign correspondent*. I mean, you don't make a secret about your disapproval of the boys my age you've met, and I couldn't agree with you more, they're positively—'

'But *Owen*?' said Lloyd. '*Owen?* Just because he claims to be a journalist and tells a good story and—'

'Lloyd,' Little Vic mimicked, scoldingly. 'Owen is your *friend*. What if he spoke about you that—'

'Fair enough. Just don't mention it to him, OK? It's all too unseemly.'

'Of *course* not,' said Little Vic, as if the whole object of falling in love were to keep the issue to oneself. 'It's a *phase*, Lloyd. Nina and I are keeping very careful tabs on our *phases*. Of course I should never tell you such a thing but you may have guessed by now, given the older-man idea, that Nina has made a conscious decision to fancy—'

'I don't want to know,' said Lloyd, believing in an almost

46

physically painful way that he already did.

Brother and sister might have continued to talk along the same lines, but there was a crash and a slam and a child's shriek somewhere in the house, which Little Vic felt she had to rush off to investigate. This left Lloyd alone with the remainder of his sandwich and a head full of conflicting thoughts and emotions. On the one hand, he had learned that the girls had decided to be keen on older men; on the other, it was a self-conscious negotiation of a *phase*. Little Vic had all but told him that Nina had decided to be keen on him for the moment; and yet she hadn't, not really. Lloyd thought he ought to go back to his room.

Just after sunset, he re-emerged. All was quiet in the house, save for the banging of pipes as the plumbing coped with after-tennis baths. Lloyd decided to brave the evening, and descended the main staircase. The front door was open, and he ventured out into the pleasantly warm twilight. He could hear voices down at the court. He walked along the path in that direction, and arrived to greet a pair of guests – one of them the merchant banker – who reported that Nina had taken both of them on and won handily. Nina herself was reported to be searching the woods for a brand-new tennis ball someone had smashed over the fence earlier in the day.

'I'll help her,' Lloyd said, which left the two men free to return to the house. Lloyd circled round the fence and entered the brambly wood. He called out Nina's name, and almost jumped out of his skin when she replied in an audible whisper from behind the trunk of the storm-damaged oak, just feet away.

'I'm terribly sorry, no, sorry, I mean, are you . . .?'

'I shouldn't have left this until dark,' said Nina, who had been playing tennis for twelve hours, interrupted only by little Peter's foot injury.

Lloyd crunched through twigs and foliage and found Nina on all fours trying to reach the yellow ball trapped inside a thick patch of undergrowth. He insisted on retrieving the ball himself, which he was able to do only by enduring several tear-jerking lacerations to his right forearm.

'There,' he said, standing up, proudly proffering the ball like a surgeon with his first kidney.

Was this, he had to ask himself, as she accepted the ball, or was this not an unmistakable look on Nina's face? It was so hard to tell, in the near darkness of the courtside wood. He took a half step closer, which was most of the distance that separated them. She took a half step back. He stepped forward once more. Nina took another step back. This dance was repeated several more times, and might have gone on indefinitely had Nina not backed into the chain-link fence. Lloyd was close enough to feel the heat of her body, and, no doubt, she his. He wanted to say something, as if to add an escape clause to what he felt he was about to do.

'Am I about to kiss you?' he asked.

His question was not one to which Nina could reply with much certainty. Her hair was tied back, and there was still a trace of perspiration on her forehead. Her lips seemed to part receptively enough. She dropped the tennis ball. Her mouth formed the hint of a smile. This was enough for Lloyd, who pressed his body against hers, which in turn was pressed noisily against the chain-link fence, and kissed her in a way that he had not kissed anyone in years. That is to say, the kiss did not feel preliminary or searching, but might as well have been the purpose of existence. It was also the first *first* kiss Lloyd could remember that was not executed under the influence of alcohol.

Encouragingly, the kiss did not go unreciprocated. He felt one hand in the small of his back, another first on his shoulder, then on the nape of his neck. The kiss felt marvellous, as did Nina's warm and slender body. Having well and truly checked his inhibitions at the door, and acutely aware that Nina could not have experienced too many outdoor kisses in the arms of older men, Lloyd set

48

about making this kiss so artful and transporting that if Nina should become eminent enough one day to write her memoirs the kiss would be singled out as an event that changed her life.

It was Lloyd's rarely acted-upon view that time spent in sensual pleasure was never wasted. Many minutes elapsed, therefore, while night descended and the birdsong was replaced by the rhythmic clink and creak of the chain-link fence. Soon Lloyd forgot himself, if he had ever remembered himself in the first place, and began reflexively to exert himself in directions with which Nina was probably even less familiar than outdoor kissing. This involved more chain-link clinking, and the raising of one of Nina's knees. A brief readjustment caused Lloyd to open his eyes momentarily, and he saw through one of the fence's hexagons the vague outline of the tennis court. He closed his eyes once more, and lapsed again into semi-conscious pleasure. He was just – just – alert enough to know that there was a definite point that would soon arrive when he would have to stand back and protest loudly and too much that things had gone too far, that he felt perfectly awful about how far he had gone, and that he most certainly did not wish to be thought the sort of chap who would do the very thing he wanted, with every nucleic acid of his genetic being, to do.

He had not yet reached that point when, in one of those inexplicable moments of extra-sensory perception that cause murder victims to turn around just as the knife plunges down, he opened his right eye and saw what amounted to a *reflection* in the chain-link hexagon: it was another eye. Lloyd's scream of fright was muffled inside Nina's mouth. Nina's reciprocal scream was likewise muted. The scream of the person belonging to the eye on the other side of the fence was recognizably Little Vic's. Lloyd and Nina fell apart from each other, Nina's tennis skirt was smoothed down over her thighs, and a routine of hair-adjustment and vocal pleas of innocence was acted out, starting with Lloyd's absurd and involuntary announcement, 'Ah, *here* it is, the *tennis* ball, the tennis ball we've been *looking* for back here in the woods, the lost tennis *ball*, I've *found* it!'

There was just enough ambient light surrounding the tennis court for Lloyd to see that Little Vic had turned and run a dozen paces, nearly to the net, before turning around again and crying out in horror.

'*God* you scared me, God, *God*! I thought there was an *animal* trapped in there, I heard the sound all the way up at the house, I thought there was a dog or a fox or a – *God*, I can't believe you were, my heart is—'

'Calm,' came Lloyd's artificially deep and purposeful voice, from the tennis-ball retrieval area. 'We were looking for a tennis ball. Ah,' he said, even more unconvincingly, '*here* it is.'

Nina held a hand to her heaving bosom and leaned against the oak. Lloyd thought he might have twisted his ankle half-stepping on a log. Little Vic kept talking.

'Come *out* of there,' she cried. 'Come *out*! *God*. Nina? Are you all right? I swear I thought it was an animal or a trapped baby or a—'

'A trapped *baby*?' said Lloyd.

'We're coming out,' Nina said. She had regained her breath.

Lloyd and Nina poked their way like blind people along the fence and out on to the court. Knowing how ridiculous it sounded, but for some reason unable to stop himself, Lloyd continued to describe the long and complicated tennis-ball search that had ended in triumph, i.e., the finding of the ball and general hugs and happiness for all concerned. He even held up the ball to show his little sister what a success their search had been.

Nina collected her racket and walked away without a word. Lloyd went on babbling about the tennis ball, even going so far as to place it in his sister's hand, as if further

50

proof of its physical existence might cause her to rethink the meaning of what she had seen on the other side of the fence. Little Vic said nothing, just stared at her brother as if his hair had caught fire. Still talking, Lloyd ascended the lawn to the house, climbed the stairs, packed his bags, descended the stairs, strode through the main hall without noticing a wailing child, crunched across the drive, got into his car, and drove with gritted teeth towards London. He was stopped not once but twice for speeding. On the second occasion the policeman asked him if he felt all right, and Lloyd replied that he felt quite certain that he had done nothing wrong.

In recalling that weekend, Lloyd was aided by Tourraine's Syndrome in realizing just how acute and elaborate his embarrassment had been. It seemed impossible now, seven years later, that he had writhed about in mortification, denied even to himself that anything had happened, avoided Nina and Little Vic, evaded the subject by burying himself in work and a slightly older woman named Joan. His psychological repression of the event was like Tourraine's Syndrome in reverse – the conscious memory had been deleted, only to return in dreams. He cringed even today, so powerful was his ingrained code of gentlemanly behaviour. And still, he thought, now that his brain spilled over with memories and he waited for Nina to return his call, it was awfully cowardly of him to have denied his true feelings. How many opportunities must he have missed over the years, as he plotted the safest emotional course through life? He had only now realized, at so late a stage, that the man who lives a controlled life, making sure to do nothing he regrets, is likely to end up regretting having done nothing at all.

CHAPTER THREE

At ten the next morning, Nina found herself hurtling northwards on the M1 in a maroon Jaguar with Chad Peele at the wheel. They listened to the radio as an edgy-sounding news-reader, in the complete absence of reliable information, tried to describe the progress of the war to an anxious public. To Nina it was all a senseless drone, verging on disinformation; to Chad it was remarkable and intensely interesting. Unsurprisingly, given his political upbringing, Chad favoured war, any war, any where. Nina wisely kept mum on the subject, and, being quite intelligent, chose not to hold a firm opinion on matters of man's cruelty to man. She was far more worried by Chad's racing-driver approach to the motorway.

Chad Peele looked older than his thirty-two years. He dressed like a banker. Someone had told him that he would look more intellectual and less like a softening athlete if he wore glasses, but his unnecessary eyewear looked as phoney as a cheap toupee. His massive thighs strained the creases in his trousers. He had privileged skin and teeth. He wore a tiny enamel American flag and Union Jack pinned in his lapel, and had asked everyone involved in CYSR to do likewise. (It impressed Nina that Chad showed such enthusiasm for his work. She considered CYSR to be doomed and absurd.) Chad had bulky forearms. Nina thought she could see the tensing of his muscles through the sleeves of his suit as he clutched the steering wheel and kept the car from swerving in the high winds. Chad was big all over, and his knuckles were hairy. Nina disliked muscular, hairy men in general, but it was Chad's overhanging brow and closely spaced eyes and quite gigantic rugby-player's buttocks that settled the matter in her mind. Chad took his eyes off the wind-blasted motorway and smiled at Nina. It was an intriguing smile – half leer and half goodwill, and not a huge amount of wit.

Chad had one good point, which was that during the six months Nina had worked closely with him she had been exposed to almost none of the usual innuendo about unprofessional after-hours conduct – the usual being overt, continual and unyielding. Still, he found it difficult to address her by her proper name. Nina's British bosses in the past had called her 'Darling' and 'Sweetheart' and 'My love'; Chad called her 'Gorgeous' and 'Darlin' ' and – worst one of all – 'Babe'.

'Please don't call me that,' she had said, the fourth or fifth time.

'Call you what, babe?'

'Babe.'

'Aw, shucks, sorry, babe.' He thought this was terribly funny, and still funnier when she had pinched his bicep as hard as she could when he had called her 'Babe' in a meeting with assorted regional CYSR operatives. Nina didn't so much dislike Chad as disdain him. The stories she had heard about his governor father made her flesh crawl. She hadn't yet dared to ask him about the pregnant woman on death row. The London papers carried the story with ever greater frequency as the date of Claudia Brown's execution neared.

Chad's main problem, in Nina's eyes, was not his American-ness, but his *bloody* Americanness. He had never been to London before his CYSR posting, and it had fallen to Nina to show him around. She had met Americans who seemed to have adjusted well enough after longish stays, but Chad was unable to modify his behaviour or retain lessons learned about ways British. He tipped lavishly in pubs. He would not modulate his booming voice. He slapped people heartily on the back when they least expected it. He talked down to people about the simplest things, as if, in one particular case, a Cambridge don might not have heard of California. He was condescending about the state of British technology, transport, communications, royalty, hygiene, cuisine, refrigeration and sport. He thought the cars were too small and the roads too narrow and driving on the left insane. He started most sentences with the words 'Back home . . .'. He was something of a racist, like his father, and dismissive of women. He thought everyone with a posh accent was homosexual, and therefore detestable. Nina's first impression had been of a man with a barren vocabulary, humourless conversation, bizarre religious beliefs parading as Christianity, and someone who boasted of never having read a book since Junior High School. All of these characteristics pointed to a fact of his character that had taken Nina all of thirty seconds to deduce in the first place: Chad was ignorant.

A healthy turnout of hacks and photographers had converged on the Northampton grove. The seven US veterans and their English wives posed for photographers before their spruces, which had grown tall and strong and had survived the great storm of '87. They were asked to reminisce about their war, and to comment on the current one. The reporters were rewarded with the good news that two of their grandchildren had been sent to the war zone with the UK forces, and that one great-niece would be fighting for the Americans. The reporters competed with one another for the best possible pun on the Special Relationship to use in their headlines. Chad stood proudly to one side and watched his PR stunt take shape. Nina found herself giving interviews on behalf of CYSR, and declined four invitations to lunch nearby, three invitations to dinner back in London, and one suggestion about what it might be possible to accomplish amongst the spruces.

The weather was cold and windy, but the aged couples gamely answered questions for more than half an hour, as the photographers called for hugs and dentured smiles. The soldiers and their wives were proud of their grove, and provided quotable comparisons between the survival of the trees and their long-lasting intercontinental marriages.

Chad carried a portable telephone, and dialled happily away while leaning one elbow on the roof of his car. He called Nina over at one point to tell her that Mr Hamish Frederick, the theatrical director, wished to speak to her.

'I had to hear your voice,' said Mr Frederick, over the phone. 'Say something.'

'I am standing near a wood in Northampton,' said Nina, 'moved nearly to tears by yet another Caesar coup.'

'Beautiful,' said Mr Frederick. 'Now listen to me. Your American actors have taken a vote. They seem to be under the impression that this production is some sort of collective. They have informed me of their desire to perform *Julius Caesar* in World War Two military uniform. The set, need I say it, will be Blitz London, all exposed pipes and bomb shelters. I resigned on the spot, of course.'

'You can't resign, Mr Frederick,' said Nina. Overhearing this, Chad narrowed his eyebrows even more than usual and reached out angrily for the phone. Nina raised her free palm, indicating that she would take care of the problem. Chad retreated in the direction of the journalists. 'I'll do my best to help you assert your authority,' Nina said. 'You are quite right that the costume idea is preposterous. We will put it to them that their brilliant suggestion is impractical and far too expensive. Think of the Special Relationship, Mr Frederick. Nowadays you could almost say it was part of the war effort.'

'Are you married, Nina?' asked Mr Frederick.

'No, I am not.'

'Will you marry me?'

'How very kind of you to ask, Mr Frederick, but no, I'm afraid I won't. You are too old and fat.'

'My dear girl,' said Mr Frederick. 'I do like you.' He rang off with a chuckle.

It was then that Nina remembered that she had not yet returned Lloyd's mysterious phone call of the previous evening. As Chad was still busy chatting with the press, Nina dialled Lloyd's home number on the portable phone.

'Hello?' came Lloyd's expectant voice, after only half a ring.

'Lloyd, it's Nina. I got your—' There was a muffled sound of receiver-dropping on the other end. Seconds later Lloyd's voice returned.

'Sorry, hello?'

'Lloyd, hello, it's Nina here. I got your—'

'Message, yes, ha, ha. Jet lag, Nina, how are you?'

'Well, I'm fine, Lloyd. I hope I'm not—'

'Don't be silly, I'm fine,' Lloyd said.

Nina held the phone out at arm's length and looked at it, as if the apparatus could be blamed for Lloyd's incoherence.

'The strangest thing has happened,' Lloyd said. 'No, I can't tell you what. No, no, this is terrific. I've asked a doctor and it's fine.'

'A doctor? What are you saying?' A dozen possibilities presented themselves to Nina.

'I can't tell you. But the doctor says it's fine. Who shall decide when doctors disagree? Sorry, I must have read that somewhere. I mean—'

'This is the strangest conversation I've ever had,' Nina said. She was unaccustomed to portable telephones, so that the peculiarity of Lloyd's remarks was magnified by the fact of her standing outdoors in Northampton with a stiff wind lashing her hair.

'Sorry, don't mean to be strange. I must see you, though. Can I see you?'

'Well, of course, yes. Are you—'

'Where are you, Nina?' Lloyd asked. 'You sound so far away.'

Nina saw Chad, over by the spruces, beckoning her. He probably needed an accent translated.

'Where are you, Nina?' Lloyd asked again.

'I'm in the country,' said Nina. 'With Chad.'

'Oh,' said Lloyd. 'I see. I *see*.'

'Now if you'd—'

The line went dead.

'Swine!' Lloyd shouted, and leapt back from his telephone. 'With *Chad*, eh? In the *country* with *Chad*? Swine!'

He began to list to himself the ways in which he would prepare for battle with the American swine. Karate lessons. The manufacture, with Dr Porris's help, of a lethal and untraceable poison. The honing of his mind to highlight the contrast in their respective intellects. The circulation of sinister rumours about Chad's political affiliations at home. The enlistment of Little Vic as loyal foot soldier and CYSR mole. The systematic discrediting of CYSR and all its works. Chad, the swine, would be packed off stateside in no time. Lloyd would *bury* CYSR.

As Lloyd calmed down, he saw that he had to make certain that he did not antagonize Nina even as he liberated her from Chad's imperialistic clutches. Rashness had never been part of Lloyd's makeup, and he decided not to allow Tourraine's Syndrome to interfere with the processes of reason. He could already tell that normal conversation was going to be difficult, what with all the intrusions of fact or wisdom that seemed to leak out every time he opened his mouth. He wanted to use his power wisely, and for peace. There was no denying Lloyd's love, and there would be no denying Lloyd.

Thinking how odd Lloyd had sounded, and wondering if a telephone fault had disconnected them, Nina returned to her CYSR duties. The American veterans and their British wives were allowed to return to obscurity. The journalists packed up their notebooks and cameras. Chad invited Nina to join him for a drink at a roadside pub, which he still called a bar.

Nina couldn't help admiring Chad's energy. He had thrown himself into this outing as if it had been a minor but crucial flanking manoeuvre in a major land battle. He was interested in everything around him, and he interrogated each person who crossed his path as if he were an intelligence operative behind enemy lines. No sooner had they ordered their half-pints than Chad embarked on a conversation with a lone drinker on the subject of the war – the war was, at that moment, exploding on an overhead television screen. Chad parroted his government's stated aims, methods and achievements. In this case Chad had landed on a sympathetic interlocutor, a pensioner with a missing hand who looked as if he knew a thing or two about war, and thought that it was about time Johnny Arab got his, etc. Nina squirmed in her chair as Chad patronizingly explained to the old man that posteriors were being kicked by American boots, and no one would ever again doubt the power and resolve of his nation to make the world safe for democracy. She could hear it coming minutes away, and Chad did not disappoint: It was the United States of America that had twice fought and won wars for Britain, and out of the goodness of her heart had kept this wet little country sheltered beneath a nuclear umbrella thereafter. Nina was shocked when the man nodded in agreement. She felt her patriotism rising in her throat. She wanted to interrupt her nominal boss and straighten out a few matters concerning power and influence in the world. Instead, she bit her tongue and sat in silence.

She wondered about Lloyd. She had always thought of him as an avuncular figure – always generous, gentle and enthusiastic; also obsessive, socially clumsy and introverted. When Chad asked her about English men, she told him he ought to meet Lloyd ('I'd *like* that,' Chad had said, making a mental note). That seven years of frequent meetings had elapsed without any mention of their passionate moment or two behind the tennis court said a great deal about the unchanging nature of English manners. Nina thought of that evening quite often. She and Little Vic had known for days in advance that something along those lines would develop. They had discussed at length, both before and after, the amazing power girls seemed to have. They could make things happen, magical and desirable things, such as kisses with older men behind tennis courts. They had felt only slightly guilty that their amusement at what had seemed a game had appeared to cause Lloyd, a fully fledged *adult*, such trauma.

And now his message, and their aborted conversation on the telephone. She wondered if it would be wise to ask Little Vic what the matter might be. Little Vic was infinitely loyal to her older brother, but might be persuaded to gossip. Whatever it was – and by now Nina thought she knew perfectly well what it was – it seemed sensible to let matters take their natural course.

Chad had finished his drink, and stopped haranguing everyone within earshot on the unstoppable wind of change whipped up by the lone superpower's devotion to justice. Even after they quit the pub and were *en route* to London, Chad continued his pedantic monologue. He said Nina would see for herself when they flew to New York the following day for a fortnight of fund-raising. The confidence, he said. The inevitability.

The horrible thought occurred to Nina that, far from being in decline, or passing the baton of imperialism Pacificwards, the American Empire had *only just begun*.

★

'How do I sound to you?' Lloyd asked, sitting across from Owen in a restaurant specializing in fish and sycophancy. 'Do I sound normal?'

'Perfectly normal. It's the way you *look* that worries me.'

'What? What way I look?'

'I'm only joking, Lloyd. You look and sound fine. Agitated, yes. Paranoid, yes. A bit goggle-eyed. Maybe the war is getting to you. Otherwise, nothing to worry about.'

'It's just that the strangest thing has happened. I'm going to confide in you, Owen. I'm going to tell you everything.'

'May we order, first?'

They ordered.

'I've consulted Porris about my condition,' said Lloyd. 'He says it's a mildish Tourraine's Syndrome. Ever heard of it?'

'Is that the one where your bones melt?'

'What? Is it? Porris didn't say anything about—'

'Of *course* I haven't heard of it. Please, relax. I'm listening.'

'Oh, thank God. No, it's fairly common, according to Porris. Won't last long. It all started on the flight home, remember? Remember how odd I felt?'

'You electrocuted yourself.'

'Correct. And the most amazing result. My memory has returned to me.'

'You'd lost your memory?'

'Not my normal memory. Everything else. Everything I had known and forgotten returned. It's almost indescribable. It's mostly French and Latin and poetry, the things one *wants* to have remembered all this time.'

'How very useful.'

'But other things as well. It's still progressing. I'm weeding through the superficial things, and now I'm remembering conversations, emotions, *moods*.'

'Give me an example of Latin, then.'

'*Nil agit exemplum, litem quod lite resolvit.*'

60

'Marvellous. So you have a disease that makes you incredibly boring.'

'It isn't a disease, and it certainly isn't boring for *me*. I quote Horace at will, for heaven's sake.'

'Not around me, you don't.'

'Owen, don't you see? I'm an intellectual. I know a huge amount.'

'That's going to be very helpful in the aphrodisiacs business, Lloyd. The clients will pay anything to shut you up.'

'I couldn't even speak coherently for the first couple of days. Information kept popping out. But none of this is important. The important thing is that a side-effect – I think it's a side-effect – has made itself evident. It all has to do with love. A memory of love, if you like.'

'If you're about to say what I think you're about to say, I'll—'

'It's Nina, Owen.'

'You've remembered that you are in love with Nina?'

'Precisely.'

'Welcome to sanity, Lloyd. Aren't we all?'

'Pah, you don't understand. You can't understand. This is not theoretical. This is physical, *unquestionable*. It's in my head at all times.'

'You asked earlier if you sounded normal, Lloyd, and I have to say that—'

'Mockery doesn't help. You have to believe me. I can't describe it to you.'

'I'm sorry,' Owen said. 'I promise to be sympathetic.'

'Thank you.'

'I want to know why you had to tell me this. This disease – sorry, what is it?'

'Tourraine's Syndrome.'

'Yes.'

'I'm practising not sounding like a lunatic.'

'I see.'

'It's just that I'll have to see Nina soon, and I don't want to sound completely barmy when I do. There is competition,

61

you see.' Lloyd leant back and folded his arms. It was with a
sneer that he said, 'From "*Chad*".'

'I'd heard,' Owen said.

'What do you mean, you'd *heard*?'

'From Little Vic.'

'OK, what are you doing talking to my sister?'

'Don't be silly. I see her now and then. Don't be a prat,
Lloyd.'

'Sorry, of course. Who am I to say? Have a go, then. *Take
my sister.*'

'Little Vic says the "Chad" fellow is quite a personality.
American in all the hideousness that term implies, but—'

'*But?*'

'But, Little Vic reports, kind of beautiful, man-wise.'

'*Beautiful?*'

'Big, handsome, rich beyond adjectives, charismatic,
sexy, rich again—'

'You're inventing this.'

'Ask your sister.'

'I think I will. Did she say anything about Nina and . . .
and "Chad"?'

'Only that she envied her for working so closely with
him.'

'They were off in the country together, you know. I
suspect the worst.'

'That's the least of your worries. She seems to have gone
off to America with him. Just this morning. Or so Little Vic
says. Off to America can only mean meeting the parents.'

'You're winding me up.'

'Not at all. I am loyally reporting all that Little Vic said to
me. We like to gossip behind your back.'

'I have to get a grip on myself. It's all such a great change.
Imagine – *Nina.*'

'Haven't I always said so? It was latent all along. Typical of
you that it took a finger in the mains to bring it to the
surface. Let's hope she's struck by lightning in America and

we can have some reciprocity.'

Lloyd searched Owen's face for signs of sarcasm. It was so hard to tell, with memories coming thick and fast, who was friend and who was foe. Owen was not the most reliable man to approach for advice. His own life had so far been an almost haphazard adventure. Owen's friends had watched in amazement as he had married, at twenty-two, a friend's Portuguese *au pair*. They had observed, with equal astonishment, his callous decision to divorce her, and the way in which he had made out his marriage to have been one of convenience for his wife. Who knew where the truth lay? Owen's journalistic career, put temporarily on hold by his 'five killed, some seriously' gaffe, had never struck anyone as realistic.

He transferred from broadcast to print, coaxing assignments out of friends from university. He was capable of such outlandish untruthfulness in this field, especially in regard to his exact whereabouts when his far-flung dispatches arrived in London, that only a man of Owen's endearing charm could have held on as long as he did.

A first brush with failure came during one of the African famines. Owen's byline appeared above two emotionally charged magazine pieces, a series that did much to contribute to Britain's awareness of a distant tragedy. His editors and readers alike were so moved by his compassion, and by his ability to make the sheer hopelessness and agony of his subjects bleed off the page, there was talk of awards, of television documentaries, of editorships. His friends worried about his safety, and thought often of him as they bedded down in cosy London; the disease, the military skirmishes, the quite evident lack of food and clean water – how did Owen manage it?

Owen managed it by staying in a bed and breakfast in Lyme Regis, and dramatically interpreting the news reports he saw on television. He might have escaped with his cruel deception intact, had a local girl not insisted that part of his obligation to her, as she had agreed to share his seaside room, was a trip to London. Typically, Owen was only too happy to arrange an elaborate overnight outing, which was to have included a picnic on Hampstead Heath, tickets to a musical, dinner at the Calliope and pressed sheets at the Savoy. They got as far as the Calliope, and then as far as after-dinner brandy, before Owen was spotted by the editor of a competing magazine. Owen still might have got away with it, had his most recent piece not appeared that same day, and had his ruddy complexion not looked more Icelandic than equatorial.

Gossip columns mauled him, held him up as one of the worst examples in *history* of journalistic cynicism, corruption and wickedness. He was attacked and disowned by former friends in the profession. His name became synonymous with deceit, as in 'to do a Hearn', or 'to Hearn it'.

Incredibly, Owen was given yet another chance. This came about because of the stirring apology he wrote for the same publication that had carried his phoney famine series. It turned out that Owen had, in fact, visited one of the camps where famine victims came in search of donated food – and where they died. Owen admitted in his piece that he had witnessed about five minutes of this horror before breaking down in tears and hysterics, and begging aid-workers, soldiers and fellow journalists to take him away. He described his reaction as a sympathetic nervous breakdown, and claimed to have been insane when he composed his fictional dispatches from Dorset. Further, he wrote, he had believed that any consciousness-raising that resulted from his impressionistic pieces – they were indubitably affecting – was all to the good.

The end for Owen came two years later. Still eager to make up for his African disgrace, Owen set out for Cerevia, where a powerful earthquake had miraculously left no one dead, injured or homeless. He was so amused by the fact that, when pronounced in Cerevian, his name meant 'to force to perform fellatio', that he immediately wrote a piece listing the ways he and others had been embarrassed during his brief stay. This was hilarious until the day of publication when an aftershock buried six hundred people in mud slides. By that time Owen was safely back in London, where he could be sacked to his face.

Aphrodisiacs saved him. Lloyd, who had never intended to get into aphrodisiacs, welcomed Owen's contribution of charisma and recklessness. Clients loved him. He held his drink remarkably well. He invented the product's name (Sex Balm). He knew the precise balance between false promises and effective promotion. Owen was, after all, a born liar.

'You still don't understand me,' Lloyd said. 'You think I'm making this up.'

'Not at all. I believe you, and I support you. We have always known how marvellous Nina is. What remains is the derailment of "Chad". I'm at your service.'

'If we have to', said Lloyd, employing one of the tongue-in-cheek catchphrases of their business, 'we'll kill him.'

Little Vic sat in her cubicle at the empty CYSR offices, reading Jean-Louis Parent's *L'Amour et la Pitié* for the third time in two weeks. It was the most meaningful novel she had ever read. It spoke directly to her, as no other story ever had. It had changed her thinking to such a degree that merely catching the bus in the morning had become an experience in contact-making with the soul. What Jean-Louis Parent's novel had taught Little Vic was that every second of her life was like a drop of water leaking – in the French author's words – from a celestial cistern. It was possible, according to the life presented in *L'Amour et la Pitié*, to drink and savour each drop as it fell.

Parent himself, not surprisingly, drank every drop and died beautifully at twenty-nine. Little Vic, closing the book and wiping away a tear – half of love, half of pity – resolved to learn everything she could about Parent and to emulate his every act. She believed she probably had no more than five years to live.

Chad and Nina had left the previous morning for America, which left Little Vic manning the ramparts. There was nothing whatsoever she could do, although the formal, meaningless description of her usefulness was 'answering the telephone'. She had not heard it ring for three days, when someone had called asking for an advertising agency.

If there was one thing Little Vic had learned from her three epiphanic readings of *L'Amour et la Pitié* it was that a girl had to *act*. Action, Parent wrote, was the *sine qua non* of existence. In the first month of her employ at CYSR, she had digested so much intellectualized despair that she now felt acutely, self-consciously, urgently in need of life-affirming *action*. If she were French, she would have to write a book. If she were a member of a long-oppressed minority group, she would have to plant a bomb. If she were Japanese, she would have to commit ritual suicide. Little Vic was neither French nor Japanese, and she could not truthfully say that she was oppressed. She had already begun to shrug her shoulders a great deal and cultivate an insouciance meant to suggest an utter indifference to fate in a universe absurd beyond the need even to be *called* absurd; she told everyone that she suffered from insomnia, because Parent was a notorious non-sleeper.

What Parent described was the opposite of what Little Vic did. His heroine, who went by the initial 'M', was a woman who sought, who pursued, who grabbed by the lapels and shook. 'M' got an idea in her head – usually at dawn, with her bare feet lapped by the sea – and relentlessly would she track down the object and satisfy the desire. Whether a man who captured her imagination, a stretch of water that begged to be crossed by canoe, a point on the map still unvisited, 'M''s name was ever *action*. Little Vic idolized 'M' more than any figure in life or literature. Little Vic wanted to *act*.

It was as she made this resolution that Little Vic was

startled out of reverie by an unexpected ringing of the telephone. She picked up the receiver and said what she had been trained to say: 'Caesar. How may I help you?'

'Vic, Lloyd here.'

'Oh, thank God. I thought for a moment *work* would be required. You can't imagine the sheer boredom of it all. How are you? You know, I thought I'd been hired as a PR lady, the type who has to dress up and have her hair done and use her feminine charms? But no, I sit here reading while the others are all off—'

'That's what I wanted to ask you about. Nina's not in *America*, is she?'

'Your information is correct. She left only yesterday.' Little Vic put on the exaggerated voice of a secretary. 'Who, may I tell her, is calling?'

'Never mind that. Dinner tonight?' The James siblings were direct with one another.

With a rendezvous arranged, Little Vic replaced the receiver. She looked down at the jacket photograph of dashing and unshaven Jean-Louis Parent. It really was true that a girl could read only so much existentialist fiction and philosophy before she had to *act*.

In his tragically curtailed *œuvre*, Parent seemed to recommend to his readers and acolytes that they ought to take a human life. Only then, he reasoned, could they pretend to know what it meant to be alive, to suck the oxygen of freedom, to carry on under the burden of guilt and sorrow that is in many ways the inheritance of mankind – to know, in a profound way, that the celestial cistern dripped. Every single action taken by Parent's characters reeked of meaning. There, in chapter fifteen: ' "M" put down the razor and turned off the tap.' If only Little Vic had discovered Parent at university – a Ph.D. thesis might have been born from that sentence alone: 'Steel and Water: Symbols of Suicide and Life.' But Little Vic was not an academic. Jean-Louis Parent had said himself, in *L'Amour et la Pitié*, that the study of literature was a waste of time; he had studied a staggering amount of literature to reach that conclusion. Little Vic recited to herself one of Parent's aphorisms: '*Plus ça change, plus c'est de la merde.*'

The central problem Little Vic faced was that so many of the life-affirming tactics suggested by *L'Amour et la Pitié* were repulsive to her. Murder, for example, did not appeal – not for murder's sake, at any rate. Ditto incest. Travel to exotic lands she could barely afford. Sexual intercourse with unshaven strangers in lice-ridden beds? No, not on second thoughts. Most of the things 'M' did between existential episodes were merely symbolic. Anyone could do them: to walk down a dangerous street in the middle of the night; to break a china plate; to stare broodingly out of a window; to lie in bed and feel a trickle of sweat through one's cleavage.

'M' sweated a great deal, now that Little Vic thought of it, which was another problem. So much of 'M' 's life had been lived in oppressively hot climes. In London the most Little Vic could hope for was the annual perspiration on the tennis court when Nina ran her to and fro with merciless back-hands. She would have to wait until then for an opportunity to lounge about, trickling.

There was nothing *sultry* about her, Little Vic decided. Men thought she was cute. Because so many of the men she knew she had met through Lloyd, they all seemed to think of her as a little sister. 'M' had no family at all, except for a father whose identity she did not know, and countless lovers – all equally faceless and sinister.

'Find out what you want,' Little Vic said aloud, alone in her office. 'Find out what you want, and get it.'

This third reading of *L'Amour et la Pitié* really had affected her profoundly. Little Vic could feel herself changing, veering towards action. 'Find out what you want.' It was Parent's line: 'I want, therefore I am.' *Volo ergo sum.* Little Vic's desires, if 'M' 's priorities were anything to go by, ought to be primarily sexual. Little Vic addressed this issue in her mind, and found a distinct affinity for this side of 'M' 's overworked life-force. She needed a man, preferably a foreigner. 'M' 's men were big and strong and anti-intellectual. Like bulls, they lurched about and broke whatever they ran into. They were blind to beauty and love, and lived for violence and sex. They were, in other words, in every conceivable way unlike the so-called men Little Vic knew, who were interested in money and sex, but money on its own would do. 'M' 's most triumphant moments came when she seduced one or several of these feral creatures, when she proved herself to be their natural mistress.

Little Vic knew that she wanted to seduce Jean-Louis Parent. That was the ideal. For two weeks now she had fantasized energetically on this point. Just to be in Parent's company for an evening, for one drop from the celestial cistern, would be to live a full decade at mortal pace; to make love to him, glory. Ah, but, *merde*, Parent was dead. He had died of so many things – drink, drugs, tobacco, love, pity, *Angst*, ecstasy – that the Mexican coroner's report had gained an ironic footnote in literary history for stating that the great young man had died of 'natural causes'. He left behind one collection of essays and criticism, one long novel, and an army of mostly female devotees who, like Little Vic, were attracted to his life and teachings like moths to flame.

'Find out what you want and get it,' said Little Vic. She wanted a big brute of a foreign man. She looked up from the photograph of Parent, and her longing gaze fell on the desk opposite. It was Chad's desk. Big, dumb, brutish, technically foreign Chad. The matter was decided. Little Vic would live at last.

The war raged on, and Lloyd's memory remained intact. Dr Porris checked in every day or two, to be told of his friend's mental pyrotechnics. Sometimes he rang up just to ask for a piece of information. Lloyd found himself brooding more than ever on the past, raking over pleasant and unpleasant recollections as if they might reveal a clue to his future. His main conclusion, after a few days of this, was that he had so far failed to live at all. This was not only because he had ignored a powerful subconscious love for Nina, but because everything else he had done – his property deals, his aphrodisiac business, his empty and repressed romantic liaisons – had been so strikingly banal and unemotional that he might as well have been locked up in prison the whole time. Lloyd felt that he had no *soul*.

He realized that he had long used the excuse of his father's ridiculous demise to defend to himself an existence devoid of meaning or passion. By throwing himself into work and providing for the supposed material needs of his little sister, he had even managed to avoid anything as time-consuming as a proper period of reflective mourning. Now, of course, he remembered the day of his father's death with painful clarity – the moist breeze in his face, the wild flowers speckling the hillside, the stench of sheep dung on the air.

Peter James had been a prominent enough member of the Bar to warrant obituaries in the national press. Those newspapers that reported the cause of his death as 'a shooting accident' had unwittingly suggested suicide. Lloyd's immediate task had been to ring his friends and distant relatives and explain to them that this was certainly not the case.

Peter James had never been one for blood sports. He was devoted to his work, extremely shy, appalled by the state of his wife's mental health, wary of his children, and wished nothing more of a Sunday afternoon than to be left alone to his library. At the age of sixty-one, a weekend shoot had been suggested that he simply could not decline: Colonel Corrant, thinking he was doing his old friend a favour, arranged for Peter and Lloyd James to join him and a potentially important client on the latter's estate. It was an admirable gesture, and Lloyd's father had to admit that if anything came of this encounter he would be in Colonel Corrant's debt.

Much as it pained him to do so, he made his preparations for the tracking and killing of wild beasts. He retrieved his own father's shotgun from the attic, cleaned and oiled it, polished its stock. He consulted shooting magazines so that he could approximate an acceptable costume. With hats, scarves, thick socks, coats, wellingtons, binoculars and shotgun stowed in the boot of his car, he and Lloyd drove away from a bickering family on a wet Friday evening. Lloyd remembered vividly that his mother's last words to her husband were obscene, and delivered in such a shriek that the neighbours almost certainly heard.

They spent the night at a convenient inn, and awoke on a misty morning in the gentle Dorset hills. The shooting party gathered, and set off with the intention of slaughtering pheasant. Colonel Corrant coached Lloyd and Peter James in a low voice on the etiquette of the informal shoot. They walked apart from the five others, who were keen and experienced, their guns broken nonchalantly over their forearms. The single dog on duty sniffed the moist air and trotted ahead. Peter James's main concern, characteristically, was that he should not be called upon to fire his weapon. Only reluctantly had he loaded it. He dreaded in equal measure both missing and hitting his target. He admitted that he had not fired a gun since his army days.

The mist turned to fog. Peter James asked if these weren't particularly dangerous conditions. Colonel Corrant shook his head solemnly, and the men drew closer to their partners so as not to lose touch. As for Lloyd, he relished the shoot, and caught up with the most zealous hunters to the fore. He clutched his own borrowed gun and practised releasing its safety catch.

Into the cleft of a deep valley they walked, where the fog grew dense. The dog had to be recalled every few minutes. It was suggested that they search out higher ground. Peter

James was not the fittest of men. The climb out of the valley winded him. He lagged slightly behind. He walked with his head down, breathing heavily, and was startled by the sudden apparition of a cow. Colonel Corrant, who had stayed with him for a time, later reported that his old friend skirted the beast as if it were a rhinoceros. Peter's fright at the appearance of the cow caused him to fall even farther behind, until Colonel Corrant had to choose between the company of his friend and the company of his friend's potentially important client. No one could blame him for choosing the latter, and no one ever saw Peter James alive again.

The shooting party, *sans* Peter James, arrived at the crest of a hill. There the fog cleared sufficiently to make a proper shoot possible. When Colonel Corrant pointed out that Peter was nowhere to be seen, the impatient hunters said they would give him five minutes to catch up, then leave him to his own devices. Lloyd peered into the soupy valley, searching for signs of his father. He half wished not to see him appear, as it would spare him even the possibility of having to take aim and fire later on. Five minutes later, the men trudged off towards still higher ground. They joked that Peter James had probably drowned in the fog.

They continued along a grassy ridge, and noted that the fog had begun to lift from the valley below them. They slowed down, thinking that Peter James might now be able to spot them on the ridge. Fifteen minutes later they heard the dull, fog-dampened report of a shotgun from the valley. The men laughed, and commented that Peter had bravely taken on the pheasant single-handed. Someone suggested that he might have been trying to draw attention to his position, and they did the best they could to orient themselves to the source of the gunfire. Down the steep slope they went, slightly annoyed but good-humoured enough to take a quick look for Peter James.

The fog had almost lifted from the valley now. Lloyd stopped every so often to listen. He found a hillside path that led down to a stream at the bottom of the valley. The voices of the men behind him were jokey and boisterous. They were going to give old man James a right talking-to. How dare he lag behind and cause all this bother. Their voices were soon dulled by the leaves of a dripping wood. Lloyd said he was sure they were headed in the right direction, called once more for silence, held a finger to his lips, listened. Just then came another shotgun report – not far away, across the stream and back in the direction from which they had come. 'How much ammunition does he have?' asked Colonel Corrant, red-cheeked and dressed for a blizzard. 'He'll kill us all, hah!' Lloyd hurried ahead to cross the stream at a rocky narrows, then doubled back on the far bank. There were no more sounds to be heard. He wanted to call out for his father, but it would have been too embarrassing to yell 'Papa!' or 'Dad!' He pressed on, zig-zagging through the wood, and at last came upon a clearing.

The scene that awaited him there, grisly and bizarre, was one Lloyd thought he might require psychiatric treatment to cope with in later life. His conflicting reflexes – to rush forward and to flee – caused him to fall over. He crawled forward now, on all fours, wincing in horror at what he beheld. When he felt he was too close to approach at ground level he stood up, rubbing his knees, and stared at the unreal tableau before him. The others had caught up now, and took their places next to Lloyd, staring dumbly.

They were staring at three things: a gun, a deer and a corpse. The deer was still alive and standing. The still-smoking shotgun lay at the deer's feet. The corpse – formerly Lloyd's father – lay two yards away, and was grotesque. No son should have to see his father that way – ripped open, pulpy – but that is the way Lloyd saw him. What was so strange, though, and what kept all the men standing mutely in line, was the configuration of animal, gun and corpse. It looked as if the deer had surprised Lloyd's father, stripped him of his weapon, and shot him in the thorax at point-blank range.

The quivering deer looked at the newcomers in that sideways, paranoid way deer have. Two of the men took fearful steps backwards. The deer limpingly turned to one side, and they could see that its hindquarters and left rear leg were covered with blood. It staggered and fell down, palpitating with rapid breaths. Colonel Corrant, the most experienced gun in the group, strode over and shot the deer in the heart. Lloyd recoiled. He felt an arm around his shoulder, felt himself being turned aside and led away. He walked a few paces, and sat down against a tree with his back to his father. He heard panicked voices urging calm, near shouts attempting to soothe him. The men were undone. They told him to remain seated, but he stood up anyway and returned to where his father lay, now covered by Colonel Corrant's green coat. He had returned not to pay respects, but as a detective. He wanted to make sure he understood what had happened. He looked at the other men with him, and realized that he was the calmest one at the scene. Even Nina's macho father, who had slain the killer deer, had blanched and begun to shake. The important client had burst into cheek-puffing tears. Two of the others announced that they would go in search of help, and darted into the trees in the wrong direction.

Lloyd surveyed the scene, and put the pieces together. He bent down and lifted the dead deer's head. There was a severe lesion behind one ear that had not been caused by Colonel Corrant's fatal gunshot; there was the chest wound that had; there were the widely spaced shotgun injuries to its hindquarters; and there was a broken, bloody right rear ankle. Lloyd dropped the head and thought over the situation. The answer came to him straightaway.

Lloyd deduced that his father had been surprised by the deer in the clearing in the same way that he had been terrified by the cow. He had seen the deer's broken leg – an injury sustained, Lloyd guessed, while crossing the rocky stream nearby. Lloyd's father would have known his duty: to put the creature out of its misery. From too far away, with half-closed eyes, he would have fired. That was the first shot Lloyd had heard on the hillside. He had wounded the deer, which was already so badly injured that it could not run away. He must have been left staring into the pleading eyes of a twice-wounded animal, and felt awful.

Knowing his father, Lloyd could very well visualize how he would have agonized over this predicament, circled the helpless and adorable beast. He would have known his duty. He would have known the animal had to be spared the agony of slow death. He would have looked down at his shotgun and reminded himself that one charge remained. He would have turned the gun sideways to place his inexpert finger on the rear trigger. He would have raised the barrel and taken aim. He would have looked down the sights and focused on the deer's big eyes and twitching ears. He would have closed his own eyes and half-squeezed the trigger, then realized that if he missed, or wounded further without killing, he would be the laughing-stock of his friends and his potentially important client. He would have made the decision to steel himself for a more certain and humane solution, also more manly, which was to grasp his gun by the barrel, walk straight up to the deer, and bring the stock down hard on the deer's fragile skull. Lloyd could remember the minutes that had elapsed between shotgun reports, and imagined his father coming to this decision very slowly. There would have been no sound in the clearing but the snapping of twigs underfoot and the drip of the deer's blood on wet leaves. He would have taken his time approaching the deer, feeling the weight of the backwards gun in his hands, perhaps automatically recalling his cricketing days as he clutched the side-by-side barrels.

Lloyd knew that his father would have closed his eyes as he brought the stock down. He was such a mild man, so completely removed from the violence of the natural world. He would be acting out of desperation and embarrassment.

He would be hoping that none of the others had heard his shot, that he could conceal the deer and compose himself before he was tracked down. He would apologize for having got lost in the fog, for holding up the shoot: he would laugh at his own incompetence.

Blindly, then, he would have swung his loaded club. The gun would have fired on impact, hitting him in the chest. He would have taken two or three surprised steps backwards, and died immediately. The shotgun lay where he had dropped it, at the feet of the quaking deer.

CHAPTER FOUR

Nina slopped through dingy roadside snow on her first day back from America, eager to get to the office for a cup of tea. The trip to America had been, according to her, a fruitless disaster; according to Chad, a triumph. The American businessmen in New York loved the idea, the concept, the presentation. But the money thing – no, the money thing was a problem. Didn't they know there was a recession on? A war?

Nina had met the President of the United States. She had met him, quite unexpectedly, on an afternoon when the war was going terrifically well and he thought he had time to meet Governor Peele's son to discuss his own potential role in CYSR. 'We're seeing the President at five,' Chad had told Nina. 'Cheese and crackers.' Nina asked him if he had ever met the President before. 'Many times,' was his reply. Chad's father was a stalwart campaigner for the President's political party. Chad had been enlisted to play golf with the President, and, more competitively, with the Vice President.

The meeting was swift and disorganized. Nina and Chad

were allowed through a White House gate, were swept down a corridor of power, were told to wait, were swept down another corridor of power, and there was the President. The President personally cut a piece of cheese and placed it on a cracker and handed it to Nina. There were dozens of people in the room. Chad spoke to the President about golf, about his father the Governor (a perceptible twitching of the President's eyebrow in response), and about CYSR. Chad gave the President one of his Stars and Stripes/Union Jack enamel pins, which the President later, in a moment of confusion, presented to Nina as a gift from the American People. The Commander-in-Chief said he thought everything sounded neat, and then he left to continue prosecuting the war. Nina finished her cracker and did the same, minus the prosecution of the war, guided by a singularly chuffed Chad.

London looked rather nice in the snow. The inevitable paralysis of the transport system kept the city streets clear. Nina reached her office exactly on time, having left home a mere ninety minutes earlier than usual. She was surprised to see Little Vic already at her desk, then doubly surprised at her friend's odd appearance. Little Vic wore a tight black dress and black stockings, had adopted an angry coiffure that would have been more at home on the head of a particularly aggressive Parisian catwalk model, had painted her fingernails red. Her costume could not have been more inconsistent with a bitterly cold day in London.

Nina's first instinct after greeting Little Vic was teasingly to ignore her friend's transmogrification, but after a minute or so of small talk she broke down and demanded to know if Little Vic had lost her mind.

'I'm a new woman,' Little Vic said. '*Volo ergo sum*. I've been going stir-crazy here, with you and the boss away. Has it ever occurred to you how utterly meaningless our lives are, here, now? Do you actually think there is just reward for toeing the line, for doing one's duty, for plodding on regardless, for playing by the rules of a society intent on crushing the spirit of its—'

'Vic, *please*. What's come over you?'

'Do you know what I did this morning? I took a *taxi* to work. Eight quid. A *taxi*. I'm not just going to close my eyes and grind out a life – marry out of desperation, procreate, stand in the park with that half-wit mother's expression on my face. I'm going to take taxis everywhere I go. I'm going to spend more than I earn, sleep with my bank manager, *bollocks* to the tax inspector – I'll sleep with him or her, too – and I'm going to take even more advantage of Lloyd's generosity. Do you think I studied the great literature of the world for nearly twenty years just so that I could sit on my bum saying, "How may I help you"? I don't want to help *anyone*. Life in London is oppressive enough. The drudgery, the expense, the routine, the filth, the congestion, the *odiousness* of—'

'Vic, *please*.'

'I mean, if you don't like the food, you send it back. I want to see the *manager*, for Christ's sake. I want to have a word with the *manager* of this stinking . . .'

Nina listened to her friend's tirade, and wondered what had come over the James family. First Lloyd, babbling, 'Jet lag, how are you?', and now Little Vic, ridiculously skinny in her tart's outfit, apparently insane. There was the history of their mother to keep in mind, of course.

'You've been reading that Frenchman's book again, haven't you?' she said, when Little Vic paused for breath. 'That isn't good for you. And I don't know how Chad will feel about your—'

'How *is* Chad?' said Little Vic, puckering her mouth. 'Was everything *wonderful* in America? Eh? Was this one of those "business" trips we little people hear about? Elbows touching at the boardroom table, unbearable tension, release at last in a motel in the on–off glow of neon? Eh?'

'Don't be silly. We met the President.'

'The president of what?'

'The President of the United States.'

'How *inconceivably* glamorous.'

'Vic, I'm worried about you.' Nina had not yet taken off her coat and gloves. 'Let me make some tea.'

'*Espresso* for me, if you don't mind. I bought a special machine and charged it to Caesar. It's right there.' Little Vic reached down for her bag and extracted a silver cigarette-case.

'Smoking, too?'

'Do you mind?'

'Look, just because you've lost your mind doesn't mean you have to be rude to me. I'm your friend. Smoke if you want. Be French in every way, if you like.'

'Soon,' said Little Vic, 'I will have hairy armpits and a kind of tangy scent to my—'

'Now, you *must* be joking.'

'Humour me,' said Little Vic. 'It's just a phase.'

It was then that Chad made his entrance.

'Girls,' he said. 'I'm surprised you're here. What a day, huh?'

'Ghastly,' said the women, in unison.

Elated by his meeting with the President, and oblivious of his failure to secure funding from any quarter in the United States, Chad plunged his tiny staff into work. The Committee, which met fortnightly, had to be briefed on the American trip, the progress of Hamish Frederick's *Caesar*, the construction of the Monument to the Special Relationship in Plymouth, the planning of the Hands Across the Water Fourth of July Goodwill Parade and the headway made on CYSR's computer database of Churchilliana. The 'Hands Across the Water' television special, scheduled for the autumn, had been delayed by the death of its first producer, but all was not lost on that front.

The war was helping. Chad could scarcely conceal his

glee. There was a huge amount of butt being kicked. Britain, lapdog to America though she had become, had managed to show herself in full possession of her military wits. The French and the Germans had behaved just abominably enough that the Special Relationship could claim unique precedence among the Allies. An outstanding villain had united the two most powerful nations of the last one hundred and fifty years in a war on evil. Chutzpah was being shown. Finest hours were in evidence. A stunning lack of Allied casualties had made everyone feel warm inside.

'If the war goes on all year,' Chad said – and at that time no one could be sure that it would not – 'it will do wonders for our profile.'

Little Vic coughed on her cigarette smoke. To compensate for this existentialist's gaffe, she sat up straight and thrust out her narrow chest. Chad had yet to remark on her transformation into a sultry philosopher's moll.

'The main thing is preparedness,' said Chad. 'We sure aren't going to *lose* this war, but if it's drawn out, messy, lots of body bags, we have to be ready with the Churchill database for inspirational—'

'We will fight the sons of beaches,' said Little Vic. 'We will fight the little shits.'

Chad and Nina looked up at their young colleague.

'Yes?' said Chad.

'Carry on,' said Little Vic, with a wave of her cigarette.

'I have to know about the Memorial. Anything new on that, Nina?'

Nina sighed. 'The artist, Sean Davidson, has been living at the site for four months, gaining inspiration. He lives in the shell of a World War Two tank, actually. He stares out to sea and thinks about lend-lease. We may have a problem.'

'How so?'

'The artist is vocally anti-American. Also anti-British, come to that.'

'Labour Party?'

'I'm afraid so. His work to date has been more along the lines of Third World-motherhood in steel and brick.'

'I knew this was a bad idea,' said Chad. 'How did we get saddled with this idiot?'

'Nepotism,' said Nina, pointedly. 'He is the son of Lord Davidson, who is all right politically but gaga otherwise. Lord Davidson chose him.'

'Well, who is Lord Davidson to appoint the Monument artist?'

'He's the elder brother of Sir Ian.'

'*Our* Sir Ian?'

'Yes.' Sir Ian was CYSR's co-chairman. 'Hard as it is to believe that there is someone older than he. The artist is Sir Ian's nephew. If we aren't careful, Davidson will build something defiant.'

'Like Eden being buggered by Eisenhower, for example?' said Little Vic, unexpectedly.

Once again there was a pause, as Chad and Nina appraised Little Vic.

'Perhaps,' said Nina calmly. 'But most of all I am worried that what he constructs, if inspiration ever strikes, will be hideous. What's wanted, of course, is a Churchill–Roosevelt monument, as if there weren't enough already.'

'Buggering each other,' said Little Vic smokily.

'Arm in arm?' Chad suggested.

'Shaking hands?' said Nina. 'I'm just afraid we're going to end up with a heap of bricks and lead pipes that some royal or other will have to unveil, grim-faced.'

'I'll speak to Davidson,' said Chad. 'Does he have a phone in his tank?'

Lloyd and Owen sat by the pool of their Johannesburg hotel, washing down toasted bacon-lettuce-and-tomato sandwiches with cold beer. Not only did they not tell anyone at home that they sold Sex Balm to South Africans, they hardly admitted it to themselves.

'I shouldn't have come,' said Lloyd. 'My place is at Nina's side. What rotten timing.'

Lloyd had grown used enough to Tourraine's Syndrome that he could now speak coherently without falling into Latin or French, or succumbing to inane logorrhoea.

'Ah, but business is good,' said Owen. '*Fin de siècle*, and all that.'

'What happened to the idealism of youth?'

Owen pondered this question for a second or two. 'I handed it over to my bank manager, in exchange for shelter.'

Owen's finances were as legendary as his reportage. His debt was massive. He thought of himself as a Third World country with no indigenous resources. Creditors in top hats and black capes turned up on his doorstep with letters written in blood. His charm had taken him far enough to become indebted on a scale that his accountants thought was probably insurmountable. Owen picked up a newspaper and read about the war, which seemed even farther away than usual, to take his mind off his troubles.

Lloyd had little use for newspapers. During the past few days he had perfected the Tourraine's Syndrome sufferer's art of 'mental reading'. He turned the pages of his memory, revisiting lost knowledge. He discovered that at one time he had been intensely interested in cricketing statistics. He flipped through an astonishing variety of pornographic magazines. There was that Bible again, Genesis over and over, begetting and begatting until Noah and then . . . and then a few psalms. Lloyd's realization that he had read so little of the Bible caused him to ponder his religious affiliation. A man possessing so much knowledge would need a system of belief, or at any rate an apologia.

With his sunglasses on, in the privacy of his mental library, Lloyd set about defining what he believed. This frustrated him at first because his 'Belief' file appeared to be empty. There were only subdirectories of 'Belief' such as 'Opinion' and 'Suitable Dinner Party Conversation'. Under

'Opinion' there was the Golden Rule, which seemed to make perfect sense. Under 'God' there were hundreds of moving quotations from those who had more fully furnished 'Belief' files, but Lloyd's brain had never taken them on as fact. He had to conclude that he was so deeply atheistic as to make the term redundant and meaningless. What he had – and this realization struck him with such force that he announced it aloud to Owen – was *Englishness*.

'I am English,' Lloyd said.

'Eh?'

'English, is what I am.'

'Of course you are, Lloyd. Don't let anyone tell you otherwise. I'm right with you on that one. Blighty's where you belong. Never mind these disgusting people, we'll be home soon.'

'You don't understand. I mean that I *believe* in my Englishness. It's all I have to cling to. Other people believe in gods of various kinds, they always have. Other people believe in reincarnation, it says so right here under Buddhism. Americans – like "Chad" – believe in just about anything at all, one thing after another. What I believe in has its physical manifestation right there between Wales and France. All wet and adorable.'

'Like a baby seal.'

'You're supposed to be supportive, Owen. I'm not a well man.'

'I believe that you believe. I'll be your acolyte. I already idolize you because you actually *own* a tiny part of wet and adorable England.'

'Ah, to be King,' said Lloyd.

'That would get Nina's attention.'

'Do you think Nina believes in Englishness? Will I be able to sweep her away by living up to my creed of nationality? Or does she believe in the satanic forces of America, heft and brawn, horns of gold, talons of intercontinental ballistic—'

'Any more talk like that and she'll be on the next plane to

84

the USA. Be yourself, Lloyd.'

'So right, Owen. I will be myself. I will be English down to my cuticles. She will be ashamed by her lack of patriotism and cultural pride. To think, a daughter of England cavorting with America like some Edwardian tart. Special Relationship, indeed.'

'Use that anger,' said Owen, returning to his newspaper.

'It isn't said often enough how big and dumb Americans are,' Lloyd said. 'They don't seem to *mind* being called vulgar, they relish that. But if we kept reminding them how big and dumb they are, how ignorant and muscle-bound, how *Chadlike* they are – without exception, mind you – we'd be getting somewhere. Are you listening to me?'

'Absolutely. Big and dumb.'

'Here they are raining death on foreign lands, which is *Britain's* rightful job. The cheek of it. When will *England* rear her mighty leonine head again? England is sanity. England is control. England is men in safari suits *administering*, for God's sake.'

'Hear, hear.'

'England is shrugging off yellow fever and building the bally bridge anyway.'

'Tally-ho.'

'Not some pet co-linguistical trained monkey, some Churchill-parroting museum display, some lackey to be ordered here and there to do the dirty work of *arriviste* America.'

'Rum do.'

'William bloody *Shakespeare* had some things to say about England, I'll have you know.'

'Do tell.'

'Do you know that "Chad's" piss-poor organization wants to stage all-American productions of Shakespeare's tragedies? On *English soil*? Why, in our own *fathers'* day, we had our priorities the right way up. *Bastards*.'

'Lloyd?'

'Eh?'

'If you don't relax I'm going to have to send you to your room. People are starting to stare. We have sex to sell.'

Nina did not bother going home before her date with Andrew Fritt. Bombs had rocked Downing Street. Heavy snow continued to fall. The war, the attack on the war cabinet, the snow: all in all, an eerie day.

Andrew was a recent acquaintance of Nina's, and a relentless suitor. While he was friendly enough, and of a shape and size that might ordinarily have appealed to her, Nina found herself dreading the thought of spending two or three hours in his company. There really was some truth in Little Vic's ravings of earlier in the day. Life had become so unspontaneous, its rituals so transparent. She tried to imagine Andrew, on his side of town, showering and shaving, applying cologne, gearing up with his favourite loud music, striking poses in front of his mirror, practising the after-dinner pitch: 'What do you think, then, darling? A *digestif, chez moi*? Eh?'

It was all too embarrassing. Nina had long ago admitted to herself that her most satisfactory liaisons were of the kind Little Vic seemed to be espousing – abroad, in warm climates, with extremely good-looking men with tans who had no stake in seeing her again and actually meant it, in a visceral way, when they called her 'beautiful'. They gave her breakfast in bed, they were wonderfully confident about their wonderful bodies, and pleasure was achieved in a straightforward and mutually agreeable manner. Andrew probably thought he was going to have to *trick* her into bed.

He was waiting for her at the restaurant, with his unfortunate teeth and chin to the fore. He began to talk about himself. They hadn't seen each other for three weeks, and it seemed as if Andrew felt he had to reaffirm his credentials as a potential sex partner.

86

Nina found herself observing Andrew as if through binoculars in a game park. The first part of the ritual was the establishment of his qualifications as a provider of food and shelter: 'Business surprisingly good, actually . . . been able to do up the flat somewhat . . . thinking of a new car . . . boss being nice to me, know what I mean?' The second part, only slightly more subtle, was the obligatory invocation of 'abroad' as an indicator of worldliness and sophistication: 'Back from New York only last week . . . thinking of Capri for July . . . never been to Goa? No? Most marvellous holiday there last year or was it the year before? . . . though for scuba diving it really ought to be the Red Sea, somewhat dangerous in these times, I suppose, but in the old days . . .' Third was an insistence – peculiar under the circumstances – that women fell into his lap like crumbs from a stale baguette. 'A girl I knew . . . a girlfriend of mine . . . in the South of France with a girl . . . sorry, a *very* stupid girl, but beautiful, know what I mean? . . .' And finally, most pathetically in Nina's view, a stab at the cultural richness in his life: 'An exhibition at the . . . plays not what they . . . most *marvellous* recording of . . . a friend who's the producer of . . .'

Oh, it wasn't Andrew's fault. Nina told herself not to be so uncharitable to this twit. It was her social role to listen to the suitor's curriculum vitae, and to make a decision deep within her genes and upbringing about the fellow's desirability. It was unfair of her to be so disinterested in her observation of courtship. She realized too, after scolding herself, that during Andrew's requisite monologue she had drunk nearly a bottle and a half of red wine.

Nina watched Andrew's rat-like mouth opening and closing around words that made even less sense as the drink flooded her system. What he said did not just annoy her, it offended her. She squinted, trying to focus on his face, trying to maintain at least a modicum of politeness before allowing his generous payment of the bill and fleeing into any taxi that might have braved the snow. The frustrations of the day – the snowstorm, the attack on the war cabinet, Chad's blind optimism, the background music of the war – all of this, combined with drink, had an odd effect on Nina. She felt dislocated. There was something ominous in the way she had reacted to Andrew's perfectly natural speech: she found that she hated him. Nina was not a woman of strong emotions, or not until now. She actually *hated* Andrew, and everyone like Andrew, which meant virtually all men. Nina thought she was about to scream, or spit at Andrew, or sweep the plates and glasses off the table with her forearm. She thought of all the occasions, during her years in London, when she had sat through a dinner like this one, listening with an involuntarily flirtatious smile to hours of fatuousness and pretence. She felt real anger now, and squinted harder to see if Andrew could tell.

'. . . not that I know all that much about wine, though I'll not soon forget a charming little man in Vilenchet whose crop that year we . . .'

No, he hadn't a clue. She picked up her cheese knife, fondled its handle, looked at a distorted reflection of her right eye in its blade. She wondered if Andrew would notice if she plunged the knife into his meatless shoulder. She put the knife down again, and picked up her wine glass. It had become full again. She drained it. It was refilled. Ah, she said to herself. Andrew thinks he is succeeding.

She looked at Andrew over the rim of her glass. She asked herself what it was she wanted or expected. Here was this . . . this *creature* sitting across from her – oblivious, conceited, one-dimensional. She could hardly remember his surname. Where had she met him? Oh, yes, of course. At the bank. He was a banker. Chad knew his boss. They were supposed to finance part of the Fourth of July Goodwill Parade, in exchange for advertising hoardings along the route. Nina couldn't remember if they had come away with any money or not. She had come away with a dinner date. What could she have been thinking when she accepted?

Her head was swimming now. Andrew had bits of cinnamon stuck to his upper lip. He was talking about what a bad skier he was, especially in deep powder in remote spots reachable only by helicopter. Had she said *anything* yet, this evening? Her glass was full again. Andrew was no doubt thrilled by his progress. This was their second dinner together, after all, and why shouldn't he think they would soon be curled up together in a warm bed after a mad taxi ride through the snow? It wasn't Andrew's fault that he was such a buffoon. Andrew was playing his part according to the rules.

Now Nina felt very odd indeed. She could no longer hear Andrew at all, and his face was distorted through her squinting eyes. She felt the most unusual sensation: it was as if part of her mind had come unstuck. She knew that she would shortly have to excuse herself to be sick – this happened at least once a year – but in the mean time her mind had a message for her. What did it want to say? What was this subconscious insistence? She closed her eyes, and the message was clearer. The unloosed part of her mind was telling her that she was in love. No, surely not. Not with this blithering . . . oh, no, not with him. With someone else. Someone she had known far longer. It should have been so obvious. She saw his face. She told herself his name. She opened her eyes and there was Andrew, signing for their dinner and saying, 'What about it, then, darling? A little *digestif, chez moi*? Eh?' His expression was so repulsive, so self-regarding, that Nina actually retched. Recovering, speaking for the first time in hours, she asked Andrew if he would be kind enough to escort her to the ladies, so that she could vomit.

The aphrodisiac trade was not a difficult business to master. A more or less constant demand from bored, fat, rich, gullible men ensured orders for the most convincing products. Sex Balm was one of these. All over the world, women paid good money for Fountain-of-Youth snake-oil; a smaller number of men threw money at products not guaranteed, but merely reputed to enhance their virility.

Lloyd justified his business to himself by arguing that his product actually worked. It *must* work, if grown men in complete possession of their faculties paid two hundred and fifty quid for a few minty drops of Sex Balm. They staged parties for Lloyd and Owen, and, being rich, had many young ladies on hand with whom they hoped to experiment. They joked to the ladies that these two young men from London, England, had sold them a liquid sex aid, and you wouldn't believe the cost. They seemed to enjoy the idea that they were being robbed. Makes you hard as a gun barrel, they would add, to Lloyd and Owen's disingenuous blushes.

Their customers were almost invariably entertaining sorts, though somewhat sinister. It took a singular brand of bloke to tell women that he used aphrodisiacs: men who were confident enough to know that women would understand that Sex Balm was merely a turbo-charger on an already powerful engine. They rarely came by their money honestly. There were arms dealers, iffy politicians, and those who had made the decision not to let their inheritances carry forward beyond themselves. There were abusers of other, anaphrodisiac substances, such as alcohol. There were men whose faces betrayed a pitiful lack of genital endowment.

Lloyd and Owen had not yet moved into wholesaling, and resisted the temptation on supposedly ethical grounds. One of the perks of face-to-face retailing had always been that their wealthy customers invited them along to the scenes of the debauchery for which Sex Balm had been purchased. In South Africa they stayed close to their hotel and kept their heads down. Their customers came to them. Their main contacts were three well-connected brothers named Van der

Poyes, who were simple-minded and rich. Like most of Lloyd's customers they insisted, as they handed over their money, that they did not believe in Sex Balm; on the other hand they bought more of the stuff, per capita, than anyone in the world. Their women, from what Lloyd and Owen had seen of them, did not appear to be impressed by the results – or perhaps they always looked stupid and bored.

After a ten-day stay, Lloyd was glad to be leaving South Africa, glad to be high over the vasty veldt. He had his reunion with Nina to look forward to, and his confrontation with Chad. As long as no new side-effects emerged from his electrified brain, he was confident that he would be victorious. He settled into his seat, closed his eyes, and reminisced hugely. He found that he could use his inner eyes like a zoom lens, magnifying images of his past and inspecting them for the minute details he would not have noticed as he had lived them. He tried to think of someone he knew who might be out in the desert risking life and limb for the Yanks' oil. He couldn't – which, knowing his friends as he did, was probably a very good thing for the Allies. He mentally read bits of Proust and Dostoevsky, and noted that some of their preoccupations in many ways matched his current condition – although in Proust's case Lloyd had only a title to go by. He allowed his mind to wander through the chambers of memory that were the narrative of his stunningly pointless life. He returned often to memories of Nina, avoiding where possible the Courtside Humiliation episode. He saw her four years ago, fresh from university, bubbling with anticipation, having alighted in London as a self-conscious member of the latest crop of *jeunesse dorée*. He remembered helping her to move into her first flat, and the way she bravely concealed her disappointment at having to live in a dank, out-of-the-way dungeon. He remembered the way she had set about establishing a life, a circle of friends, a social identity. It was sad – pathetic, even – for Lloyd to recall the hopeful enthusiasms of London's Ninas and their male equivalents, who seemed to expect such glamour and magic in their privileged lives, and ignored as long as they could the mundane oppressiveness of the city. Just as he had kept a fogeyish, parental eye on Little Vic's romantic progress – only a painful act of will allowed him to look on without interfering – he had studied the men in Nina's life with the horror of a neurosurgeon charting the growth of a tumour. He was retrospectively jealous. Young, overpaid chaps with expensive motors were pretty thick on the ground in those days, and they quite understandably beat a path to Nina's door. He wondered why she had never accepted a marriage proposal, and decided the answer was that the men were repellent. This thought cheered him for a moment, until he remembered how repellent he was. All of that would change. He would find out what a good man was, and he would become that good man. 'Be yourself,' was the accepted wisdom in situations like this; Owen had said so too, but that wasn't nearly good enough. He had to become someone else. So much of life – especially Lloyd's life, given the nature of his occupation – was counterfeit. Why shouldn't his *character* be superficially fraudulent? Lloyd saw no ethical problem here. After all, if he weren't at all times *acting* the role of a well-adjusted businessman who enjoyed society and believed in its perfectibility, he would rant and shriek every waking hour – stopping only to copulate and drink – about pointlessness and emptiness and the cruelty of existence.

Oh, Nina. Nina would be the point of it all. Lloyd remembered a day, three years ago, when Nina had joined him and Little Vic for a drive in the country. The girls, full of themselves and the magic they perceived in their London lives, pretended never to have seen cows or sheep or hedgerows before. They took a walk in the park of a stately home, each girl taking one of Lloyd's arms. Everything, according to their game of the day, was a novelty – ducks, deer, fallen trees. Lloyd could see their windswept faces so clearly now: Little Vic's slightly drawn from the working-week's labours, but bright with hopefulness and enthusiasm for their adventure in the country; Nina's so pretty and assured and . . .

'All right, Lloyd? Eh?'

'Sorry, what?' Lloyd opened his eyes.

'You all right, then?'

'Sure. Sorry, why?'

'You're crying, mate.'

Now, this wouldn't do at all. Lloyd could not very well go around in a haze of nostalgia, going soft and misty and regretful. It was one thing to be in possession of a perfect memory for facts, such as they were; quite another to live under the burden of total emotional recall. Lloyd went to see his friend Dr Porris to get himself sorted out.

'Good to have you in my clutches,' said Porris. 'Do you feel up to a battery of tests?'

'A cup of tea and a chat, more like,' said Lloyd. 'I am assuming, of course, that there is no cure – providing I could be convinced I wanted one.'

Porris, tall and stooped, had wrists so thin he wore a woman's watch. Even without Tourraine's Syndrome, he knew more than Lloyd did.

'No cure but time,' he said. 'If that.'

'I suppose you had better tell me what happened to Monsieur Tourraine.'

'Long version or short?'

'Short.'

'Tourraine ran for mayor of his city, was narrowly defeated. He became a minor celebrity, left his wife and children. He joined the *Front National*. Because he lacked an education, the things he remembered were juvenile. He was a disgraceful person, and his Tourraine's Syndrome only highlighted the fact. He began to believe that his father had murdered his mother by pushing her in front of a bus – when Tourraine was six. He brought charges. His father was acquitted. Tourraine murdered his father, then committed suicide. The end.'

'How ghastly.'

'There's no telling how much of this can be attributed to Tourraine's Syndrome. He might have come to the same end without it. The main thing is that Tourraine's Syndrome seems to have given him extraordinary *conviction*. He felt that he knew the truth about everything. You can imagine how dangerous that would be.'

'H'm.'

'Any of this ring a bell for you, Lloyd?'

'No, oh no. No, no, no,' said Lloyd, his field of vision superimposed with a mental holograph of Nina. 'So far the most dramatic effect has been that I can tell you that Paramaribo is the capital of Surinam.'

'That is useful, yes,' said Dr Porris.

Lloyd looked down at himself and noticed that he wore a dark grey suit and white shirt, but no tie. He looked like a recently released prisoner. How could he have forgotten to wear a tie?

'I'm not Tourraine,' he said quickly, looking up. 'I have no real convictions. You'll be glad to know that all is still mystery. I don't *know* anything. I just know what I've been told.'

'I suppose', said Dr Porris, 'that referring you to a psychoanalyst would be out of the question?'

'Of course. I'll leave their couches free for people who are mentally ill. I'm coping quite well, don't you think so?' Lloyd narrowed his eyebrows threateningly. '*Don't you think so?*'

'Erm,' said Porris, 'yes. So far.'

Lloyd almost told Porris the truth. He started the confession – 'I've become obsessed with a' – then shut his mouth.

'Yes?'

'Nothing to do with Tourraine's Syndrome. This is personal. I shouldn't have brought it up.'

'As you wish.'

'It's just that I'm about to get married, and I hope Tourraine's Syndrome won't interfere.'

'Married? How nice for you. Do I know her?'

'Nina Corrant. I don't think so.'

'No.'

'An old friend of the family. I suppose it was inevitable.'

'No doubt,' said Porris.

'I'm glad to have had this chat. Sorry to have wasted your time.'

'Not at all. Fascinating. Just remember one thing.'

'What's that?'

'Tourraine thought he was perfectly sane. Right up to the point when he—'

'I don't want to hear it.'

'You already know most of what happened.'

'Anyway, the volatile French. With me it's just knowledge, alphabetical and petty.'

Lloyd rose to go.

'How's Owen?' Porris asked. 'Owen Hearn? Haven't seen him in ages.'

'Owen? God, how do you think he is? Just blunders along. Been ever so helpful. Sells the Balm by the gallon. Force of personality – that's his strength.'

'Business is holding up?'

'Ticking over. The war doesn't help. I lie – nothing has changed. You? Getting any wounded in?'

'Nothing of the kind. A downturn, as you'd put it. People are watching the war and forgetting to be ill. As for casualties – well, you've seen the score so far.'

'Owen says we have to remember everything about the war. For the sake of our grandchildren.'

'I'll concentrate if you will,' said Porris, seeing Lloyd to the door. He wore oval rimless glasses and looked to Lloyd like someone who carried around a disproportionate amount of sadness. No one ever asked Porris how *he* felt.

'How do *you* feel?' Lloyd asked him.

Porris looked at his woman's watch. 'Spiffing,' he said. 'Now you take care of yourself.'

At the door of Porris's flat, putting on his overcoat, Lloyd felt a sudden pain in the region he would normally have associated with his bowels. It was so sharp and severe that he dropped his coat, clutched his belly and doubled over.

'What's this?' said Porris, guiding Lloyd back towards the sitting room. 'Tell me where it hurts.'

Lloyd contradicted his dismissive hand gestures by groaning. He found himself sitting down. Eerily, he knew what the problem was. He sat up straight in his chair and said, 'It's fine, it's OK, I didn't tell you the truth. I told you I was getting married—' Lloyd spoke through clenched teeth, but already the pain had begun to subside. 'What I ought to have said is I *hope* to get married. I *want* to get married. I am in love. It is Nina, as I said. She has no idea.' The pain had disappeared.

'I'm worried about you, Lloyd.'

'No need,' he said. 'I seem to have a bit of a lie-detector in here.' He pointed at his stomach. 'Built in.'

'Fascinating,' said Porris. 'Tourraine and the others never mentioned a—'

'Maybe they never lied,' said Lloyd. 'I must be going.'

'Keep me apprised, won't you?'

'Of course.'

'This is fascinating.'

'Not at all,' Lloyd said. 'Highly desirable. A challenge, that's all. I know enough now to be able to tell the truth.'

'Fascinating,' Porris repeated. 'You know the way out.' The young doctor made no attempt to conceal his rush to commit his discovery to paper.

Little Vic thought Chad was actually quite good-looking, if you didn't mind broad shoulders, perfect teeth, thick and neatly parted brown hair and blue eyes. She disagreed with

96

Nina on this score. She was going to enjoy the role of seductress. She was living now, all right – Jean-Louis Parent would have been proud of her. Skinny English girl no longer, not Little Vic, no sir. Nina was in Plymouth, talking Sean Davidson out of his tank. Little Vic had Chad to herself.

Chad had been on the phone for hours, trying to make golfing reservations at the Royal and Ancient. He had been told this was impossible. Chad didn't know the meaning of the word. Little Vic watched in fascination as Chad wheedled whatever unfortunate Scot was on the other end, landing body blows of dropped names, counter-punches of bribery. He had his reservations. Little Vic invited him to the pub across the street from their office building. Chad stretched his broad upper body behind his desk, and accepted.

They found a table in a nook of the pub, and sat close together. Chad drank beer. Little Vic drank a double Martini. She wanted to see this seduction through.

Little Vic's romantic life had been disappointing to her, even before it had been thrown into depressing relief by the example of Parent's protagonist. She tried not to blame English men for the state of her affairs but . . . but then she did. The word *pathetic* sometimes came to mind. Lloyd's friends were so *Lloyd*-like. As Little Vic learned the ropes, she became convinced that these English men – five, seven, ten years her senior – needed romantic and sexual basic training. They ought to be shipped off to a hot island somewhere and reprogrammed, whipped into shape, stripped of their childhood memories. Her one satisfying love affair had ended two years previously, when her Argentine lover had been called back to Buenos Aires to take his place in his family's political dynasty. He had been named Jesus, which made for a vocal two-birds-with-one-stone effect in the bedroom. She hadn't really minded when he left – she'd just stood, weak-kneed, beneath the flight path of a

97

jet chosen at random in the sky, thinking what a lucky girl she was to have known a man with a smile composed of such beautiful lips and eyes that drenched her in adoration . . .

Anyway, here was Chad. Little Vic loved the knowledge that he had absolutely no idea what was about to happen to him. She relished this feeling of power. She felt very much like 'M'. There was no man in the world who could resist the attentions of a slim woman in a short skirt.

There was a television mounted on the wall above their heads. On it, at low volume, men in suits disagreed with one another about the war; the war itself carried on regardless. Chad glanced up at the occasional coverage from the war zone, at reporters in camouflage uniform, at safari-suited correspondents speaking to camera in front of palm trees, at footage of the relentless takings off and landings of bombers. Chad was a proud man, a proud American. Chad asked Little Vic, whom he called Victoria, if she didn't think it was a fantastic thing that the United States had reasserted itself, shrugged off its malaise, shown who was boss.

'I couldn't be less interested,' said Little Vic. 'It has nothing whatsoever to do with me.' She tossed her head, bringing a French coiffeur's handiwork down over one eye. Others in the pub stared up dumbly or drunkenly at the television screen, showing neither alarm nor concern. Some held newspapers bearing front-page headlines of nostalgic Second World War vintage. 'The war gives me a headache,' said Little Vic. 'It isn't sexy.'

Chad loosened his tie. He made a reference to one of the CYSR projects that he had reluctantly cancelled that day.

'No shop talk,' said Little Vic, with a dismissiveness well above her official station. 'Tell me about you.'

'What you see,' said Chad, then completed the cliché.

'Your father must be so proud of you,' said Little Vic. 'I can't pretend not to have read about him and his job, and about his . . . predicament.'

'The old man is strong,' said Chad. 'He'll pull through

this. The election is years away.'

'Does he want to be president?'

'Not a chance,' said Chad.

'Why not?'

'Too, uhm, *rich*, to tell you the truth.'

'I thought rich people were supposed to be in charge.'

'In charge, yes. President, no. Think about it. They hire people to be president.'

'But your president now?'

'Careerist. *Dirt* poor, relatively speaking.'

'This *is* interesting,' said Little Vic, edging her chair closer to Chad's. She recrossed her legs. She held up one foot, shod in what her reading had taught her was the kind of flat-soled Bohemian sandal an individualist would wear. She hoped she wouldn't lose her nerve.

'Do you always drink Martinis?'

'Always,' said Little Vic. Then she saw his expression of distaste. Another tack would be advisable. 'Actually, never. I'm trying to change my image. No more nice Little Vic.'

'That's why the clothes?'

'You noticed?'

'Nina mentioned, actually, the attitude change.'

'Nina? Nina *what*?'

'I just asked her what was going on. I didn't think I could very well have you *swearing* at meetings, you know. She said— Aw, I shouldn't have said anything. It's not important.'

'Tell me exactly, word for word, what Nina said.'

'Relax. She only said you'd been reading a book, whatever it is.'

'*L'Amour et la Pitié*. It is a modern masterpiece.'

'Right. And that you'd – she said you'd "taken it to heart".'

'She's not wrong there.'

'I'm not too up on these books.'

'That's a start, actually. The author is against books.'

'Isn't that a bit . . . what do you call it?'

'Contradictory?'

'Right, contradictory.'

'You have to *write it down*, when you have an idea like that. He never wrote again.'

'What does he do now?'

'He died, actually.'

'Shame. He could have done something he thought was useful.'

'Yes. Promiscuous fornication with nameless strangers.'

'Is that what he's about?'

'Mostly. That and drugs.'

Chad rolled his eyes. He picked up his pint glass with hirsute fingers. With his other hand he raked back his plentiful brown hair.

'That doesn't strike you as interesting?' Little Vic asked. 'Or titillating?'

'Sounds impractical,' Chad replied. 'A guy could run out of money, just fornicating. Was he rich, this writer?'

'Of course not. He was an artist.'

'So when he . . . when he fornicated he'd have to do it in the girl's house? Was he a gigolo?'

'You don't understand at all. Money has nothing to do with Parent's lifestyle. A lot of it was in his head.'

'Well, he had to eat. Even artists *eat*.'

Little Vic sighed. 'He had some income. He lectured. He wrote essays.'

'But he didn't approve of himself, when he wrote?'

'He wanted to be purely – purely *wicked*.'

There was not the slightest sophistication that Little Vic could detect in Chad's blue eyes. Why, then, was he trying to take issue with a great French genius? Little Vic thought she might be losing the focus of her mission.

'I want to know about you and Nina,' she said, with intentional suddenness. Part of Parent's approach to life was a reliance on direct provocation – not an easy style for a well-brought-up English woman to adopt.

'Now, what do you mean by that?' Chad's accent contained more than its usual share of twang after half a lager.

'She's my oldest friend. Normally we would discuss this sort of thing. She's grown distant. Are you sleeping with her?'

'My goodness, girl. Aren't *you* something.'

'You don't have to answer my question.'

'Oh, but I can. Absolutely not. What I don't get is why you'd ask.'

'Just curious,' said Little Vic, who had been hoping for the opposite response, just for spice. 'Are you going to take me home?'

'Gracious,' said Chad. 'Do you mean am I going to *drive* you—'

'No,' said Little Vic. 'You know what I mean.'

'Gracious,' Chad repeated, taking her meaning on board. 'I don't suppose that I am.'

Little Vic thought she would have to retrench. More people had come into the pub. They had turned up the war. It was hard to be seductive with coarse journalists' voices raised on the subject of desert land battles.

'Say, how about that,' said Chad, pointing up at the screen. 'Looks like the war's wrapped up.'

Lloyd had travelled so much of late that his flat hardly felt like home. He seemed to use it only for telephone calls and packing. He looked at his diary and saw with relief that an uninterrupted two weeks in London awaited him. He turned on the television and noticed, abstractedly, that an entire war had been fought and won without his having laid eyes on Nina. He dialled her number, remembering that it would be necessary to tell the truth at all times. When her machine answered, he elected not to leave a message, fearing that he might utter an irrevocable, tape-recorded lie. That could kill

101

him. Instead, he dialled the CYSR number. Again, no answer. He wondered where Little Vic was. He missed his sister. He called her, and again was greeted by a tinny recording. He assumed she would be making her way home from work. She lived only twenty minutes' walk from his flat. Lloyd decided to trek over there and invite her to dinner. He had already toyed with the idea of confessing.

Lloyd put on his heavy overcoat, a wool hat and leather gloves. Before leaving, he took a last look around his flat, and thought how undignified it was for him to live alone. This had never occurred to him before. He had always revelled in his privacy and independence, worked for it, subtly lorded it over his married friends. Now he saw sterility, lost opportunity for laughter, the peculiar inaneness of order.

He closed the door and walked outside, down the steps to the quiet pavement below. It seemed to be raining on one side of the street, and not on the other. There were noticeably fewer people about, now that Lloyd's neighbours' debts had caught up with them. Forlorn maître d's fronted empty restaurants, where only a few months before reservations would have been *de rigueur*. Schools of empty, yellow-eyed taxis swam along the same road where Lloyd could remember walking backwards for half an hour in search of a cab. Lights shone in windows as people dined at home, focusing their conversation on sackings, recession, depression. Lloyd's neighbourhood was, in short, a far more pleasant place to live.

Chad's car nosed through filthy rain. Little Vic tried to convince herself that she hadn't given up. Jean-Louis Parent's spell was still upon her. She watched Chad's exaggerated profile flickering in the passing streetlights and told herself to get on with it. She liked the way he drove too fast. It was almost a matter of honour, now; she did not want to have to

102

live with the knowledge that she was unable to seduce alien residents, should she ever decide to do so in earnest.

Chad still tried to talk about work. Now that the war appeared to be over, he felt he had less capital to draw on, Special Relationship-wise. He said he wanted to avoid stressing the academic side of the project, fearing that the public would be turned off by historians and biographers and military experts swapping tales of political intrigue in bygone times. He wanted a fresh, new Special Relationship, but the generally rotten times were making it increasingly difficult to generate enthusiasm. What was needed, Chad confided, was a common enemy. The Soviet Union had imploded at last, but – while that was good for a few mutual pattings on the back – it wasn't like the heady days of the Cold War. It looked more and more to Chad, who had been thinking about this as hard as he dared, that France would have to be enlisted, at least temporarily, as the whipping boy of the Special Relationship; to a lesser degree, and for different reasons, Germany could probably fill in the gaps left over.

Little Vic wondered if it could be Chad's religion that prevented him from looking over and noticing her legs, her lips, her small but thrust-out bosom. Americans were said to be puritanical, if not downright loopy on that score. They were supposed to have personal saviours, to believe in an apocalypse, to lay hands on each other only in a healing way. Could that be Chad's problem? Certainly he showed signs of being rather *too* American in other respects – loud and gung-ho and pathetically optimistic. His father sounded like a religious lunatic, and a powerful one into the bargain.

'Chad, do you believe in God?'

'Nope,' he replied, without hesitation. 'Don't tell anyone. Anyway, if Sir Ian and the Brits don't decide in a hurry we're gonna have to . . .'

Little Vic found this infuriating. They had reached her

neighbourhood. She had so little time. It would all come down to her asking him inside for a drink.

Lloyd walked slowly, practising not lying. 'I am thirty-five years old,' he said, without noticeable ill-effects. He walked on, until he was out of earshot of a passing couple. 'I am a firm supporter of the British monarchy,' he said, and immediately felt a stab in the bowels that sent him collapsing into a railing. Through clenched teeth, he managed to speak: 'I *hate* the bloody monarchy. It *embarrasses* me.' The pain vanished, and he was able to continue on his way. 'I am in love with Nina Corrant, English woman,' he said, and felt just fine until he heard a voice behind him say, 'Good for you.' The policeman passed by on silent rubber-soled shoes, and winked. Lloyd pressed on.

'Won't you come inside?' asked Little Vic. 'Please?'

'I ought to get home.'

'You haven't eaten. I have a microwave and wine and everything.'

'I really shouldn't.' Chad had not parked, had not turned off the ignition. He got out, rounded the front of the car, and opened Little Vic's door.

Little Vic stepped out of the car in an existential panic. What if Nina heard about this? She looked down in horror as she saw that Chad had extended his right hand to be shaken. The gesture seemed absurd. She had no choice but to reciprocate, but in her Parent-inspired desperation she pulled herself closer to him and reached up to his shoulder with her left hand.

'Oh, Chad,' she said, feeling wretched and ridiculous.

'I sell aphrodisiacs for a living,' said Lloyd, rounding a corner into the street that led to Little Vic's mews. 'And highly effective they are, too. *Uhng!* They are *useless!*'

He decided he'd had enough of this painful exercise. He

was grateful to have so few secrets from Little Vic, otherwise their dinner together would consist of nothing more than long silences punctuated by shrieks of inexplicable pain.

Here was Little Vic's mews. Lloyd recalled with pride the day he had handed his sister the keys to her very own London house, tiny though it was, two hundred yards from a police station. It had cost Lloyd three-quarters of his pile at the time, but he wanted Little Vic to own it outright. She would never want for shelter nor, the way London rentals ran, for steady income should she decide to live abroad. It was the best thing Lloyd had ever done.

Lloyd turned into the cobbled mews, and froze. There was a maroon Jaguar idling in front of Little Vic's doorway. He squinted through the light drizzle at the couple standing next to the car. There was no mistaking Little Vic, so slender and dark. She was with a rather large man. Lloyd had learned over the years to rein in his natural urge to have his little sister's suitors killed, so he did not at once rush down the mews and strangle the man who, yes, appeared to have his hands on Little Vic's shoulders. Lloyd clung to the shadows.

'You have to see it this way,' Chad said. 'We're colleagues, you and I. It would be improper.'

Little Vic could not believe what she was hearing. Chad had his enormous hands on her shoulders, and was lecturing her as if she were a truant. She wanted to explain that it wasn't *Chad* she was attracted to, it was a *school of thought*. She was secretly in love with someone else, but wanted to live out at least *some* of the life-affirming actions of heroines like 'M'. It mortified her that her flirtatiousness was irrevocable, that Chad would think for all time that she had wanted him, as an individual, as opposed to a remote or abstract conception of the way life ought to be lived. She was embarrassed, something Parent's most symbolic character

105

never was, never could have been. She felt herself blushing, averting her gaze, as Chad continued in avuncular tones.

'It's not', he said, predictably, 'that I find you unattractive.'

'Oh, *God*,' said Little Vic. She had to backtrack. She had to get out of this. She had to distort the truth. 'You've misunderstood *completely*,' she said, turning the tables as quickly as she knew how. 'You don't think for a moment that I . . .? Oh, *Chad*. Look, these little misunderstandings. It's happened to me before. I don't want you to feel badly. I don't want you to be embarrassed about this. We have to work together, you and I. I don't want you to think you've done something wrong, something illegal, even, that I'll think you were trying to take advantage . . . No, not at *all*, Chad.'

Little Vic looked up uncertainly at the American from beneath her *faux*-Parisian fringe.

Lloyd was too far away to hear his sister's conversation, and he didn't want to. He knew he ought to retreat and leave her alone to her fun, and he was just about to turn on his heel and go home when something about the man struck him. Something foreign. Something . . . American. Only American men, Lloyd thought, had *hips* like that. Only American men were that big all over. The man had a jaw line that stood out at fifty paces. Granted, sometimes Australians looked like that man, but Little Vic had better taste than to . . . Now, now, Lloyd said to himself. She is her own woman. Time to go home.

Then he heard the man laugh, saw his head rise into the light from a house opposite, and knew, without having laid eyes on him before, that this was *Chad*.

Chad laughed, Little Vic knew not why. 'All right,' he said. 'We'll call it a misunderstanding. No hard feelings.'

'Fair enough,' said Little Vic, who thought she might have

pulled off a minor triumph and spared herself years, decades of shame.

Chad leaned down and gave her a friendly good-night kiss on the cheek.

'Swine,' said Lloyd in a hissing whisper.

CHAPTER FIVE

'I might as well be a pimp,' said Lloyd. 'Or a lawyer, or a time-share salesman. Don't take this the wrong way, Owen, but – and I mean this very seriously – the aphro trade is beneath my social station.'

'I'm not offended,' said Owen, one arm on the bar. 'You're an arsehole.'

Lloyd hesitated to express alarm at this remark, lest his lie-detector contradict his disagreement. 'You can't imagine what goes on in my brain. I know – I can *recite* – Thucydides. For example—'

'No offence, but if I wanted to learn the story of the Peloponnesian War, I'd look it up.'

Momentarily taken aback that Owen remembered who Thucydides was, Lloyd quoted a few lines of Milton to the effect that genius would never be understood or recognized in its lifetime.

'Bosh,' said Owen, in a friendly way.

'You've given me no advice at all. I have a power. It has been suggested between us that there might conceivably be profit to be made from my gift.'

'I can't think how. Unless you want me to go to the tabloids, which is beneath even *my* station in society.'

'With all this information at my immediate disposal, I thought perhaps that a unified theory of the reasons for existence might be winkled out of the old synapses.'

'The world awaits your pearl of—'

'It may come. Naturally I'll cut you in.'

'Can't wait.'

'You will be my manager and agent. I will speak at Oxford first. That ought to show the bastards a thing or two about—'

'Calm,' said Owen. 'You were by no means the worst student in the history of the place. I, for one, distinguished myself to a slightly lesser degree.'

'Then it would have to be off to America. I know all about this. Some Californian chappie gives you two hundred million dollars to make a ninety-minute film about your recent experiences. Then I will be knowledgeable *and* rich, and the rest will be—'

'You're already rich.'

'Hardly. As I keep trying to explain to you.'

Lloyd's portfolio was a sublimely balanced entity, which might have been described by an oenophile as conservative yet daring, short yet long, dry yet fruity. Lloyd owned a freehold flat worth three hundred thousand pounds, shares worth two hundred thousand, gold coins worth thirty-five thousand, and had paid himself forty-eight thousand pounds in the previous year. He had no debts. He expected no further inheritance to speak of. He had settled his tab with Her Majesty's tax inspector. And yet he did not feel safe.

Lloyd had spent thirteen years consolidating his financial position and that of Little Vic. He had capitalized on an unprecedented period of economic growth in the South East. He had been luckier than he had been shrewd. Whatever aggressiveness he had mustered had been rewarded; likewise his recent caution. This run of good fortune was unlikely to continue. It was a younger man's job to make money out of the new era. Lloyd doubted that he had the energy to begin anew in any field, and feared that the stable aphrodisiacs market would be his lot in life. This was unacceptable.

'What have I *done*?' he asked his friend. 'What have I achieved of a . . . of a—'

'Of a permanent nature?' offered Owen. 'If you start whingeing, I promise you—'

'Quite right. No complaints. Privileged. Life is what you make a hash of. No re . . . re . . .'

'Regrets, Lloyd?' Owen asked.

'No regrets,' said Lloyd, raising his glass, then doubling over in agony. 'Uhng!' he said. 'Er, regrets, yes, I have them. Plenty. I am full of regrets.' The pain in his abdomen subsided.

'All right, Lloyd?'

Lloyd recovered, and looked up at his old friend's face. He sensed a certain impatience in its familiar features, as if Owen had decided that all this Tourraine's Syndrome nonsense was nothing more than a self-indulgent psychosomatic mid-life crisis.

'Fine. Of course. A bit upset about last night's discovery.'

'You shouldn't spy on your little sister. She's a lovely girl, and sensible.'

'Sensible? *Sensible?* Consorting with that . . . that "*Chad*"?'

'You ought to meet him. How bad could he be? We already know he's richer than . . . than how's-your-father.'

'Croesus,' said Lloyd, automatically. 'The last king of Lydia.'

'All right, yes. Surely there are less suitable chaps prowling about.'

'Oh my God, you don't mean *marriage*? I was simply suggesting that I didn't want this American *ogre* popping across the pond and snapping up a Jaguar – a *maroon* Jaguar, if you please – and stroking my little sister's—'

'You're getting exercised over nothing. A few weeks ago it was Nina you were worried about. He gets around, our American.'

'Swine,' said Lloyd.

'You're a bigot.'

'He is poaching our women.'

'*Our* women? Vic is your sister, Lloyd.'

'Same thing. Unacceptable.'

'Let's get drunk and go over to Jane's.' Jane was a mutual acquaintance, who had many friends.

'Certainly not. The thought of one of Jane's friends, at a time like this. It makes me sick. I'm not interested.'

'No?'

'Certainly not. Uhng!'

They went to Jane's.

'Tiger penises,' Owen said, to one of Jane's friends. 'Dried, ground tiger penises. I am absolutely serious. Rhinoceros horns, whale penises, you can't imagine. You could say', said Owen, sizing up the young woman as someone unduly concerned about such things, 'that we are in the business of protecting endangered species.'

Lloyd listened without comment.

'My friend here, the chairman of our company, campaigns strenuously for the protection of rare animals slaughtered for frivolous trade.'

While this was not strictly true, Lloyd did in fact donate an annual sum to a wildlife preservation organization, the amount depending on how much his accountant thought would have the most favourable effect on his tax position.

'Hummingbird tongues', said Owen, fluttering the fingers of one hand, 'for energy. Elephant toenails', stamping his feet, 'for power. Grizzly-bear thyroid', shaking his head in pity, 'for endurance.'

The young woman looked as though she might burst into

111

tears or, conversely, tear Owen's shirt from his back and plead for ravishment.

'Bull pricks,' said Owen, slapping a forearm into his palm. 'Androsterone, from the saliva of wild boars.'

Another of Jane's friends was attracted to their circle by this last remark. During two or three minutes of interactive observation, Lloyd was able to discover that she was a perfectly enchanting, intelligent, gainfully employed, thirty-one-year-old woman who lived on her own in Bayswater and had not had a meaningful boyfriend since an ad man had died in a suicide car-crash three and a half years previously. In her eyes there was the obvious message – which Lloyd encountered only when he was not himself on the lookout for such things – that she thought it would be rather fun for them to share a taxi back to his flat. Her name, Lloyd had not quite heard.

Lloyd attempted to make himself out as the most boring, unhygienic, possibly sociopathic man she was ever likely to encounter; because he could not lie outright, the woman was charmed by what she took to be his attempts at self-deprecation. Out of the corner of his eye, Lloyd could see that Owen was enjoying his friend's supposed good fortune.

'Never mind the trade in' – Owen looked furtively over his shoulder and leaned down to whisper – '*human products.*'

He was well into his routine. He began to make suggestions about where he and Lloyd and Jane's two friends ought to go, with the usual apology that London wasn't exactly Rio, after hours. Lloyd moved into a position where the women couldn't see his face, and shook his head vigorously, bulged his eyes, drew a finger across his neck, mouthed the word '*Nina*' several times as if trying to loosen a stiff jaw.

'Let me have a word with my boss,' Owen said, winningly. Smiling, he led Lloyd to a quieter corner of Jane's drawing room.

'Exactly *what* is the matter?'

'*Nina*,' said Lloyd, continuing to masticate the word. 'I'm choking. I can't breathe.'

'You're not seriously telling me that you can't . . . that you can't . . .' Owen could hardly believe how terrible this news was going to be.

'I am', Lloyd announced, crossing his arms defiantly, 'prematurely monogamous.'

Owen slapped himself on the forehead. 'Our friendship is over. You'll stop travelling. The business will fail. My flat will be repossessed, just when I thought I had the bastards off my back.'

'Nonsense. As for tonight, I will claim illness.' Lloyd had forgotten for a moment that he was incapable of lying. 'Anyway, there isn't a problem. Jane's friends are . . . *charming*. Have a good time. I'll make my excuses.'

'Have it your way,' said Owen.

In trying to make his excuses, Lloyd lied twice, doubled over in agony twice, blurted out the truth twice, and forty-five minutes later found himself pinned to his own bed by the powerful thighs of Jane's enchanting friend.

This was not normal. It was as if Lloyd's having mentally taken himself off the sexual market had created an irresistible magnetic field about his person. This woman, whoever she was, had become almost violent. 'Rape!' Lloyd shouted, which seemed only to invigorate his partner. 'Fatal disease!' he cried. 'For God's sake, whatever you're called, stop. You're hurting me!'

She *was* hurting him. It was painful not to be with the love of his life. He stared at the ceiling, felt the woman's breath hot on his neck, was tickled annoyingly by her hair.

'I refuse', he said, his voice partly muffled by the finger the woman was trying to insert between his clenched teeth, 'to become aroused.' The woman ground her naked body against his, and laughed wickedly. 'That won't get you anywhere,' Lloyd said, fearing at the same time that it probably would.

113

'Sex Balm,' hissed the woman, straight into Lloyd's incisor-abraded ear. 'Your friend gave me some.'

'But it's—'

'*Fantastic*,' said the woman.

'For *men*,' Lloyd said, or tried to say. He didn't really know if the woman could hear him. 'And it's harmless minty stuff. No effects. All in your—'

'I want you, Owen,' said the woman.

Lloyd froze. 'What did you call me?'

Nina had spent an hour trying to persuade Sean Davidson to come out of his tank. She had rapped on the lid with a spanner. She had tied a note to a stone and shoved it down the barrel of the tank's gun. She knew Sean was in there: she could hear him sculpting.

Just after noon the tank's rusty lid squeaked open and the artist, blinking like a mole, clutching a bent screwdriver, emerged into daylight. Greasy blond hair parted in the middle, silver wire-rimmed glasses, a pallor Nina would normally have associated with severe anaemia, a tattered black turtle-neck – this is what Nina saw as the Official Artist of the Special Relationship crawled on to the bonnet of his antique fighting machine. His sculpture was already overdue, but judging by what she had seen so far, Nina could not imagine that time alone would improve Sean Davidson's creation. She thought it must be a very small sculpture, to have been fashioned inside so notoriously cramped a space.

Sean was annoyed. He looked as if he smelled as if he had not left the armoured confines of his tank for weeks.

'I know who you are,' said Sean. 'My uncle showed me your picture.'

'My picture?'

'A *photograph*. From Caesar headquarters. He said I ought to marry you.'

'Sir Ian said that?' Nina had met him just once, on the

114

photographic occasion now referred to by his nephew.

'He was wrong,' said Sean, loosening some grit from beneath his thumbnail with the tip of his screwdriver. 'You're too tall.'

'I do apologize,' said Nina, confident that someone like Sean would not recognize sarcasm if it shot him out of a cannon.

'My father insists that I get married this year. My uncle agrees.'

'Well, I suppose that's all the more reason to polish off the season's *work*, then, isn't it? May I ask how the sculpture we commissioned is coming along? It is my job to find out. No offence meant at all, of course. Just that it would help us all terrifically if we could find out your assessment of the progress you have . . .'

Nina went on for a minute or so with this droning protocol. She would give Sean a minute more to answer before she stormed the ramparts of his tank and had a look for herself.

'I'm having second thoughts,' said Sean, climbing down from his tank and squishing barefoot into the clifftop sod.

'Oh, my,' said Nina, with mock sympathy. 'Second thoughts about your . . . your work of art?'

'Of course not,' Sean replied, flipping his screwdriver at the ground like a throwing knife. 'About the Special Relationship. I am conflicted in the very worst way.' Sean looked at the ground, where his screwdriver was stuck in Blighty.

'I thought,' began Nina, 'that is to say we at Caesar had thought that this might be the case. So horrible to rush an artist of your . . .' Sean looked up at Nina, thrust his hands into clay-stained pockets. Nina looked up at the barrel of the tank's gun. 'Of your calibre.'

Nina didn't have the heart for this. The decision to commission a sculpture had come, nepotistically, from on high. These things happened, and a professional made the best of the situation. It occurred to Nina that it was Lloyd who had once said that if a country started from the premiss of hereditary monarchy, no one ought to be surprised when privilege was rewarded in less exalted walks of life. Looked at in the proper perspective, Sir Ian's nephew was handicapped by people's expectations, and by the unlikelihood of his possessing the talent a star-struck society deemed his birthright. He was, Nina decided, looking at the mud between his toes and the befuddlement in his grimy features, a pitiable figure. To expect such a man to meet deadlines was almost inhumane.

'Not to worry,' said Nina, who thought that in an emergency she could knock off a Special Relationship sculpture of her own. 'Care to show me what you've accomplished so far?'

'Are you really interested? I mean, aside from its being late?'

'Of course I am.'

'All right, then. Won't be a moment.'

Sean clambered back on to his tank, and popped down through the hatch with the practised agility of a man who urinated several times a day. Nina gazed out to sea.

Minutes later, and after a certain amount of clanging and scraping, the sculpture poked out of the open hatch, followed by the artist.

'It's all right,' Sean said. 'I simply sized it down. Couldn't very well dismantle the tank to get it out, ho ho.'

Sized down or not, the sculpture looked unhappy in the open air. It appeared to be made out of iron bars and unfired clay, with bits of local turf and grass stuck into its sides haphazardly.

'It goes here,' said Sean, placing it on the bonnet of his tank. 'There are two of them, of course.'

'Of course,' said Nina. 'So the tank is . . . is *incorporated*.'

'Naturally,' said Sean. 'The whole thing is about war, isn't it?'

'Your sculpture?'

'No, the Special Relationship. It's about throwing joint wars. Am I right about that?' Sean looked suddenly worried, as if he might have misunderstood his brief. What if the Special Relationship turned out to be not all about throwing joint wars, but about language, culture, democracy, not being French?

'You're quite right, Sean. And I'm so happy that I will be able to report that you are finished. You are finished, aren't you, Sean?'

'Oh, yes.'

'Marvellous.'

'You really like it?' Sean wiped his nose.

'Of course I do,' said Nina. This was true. His iron, clay and turf monstrosity was the Monument to the Special Relationship. It was Nina's job to like it. It was her job to arrange for it to be transported into the centre of town. It was her job not to laugh when the Prince of Wales or some other victim pulled the velvet rope to unveil Sean's masterpiece.

'Listen,' said Sean, who had relaxed enough to attempt a smile. 'I take back what I said. You wouldn't consider marrying me, would you? My uncle was probably right all along.'

'I don't think so, Sean,' said Nina. 'You're too short and flighty.'

'I suppose you're right. But I am frightfully rich. Or I will be if I get married. Keep it in mind, won't you?'

'Of course.'

So far, every man Nina had encountered through her work, other than Chad, but including the already married Hamish Frederick – and, come to think of it, Sean's father and uncle both – had proposed to her. Even a woman from the T. S. Eliot Society had suggested cohabitation. In her private life she had been realistically proposed to three times;

only once had she not laughed out loud, and even then her reply ('Not if you were the last . . . Sorry, no, John') had been somewhat less than sensitive.

'You don't think it's too complex, do you?' Sean asked.

'Marriage? Well, I suppose—'

'No,' said Sean. 'My sculpture.'

'Not at all. That is, the layman will appreciate its stark, er, beauty. The expert will fathom your depths, Sean.'

'I certainly hope so. I'm in love with you.'

'I know you are, Sean. Now I must be getting back to London.'

'I've never been there,' said Sean.

'To London?'

'I realized, at eighteen, that I'd never been there. For ten years more I restrained myself. It's become something of a campaign, if you see what I mean. Artists have to be notorious for something, you see. I am going to be notorious for not having gone to London, every day of my life.'

'Well, then, marriage really is out of the question. London is at the core of my being.'

'I take it all back. I would go to London for you.'

'Don't spoil your record on my account, Sean.'

'I've been lonely in my tank,' said Sean.

'I'm sure you have.'

'I'm living for my art.'

'You're living *in* your art, Sean.'

'What a lovely way of putting it. Inspiring. You will tell my uncle that, won't you?'

'Of course.'

'And if you hinted that we might be married?'

'Out of the question.'

'There's someone else, I suppose.'

Nina gave this a moment's thought. 'Yes,' she said. 'As a matter of fact there is.'

'It's cultural imperialism,' said Lloyd, to a small audience of strangers at what would have been his local pub, had he lived in Acton. He had walked for hours before striding into this establishment, overcome by the urge to share his unoriginal conviction that all that was crass and undignified, all that was brawn over brains, all that was empire-building in the guise of freedom-fighting, was American.

'The United States of America', he said, to the pub at large, 'is a monstrous, terrifying force of evil. Britain – no, to hell with them, *England* – has lost sight of this in its own pathetic, self-pitying wallowing-in-the-nostalgia-of-long-lost-glory. Ask me *anything*,' he said, surpassing himself in *non sequitur*. 'I know all the answers. I am the chap with the facts.'

In this corner of the pub there sat six men, one furunculitic woman and two scurfy dogs. The men's ages ranged between twenty-six and seventy-five; the woman was obese and florid; the dogs were miserable and near death.

'Are you married?' asked the oldest man, who held a walking stick in one hand and his crutch in the other.

'No. And that wasn't what I meant by ask me anything. Ask me who reigned in 1516.'

'You wouldn't propose that if you didn't know,' said the woman.

'Anyway, who cares?' said the youngest man.

'For goodness' sake,' said Lloyd. '*Try* me. This is like a game, all right? I know it *all*.'

'All right, then,' said a bald man with very few teeth and a herpetic sore at the corner of his mouth. 'How long did it take Lindbergh to cross the Atlantic?'

'How long?' said Lloyd. 'How long? Oh for God's – all right. May 31, 1927, New York to Le Bourget, *Spirit of St Louis*, all right? All right?'

'No good,' said the man, with a taunting, bronchial laugh. 'How *long*?'

Lloyd didn't think he knew. He calculated. A man could only stay awake so long. It was about three thousand miles. He would have been travelling at . . . how fast? Less than

119

thirty hours, surely. Less than twenty-four? More than fifteen?

'Twenty-one hours and . . . and eighteen minutes,' Lloyd guessed randomly, with an arch look at his interrogator.

'Bloody hell,' said the almost-toothless man. 'You *do* know everything.'

Lloyd beamed. 'That's what I said. *C'est ce que j'ai —*'

'Hang on, then,' said the woman. 'What about the Americans?' She appeared to be drinking chartreuse with bits of orange rind floating on top. 'What have you got against them?'

'I think we can agree that we all basically hate the Yanks,' said Lloyd, forgetting, despite his condition, that he hated the British working class slightly more than his distant cousins across the Atlantic.

'Right,' said his audience, almost in unison.

'Bloody Yanks,' added the youngest man. 'All money and no . . . bloody Yanks.'

'History has made them our allies,' said Lloyd, pedantically. 'It could have been the Dutch, the French, the Spanish. But it's us.'

'What's us?' asked the oldest man.

'We have the burden of a common language, or most of one. We have to watch their vile films, don't we? Read their parochial novels? Have to soak up their excuse for glamour? Have to bow and scrape and agree with everything they say? Have to fight their wars? They say "Fetch", and off we go like a country of golden retrievers. It is', said Lloyd, '*intolerable.*'

Lloyd thought his proselytizing was going awfully well. He felt messianic. He would take his message to the masses in pubs from Hull to Penzance. The people – Lloyd had forgotten also that he despised the people – would adore him. A few Tourraine's Syndrome party tricks, and he would be considered the Sage of England. The rest would be easy. Lloyd was a man of conviction: England good;

120

America bad. It was so obvious: England good; France impossible; Germany vaguely evil; but America definitely *bad*.

'Just look at those shellacked-haired wallies who run the place,' said Lloyd, thinking of Chad. 'Are these people of substance?'

One of the men said something about the current Prime Minister that Lloyd chose to ignore.

'Awash with debasing American mono-culture,' Lloyd continued. 'That's what we are. Do you think for a moment that *Shelley* was American?'

'Yeats,' said the woman, who suddenly sounded Irish.

'Never mind,' Lloyd said. 'The new world is not a better world.'

'Bastards,' said the youngest man. One of the dogs growled in agreement.

'Precisely,' said Lloyd, who realized with some regret that he was drunk at four in the afternoon.

Little Vic lay in her bathtub, lazily soaping her arms. On the wall opposite, framed in steamed glass, was the official photographic portrait of Jean-Louis Parent. What was most moving about the picture, and most arousing from the point of view of Little Vic and her ilk, was the near smile in the left tenth of Parent's pale, scornful, almost unnecessarily sculpted lips. His narrow nostrils flared disdainfully at the end of a contemptuous nose. Dark hair shone in a tropical sun and fell dramatically over one brilliant eye. His slender, intellectual neck sloped into the shoulders of a man who could fight with his fists as well as his wits. His hairless chest glistened in a healthful way between the second and third buttons of his rumpled cotton shirt.

Little Vic exhaled steam. She felt her latest radical coiffure dissolving on her head and neck. She forced herself to think in French, which caused her mind to conjure up some of Parent's most bombastic phrases. 'Poetry,' she thought, still in French, 'that feeble Anglo-Saxon excuse for forfeiting life.' Also, 'Poetry? *Bah!*' (Parent had never quite succeeded as a poet.) 'The examined life', he had written, when he had still believed in writing, 'is merely half a life: half lived, half commented upon. To turn observation into art is to render life transparent, formless, secondary . . .'

Was that what Parent had said? Little Vic could not exactly remember. It sounded – she could scarcely bring herself to think this, lying naked and steamy beneath Parent's arrogant gaze – it sounded like a load of tosh. Still, she did seem to spend most of her time observing rather than living. The idea was to draw conclusions on the question of how life was supposed to be prosecuted, then to *act* with concentrated daring. She had allowed her powerful attraction to Parent's spirit and intellect – and her lust for his black-and-white image – to channel her life into seas she was not quite prepared to navigate.

Little Vic bent her knees and dunked her head backwards into the hot, soapy bath water. She smoothed back her hair and surfaced with a spluttering sigh. She listened to the sounds the water made as it dripped and levelled around her body. Parent could have written a book about those sounds, about this moment, about water finding its level.

As her ears cleared, she heard her telephone ringing in the bedroom. She felt altogether too languid – too Parentian – to jump from the bath and answer it, rare as telephone calls were. She listened as the answering machine requested name and number in a voice calculated to sound bored and technologically naïve. She heard the caller clear his throat, then say hello. It was Lloyd. It was a drunk Lloyd, which was odd in the extreme. It was a drunk Lloyd saying something about a plot to sink England, to rape her country-side, to sodomize her cultural—

What was he talking about? Little Vic gripped the sides of her tub, looked up into Parent's brilliant eyes. Lloyd's words rolled formlessly on. America, cultural imperialism – something about registering his company as an environmental charity, Britain as a senile great-grandmother. It was, Little Vic thought, quite bizarre.

'I have the answers,' said her brother, almost winded by his tirade. 'I'll call you back on that.'

Little Vic reclined in the steamy silence, perplexed. She asked herself what Parent would do, in her position. Pursing her lips, giving Parent's photograph a cruel look, she reached for a small glass vial of scented oil.

Lloyd sat in his favourite swivelling armchair, talking to the painting over his mantelpiece. Lloyd had bought this particular painting in his property-dealing heyday. The painting was a forgery of a copy of an oil that had once been falsely attributed to a student of an apprentice to Clerian. It depicted a young woman picking strawberries in a wood that was said to be inside the borders of France. The young woman wore peasant garb, held a basket in the crook of her left elbow, and leaned forward in a way that allowed the artist/apprentice/copyist/forger to revel in her strawberry cleavage. There was a speck in the background that Lloyd suddenly realized was a rabid fox. This reminded him that Britain – no, to hell with them, *England* – was under siege.

'The truth is', Lloyd said to his painting, 'that I am in love. She'll ring any minute now. My beloved works too hard. Never mind. All will be resolved.'

Lloyd was surrounded by his inherited library. He used binoculars to read the titles of the books from the comfort of his swivelling armchair. He wished he had read more than one in ten of his father's books before the onset of Tourraine's Syndrome; still, the ones he had read were awfully good, awfully English. There were even one or two written by heterosexuals that had titillated Lloyd's youthful imagination.

Lloyd spun his chair around, and watched through his binoculars as the bindings raced past his field of vision. He spun again, accelerated, almost enjoyed the nausea. Hundreds of years of knowledge and wisdom sped and blurred alphabetically through the infinity sign of the lenses. Each title that registered in his mind opened a different vault of recollection. Superficially these were pleasant, even thrilling in their concrete factuality. On another level they were disturbing reminders of a wider ignorance. Some of the books, of which he had no deeper memory than their bindings held up in firelight, reminded him of his father. These memories could be painfully specific, and called into doubt the desirability of his new power. It was one thing to know Gibbon by heart; quite another to recall with heart-breaking accuracy a twenty-year-old gesture – calmly inserting a bookmark, placing the heavy volume on a side-table, removing reading glasses, rubbing eyes – in response to an angry shout from the kitchen.

Lloyd searched the mental coffers for memories of what his father might have had to say about Americans. Always judicious, and seldom if ever rash in opinion, the closest Lloyd could get to a blanket condemnation was his father's remark that an American professional acquaintance was 'like an eight-year-old bully.' This was not a lot for Lloyd to go on, but he believed that Peter James would have supported his son's anti-American crusade. Lloyd hoped that the Britons on the CYSR team – his sister and beloved included – would not forget that it had long been England's role to civilize that vibrant, violent and obscenely wealthy semi-continent across the Atlantic. Britain had relinquished power with the grace of a clean-bowled batsman retiring from the crease; that did not mean she had to sit humiliatingly in the pavilion, weeping into her tea.

Lloyd stood up, put his binoculars on his desk. He walked over to one of the two tall windows that gave on to a fenced-in square. Quiet, prosperous London lay iron-hard beneath a vindictive rain: spring had arrived. Lloyd's reflection in the rain-spattered pane showed a familiar London pallor, and an open-collared look that reeked of indecision. Here was a man who had courted and achieved independence, yet who dreaded being alone. Now that he shared his physical isolation with a head full of unwanted memories, he felt dwarfed and subsumed.

He turned and glared at his telephone. He knew what he wanted now. Enough procrastination. Either Nina would call in the next minute, or he would leap into action, trawl the city, track her down like a bloodhound – go to Fulham, if necessary. He believed that the conquest of Nina was now inseparable from his campaign to rid Britain of her dependence on vile America. He clenched his fists and focused his supercharged brain on the telephone. He was not surprised – none of his mental powers surprised him any longer – when the telephone rang.

'You don't sound pleased to hear from me,' said Owen.

'How right you are, how very perceptive. I was hoping to hear from my future wife.'

'She's back in London, is she?'

'So say my spies.'

'Look, I won't stay on the line long. I simply wanted to tell you that if you don't give me a pay rise I'm going to have to burn down my building.'

'Oh?'

'Unfortunately, yes. Arson is the only answer. Insurance fraud, that most sympathetic crime.'

'I've been meaning to tell you that you ought to sell your flat, start again a little lower on the ladder.'

'That would work only if I could find someone stupid enough to pay as much as I did. Not likely, in this climate.'

'A pay rise isn't on the cards, Owen. Not until Porris gets going on the BC.' The BC was Lloyd's dream product, a baldness cure. Porris said it was impossible, and that anyway the world's pharmaceutical giants were somewhat ahead of the game. Lloyd told Porris that he had missed the point.

He did not want a cure, he wanted snake oil. There were armies of thinning men out there who needed BC just to give them the self-confidence to approach women – additionally armed, of course, with a few expensive drops of Sex Balm.

'Don't make me grovel, Lloyd. There's a woman downstairs who hasn't left her flat since the war, and she would almost certainly die in the blaze. You don't want that on your conscience, surely?'

'Kill her if you must, Owen.'

'What a gloomy old sod you've become. Any ideas on marketing your disease?'

'It isn't a disease. And no, I've thought of nothing practical. I'm vaguely worried about something Porris told me. About the original Tourraine. It seems the man turned into something of a Nazi, began spouting off about superior races and whatnot, killed his father, then himself, et cetera.'

'Now about this will of yours, Lloyd. I've been meaning to ask—'

'No suicidal instincts yet, thanks so much for your concern. But yesterday I burst into a pub and began ranting about America. In a negative way.'

'That puts you in the majority of pub-goers, in my experience. Why worry?'

'It's the wanting to murder "Chad" that has me concerned.'

'We could arrange for him to die in a freak fire at my place. Gas explosion, the lot.'

'Don't give me any ideas. I'll feel better after I speak to Nina.'

'Of course you will. Look, an extra fifty a week would just about do it.'

'Beg for it.'

'I am begging.'

'All right, Owen. Fifty a week it is.'

'Retroactively to the first of the year.'

126

'You are testing my patience.'

'Can you honestly say that I don't deserve it?'

Lloyd knew only too well that he could honestly say no such thing. 'Retroactive, then. And in return you will be my slave.'

'Done. You *are* a good man. Now I must be off. I'm trying to interest a quality Sunday in serializing my memoirs.'

'What an *excellent* idea, Owen. Goodbye.'

Lloyd put down the phone. To kill time he recited the first act of *Twelfth Night*. Having cheered himself with this diverting play, he reached out for the receiver. The telephone rang as he touched it.

Lloyd had been waiting weeks for this moment. His travelling schedule and Nina's, along with several failures of nerve, had conspired to keep them apart. When he heard her voice, assured and mirthful, he felt a fizzing in his belly reminiscent of pre-exam butterflies. He sat down in his swivelling armchair, covered the mouthpiece, cleared his throat, withdrew his palm, and uttered the words, 'Hello, Nina,' in the voice of a choirboy with tonsillitis.

'Are you there?' said Nina.

'Ahem, yes,' said Lloyd. 'I was just . . . cleaning the windows.' (Terrible pain shot through his body.) 'No, sorry, not, I was *not* cleaning the windows. I wish I had been cleaning the windows, but I was not.' The pain seeped away. 'No sense cleaning the windows in the rain, what? On the outside, especially, anyway . . .' Lloyd slammed his eyelids shut and bit his lower lip. He knew he could do it; he could engage Nina in conversation. Gathering his strength, he spoke. 'In Plymouth, were you?' He exhaled loudly with relief.

'Until this afternoon, yes. Coaxing an artist out of his tank.'

'I heard about him from Vic. Sir Ian's son, is he?'

'Nephew, yes. He's made a sculpture out of the materials

127

to hand. A monument to the Special Relationship. You're going to love this, Lloyd.'

'Oh?'

'I seem to recall your taking pleasure in the humiliation of the Royal Family.'

'They are involved?'

'Unless something goes terribly wrong, something is going to go terribly wrong on the Fourth of July.'

'I can't wait.'

'I've made my report to Chad. All systems go. The sculpture will be ready in time.'

The mention of the American's name made Lloyd's eyes bulge. He felt such pressure in his skull that his right ear popped. He had to remind himself that he was speaking to a person whom he adored.

'Can you have dinner with me tonight?'

'Tonight? I suppose so. Yes, of course.'

'I'll send a car for you.'

'There's no need for that, Lloyd, if you simply—'

'I insist. I'll be in the car too, of course.' It was so difficult, being in love. 'Eight o'clock?'

'Lovely,' said Nina.

Lloyd put down the telephone and performed an athletic war dance around his armchair, adding a fighter's shadow-boxing warm-up plus rope-skipping mime followed by frantic head-down arm-pumping running-in-place. Winded, he collapsed back into his chair.

Not since his late teens had Lloyd paid so much attention to his wardrobe. He donned, then hurriedly stripped off, a blazer-and-tie ensemble that *screamed* marriage proposal. His subsequent efforts to look natural nearly reduced him to tears of frustration: he looked by turns like a distant relative at a funeral; like an English tourist washed up unexpectedly on a Hawaiian surfing beach; like a Tanzanian game warden; like the father of a rebellious teenaged boy rummaging

128

nostalgically in his son's wardrobe; and most of all like a recently released long-term prison inmate unaccustomed to modern mufti. As time ran out, he settled on an open-necked, button-downed, khaki-trousered, loafered, unjacketed Fifties American movie-star get-up, and left it at that.

His hair, which had been so good to him recently, sprouting as it did from an electrified head, had decided not to cooperate. His hair sulked and would not be revivified even by severe brush-beating. When he had finished trying to make his hair look good the hair looked as if it had been around fifty circuits of a racetrack inside a sweaty crash helmet. Lloyd stripped and showered, started all over again, and finally tripped down his stairs to the waiting car looking exactly like someone who had spent three hours trying not to look as if he had spent three hours trying not to look tormented.

'Don't be an arsehole, don't be an arsehole,' Lloyd instructed himself, forgetting that there was no barrier between him and his chauffeur.

'Sorry, sir?' asked the suited driver, tensing his hands on the wheel.

'Oh, Christ, Jesus,' said Lloyd, further alienating the devout Brazilian Catholic in charge of the vehicle. A ceramic statue of Jesus the size of a rhesus monkey was affixed to his dashboard. 'Sorry, Christ, *arsehole*,' said Lloyd.

Thereafter the driver kept one eye in the mirror, while Lloyd continued to mumble blasphemous apologies and self-excoriation. He watched a soaked London pass by, deteriorating as its wealthier districts were left behind. To someone like Lloyd, anything west of Kensington or east of Mayfair was dangerous, filthy territory, inhabited by dole-fed layabouts and disorientated immigrants and IRA-sympathizing construction workers and . . . and Nina.

Lloyd's driver was not impressed by Nina's address. He opened Lloyd's door with two dainty fingers, as if his precious motor had been infected by the seedy atmosphere down an underdeveloped street. Nina's was the lower-ground-floor flat, and Lloyd had to sidestep orange rind and broken glass as he made his way down to her door: this was where the dustbins of the upstairs occupants were kept. Trying not to breathe through his nose, Lloyd made one last stab at his hair, then rang the doorbell. He wished he had asked Porris if his head might explode when he finally laid eyes on Nina, or if he might be expected to blurt out a semi-obscene list of the things he wanted to do to and with her during the short buildup to their wedding. It was too late now; Lloyd had committed himself.

The door opened, casting light into the rubbish tip that was Nina's outer vestibule.

'You must be Lloyd,' said Chad, extending a furry paw. He filled the doorway. Backlit, hulking, American Chad, silhouetted in Nina's light, a perfect set of teeth and a hand extended in greeting. A grey summer suit, an easy, athletic posture, a man who looked *at home*: here was Nemesis. 'Great to meet you.'

'How do you,' Lloyd heard himself say, 'so much about you.' He put out his hand, which was gripped and shaken like a Test-Your-Strength machine.

'Wanted to tell you what an *outstanding* job your sister is doing. Great to have her on the team.'

'Nice,' said Lloyd, still being shaken. He could scarcely see Chad in the darkness, and could not himself be clearly seen. 'Of you. To say. So.'

'Listen,' said Chad, hitting Lloyd extremely hard on his left shoulder, so hard that Lloyd had to put out his right hand and stabilize himself against the door frame. 'Listen.'

Lloyd listened, unaccustomed to being shorter than someone.

'I'm out of here. Have a *great* time, OK? See you soon, I hope, right?'

'Right,' said Lloyd, getting out of the way, pumping the

130

air effeminately with his sore left arm.

Chad ascended the ten steps in two muscular bounds, and was gone.

There, suddenly, was Nina, a hairbrush in her hand, apologizing, ' . . . drove me home, such a rush, terribly sweet actually . . .' Lloyd could not take his eyes off her lips. She seemed to him as beautiful as a woman could be. A great stack of Tourraine's memories fell upon him, raced across his consciousness, made the present into a sum of past parts.

'Aren't you going to kiss me?' Nina said, and for a terrible moment Lloyd thought he would throw his arms around her, lean her over to one side and plant the mother of all kisses on her English lips. When an English cheek was proffered instead, he recovered himself and delicately made a mouth-noise in the vicinity of her jaw, taking in a scent-memory of grass tennis courts and lemonade.

Nina wore jeans and a grey crew-neck jumper over a white cotton blouse, which meant two things to Lloyd: first, that she looked as fresh and pure as he had most fondly remembered; and second, that she had changed out of her office clothes in Chad's presence, in a very small flat, knowing and not minding that Lloyd would witness or deduce this event. Nina's enviable physique was such that even men who lived well down her street must have felt an eerie, telepathic arousal when she lifted her shirt over her head.

Lloyd had not yet spoken, nor did he choose to do so as he was ushered inside Nina's immaculate little bomb-shelter of an abode. She offered him a drink, which he declined by making steering-wheel gestures and nodding his head in the direction of his chauffeur upstairs. Nina put away the one object that was not obviously in its proper place – a tall glass that must recently have been raised to Chad's gung-ho American lips – and said she was ready to go.

'It isn't raining too hard, is it?' she asked.

Lloyd replied in the negative by frowning, shrugging his

shoulders, making Continental hand gestures indicating a merely annoying drizzle, as opposed to the insulting downpour one might have feared. He finished off this flurry of upper-limb and face movements with an open-palmed, pleading attitude and what he thought was probably a stupid-looking smile. They departed in silence.

The driver guided Nina into the back seat with an ungentlemanly look over his shoulder at Lloyd, which suggested that he had seen the previous tall, handsome fellow departing moments after sir's arrival. 'You are dating a prostitute, no?' said his look. 'I am not one to judge, but it is a filthy, immoral thing that you do.'

Doors slammed, a restaurant address given, and Nina's depressing neighbourhood was left behind. Nina was in a talkative mood, so that Lloyd could maintain his cringing silence and listen to the achingly true Englishness of his future wife's voice. Chad? *Chad?* He half wanted to wheel on Nina and instigate a premature lover's tiff on the issue of Chad's informal presence in her flat.

'. . . most insecure little man,' Nina was saying, in reference to her Plymouth artist. 'You wonder where people like that end up, don't you?'

Lloyd nodded energetically, used his hands again, tried to look secure and destined for predictability.

'It *is* good to see you,' said Nina, touching his knee. 'We haven't seen each other since – when, New Year's Eve?'

Lloyd nodded again. How well he remembered. One-fifteen on the first morning of a perilous-sounding New Year; Nina being paid attention to by an assortment of men; Lloyd apathetic; Owen explaining to all who would listen that this was going to be *his* year, the Year of the Hearn; Little Vic looking wistful at his side, clutching a tattered paperback to her bosom; old people's music from the Seventies. Owen had delivered an extended toast on the company's duty to see to it that Britain's sovereignty was not

132

dissolved like aspirin tablets in the water of Brussels – that had been his simile. There were patriotic cheers. There were suggestions that the war would be prolonged and nasty, which to this crowd meant only one thing: no foreseeable improvement in the London property market. The word 'recession' was bandied about between sips of champagne and bites of salmon pâté.

Lloyd knew that he had to speak, but he was frightened by the thought of what he might say. Close proximity to Nina had rendered him not simply mute with adoration, but in a similar frame of mind to that of his first days under the influence of Tourraine's Syndrome. He was afraid that if he opened his mouth he would recite the first paragraph of *Middlemarch*, which he had read on five occasions in five futile assaults on the novel. The other equally dreaded possibility was that he might say, 'Christ, Nina, I love you.'

'Christ, Nina,' said Lloyd, 'I—'

The driver braked hard at a red light, and apologized to his passengers.

'Yes, Lloyd?'

'I was just going to say that . . . that so much has happened. My goodness, a whole war, trips far and wide, me to South Africa, you to the States. It's a busy old life. Must slow down and take stock, don't you think?'

'I love it, actually,' said Nina. 'It's the best job I've ever had.'

'Is that true?'

'I know I joked about it in the beginning. But you would be surprised. Chad is surprisingly dedicated. He turns out not to be at all as I first saw him. He has great energy and spirit. Do you know that we met the President during the war? That's something to tell one's grandchildren about.'

Inside the restaurant, which specialized in rich sauces and naked flattery, Nina abruptly changed the subject.

'You didn't want to talk about my job and Chad, did you?' she said.

133

'Didn't I?' croaked Lloyd, his throat constricting, his butter knife clattering on the floor.

'I haven't known you all these years for nothing.'

'Haven't you?'

'I know I should have spoken to you sooner. We've both been so busy.'

'Yes.' Lloyd felt his fingers tensing around his empty wine-glass. He had not been prepared for so swift an understanding of love.

'Anyway, I don't think there's anything to worry about. Just another phase.'

'A phase?' Lloyd would not have called his unquestionable, overwhelming feelings a phase.

'Hasn't it always been that way?'

'Has it?' Lloyd thought that under the circumstances he would have remembered.

'The boy-next-door phase, the older-man phase, the headmaster phase, now this.'

Lloyd tried to digest Nina's remarks as he watched their waiter approach, an effete Frenchman whose sadistic brief was to expose the weaknesses in his customers' command of his native language. Screwing up his courage, and his newly renovated French, Lloyd launched into prolonged banter on various subjects including the war, the weather, the availability of snails, the relative inexpensiveness of Scottish salmon, the recession, the superiority of the French public-transport infrastructure and the beauty of Italian women. Nina, who spoke better French than Lloyd even without Tourraine's Syndrome, looked by turns horrified and impressed. When at last they ordered their food, she left the process entirely in Lloyd's hands.

'How can it be that I had no idea you spoke French?' she said, when the waiter had backed away.

'Just one of those things,' said Lloyd. 'One of my New Year's resolutions was to become more extroverted.' He just managed to stop himself from quoting Plethicus on the

134

subject of inhibitions as impediments to the enjoyment of life.

'Yes, but French?'

'A hidden talent.' Lloyd knew that he would have to confess to Tourraine's Syndrome sooner or later, and worried that he had come close to lying by keeping this news from Nina. 'Now, about this "phase" you were talking about? I'm not sure I understand.' Lloyd was certain that he did not understand at all.

'I know how close you are to Vic,' said Nina. 'And how you worry.'

Lloyd narrowed his eyes. 'What is it I should be worrying about?'

'I thought that was the whole . . . the whole point,' said Nina, looking at Lloyd sceptically.

'Remind me.'

'Just Vic's little . . . crush.'

'Vic has a crush. No – let me guess. A crush on—'

'Jean-Louis Parent, yes.'

'I beg your pardon? A Frenchman?' This was almost worse than Lloyd had feared. 'A *Frenchman*?'

'No need to worry. He's dead.'

'My sister has a crush on a *dead* Frenchman?'

'Let me explain. Jean-Louis Parent, the author.'

'Ah,' said Lloyd, his memory triggered at last. '*L'Amour et la Pitié*. Also the essay – what was it? – *Craignez Bien la Vie*?'

'I'm surprised you remember. Anyway, yes, she is infatuated with a dead French author-cum-philosopher and it is affecting her life and her work. I'm so sorry, I thought that was one of the reasons why you wanted to see me.'

'I had noticed a change,' said Lloyd. 'But I had no idea . . . do you think this is serious?'

'Absolutely,' said Nina. 'And healthy. You've known us both for ever, haven't you? And you've seen how – no, I shouldn't say that.'

'Go on.'

'You've seen the dearth of men.'

'The dearth of men? You must be joking. You're both—' Now hang on a minute, Lloyd said to himself. This was not the conversation he had expected. This was counter-productive.

'All I meant to say,' said Nina, 'is that you ought to prefer Vic's fantasy to the real thing directed at someone . . . unsuitable.'

Chad, thought Lloyd, biting his lip to prevent himself from speaking the man's name aloud. 'I'm not sure I know whom you mean.'

'*Whom* I mean?'

'Yes.'

'No, that can't be right. Grammatically.'

'I'm afraid it is. I'm not sure I know *whom* you mean.' This came automatically to Lloyd. This was the sort of benefit he had hoped to derive from Tourraine's Syndrome. He was a well-spoken man, when he could speak at all.

'I meant Chad Peele. I'm sure you suspected that. You have your spies, after all.'

'I suppose the possibility had crossed my mind.' Lloyd hated being diverted on to this subject. His duties to Little Vic had their limits. Her involvement with Chad, no matter how appalling, was not something even the most paternally inclined older brother could influence her to abandon. 'Why on earth would you call Chad unsuitable?' Lloyd asked, cheerfully.

'His father is a murderer, for a start.'

'The Governor? That is one interpretation.' The newspaper photographs were increasingly gruesome: Claudia Brown, seven months pregnant, staring disdainfully at the camera; Governor Peele, refusing to budge. Reports suggested that he was relying on Supreme Court intervention, which would allow him to throw up his hands and blame the bleeding hearts in Washington if Claudia and her foetus were allowed to survive. 'What does Chad have to say about it?'

136

'I think he's sickened by the whole thing. He agrees with his father in principle – there's unsuitability for you – but regrets the practical matter of having to . . . *dispose* of these people so publicly.'

'I'm not worried,' said Lloyd. 'About Little Vic, that is.' Lloyd felt so relieved that it was not Nina who pined after Chad that he could almost visualize a happy life as the American's brother-in-law.

Their first course arrived with a flurry of knife-and-fork replacement and the subalterns' simultaneous whisking-away of silver plate-covers.

'Enough about Little Vic,' said Lloyd. 'Christ, this is delicious. I wanted to talk about something else.' The first glass of wine had untied his tongue. 'I've done a lot of thinking, recently. It's hard to explain to you, but it's as if . . . as if my life had passed before my eyes. A function of age, no doubt.'

'Don't be silly.'

'You'll see,' said Lloyd. 'A time comes when there are certain priorities to be addressed.'

'I feel that way already.'

'Oh, good,' said Lloyd. 'Perhaps you will know what I mean, then, when I say that one is prone to *regret*, at a certain stage.'

'Sometimes.'

'And that one is tempted to explore such experiences as are still within one's grasp.'

'Absolutely.'

Lloyd thought this part of the conversation was going perfectly, just as he had subconsciously rehearsed it; encouraging also that Nina's answers were so far almost exactly what he would have scripted – provocative, flirtatious, expectant.

'And that some of these – shall we say – *missed opportunities* are of such a magnitude that one's life could be irrevocably altered, rendered inconsequential, even, without reversing courses and playing out the life that fate had intended.'

'Sorry,' said Nina. 'Say that again?'

'Just that it's possible not to make the mistake of thinking that happiness is irretrievable, simply because one has taken a path leading to a *cul de sac*.'

'I think I know what you mean. This sort of thing has been on my mind. It occurred to me not long ago – at dinner with that – well, you don't know him. It occurred to me that I had been missing the point, in many respects. Hesitating to admit to myself . . .'

Nina raised her eyes to Lloyd's. He dabbed quickly at his face with his napkin on the off chance that a shred of cold langoustine might be dangling unhappily from his lip. Nina's look in itself amounted to a moving experience to the hyper-sensitive Lloyd James. When she grinned, a sideways grin full of warmth and familiarity, Lloyd had to look down and busy himself with what remained of his food.

'I think we understand each other, Lloyd,' she said. 'Amazing that we should have become preoccupied with the issue at the same time.'

'Amazing,' Lloyd pretended to agree, looking up again. He did not have the courage to broach the point explicitly, so he left it in Nina's court. 'Tell me', he said, 'how these feelings manifest themselves?'

Nina sat up straight, looked up at the ceiling, smiled again. 'You certainly sound odd,' she said, looking down again and settling her confident gaze upon him.

'Oh?' he said. 'In what way?'

'Dependent clauses, mainly. And you have been addressing yourself to issues of unusual . . .'

'Of unusual?'

'Of unusual *moment*. In my opinion. I have to say I think you've put me on the spot.'

'Perhaps I have,' said Lloyd, with eyebrow-work.

'I don't mind. I'm happy to tell the truth.'

138

Lloyd, who could *only* tell the truth, made his hands say, 'Go on.'

'One carries on,' said Nina, 'one wonders, one fears. And a point comes when one feels that the truth has a kind of momentum of its own. The truth speaks, if you follow.'

'Oh, yes,' said Lloyd, who had begun to feel his life wheeling into its rightful trajectory.

'This has happened to me, I believe.'

'Has it?'

'I think so. I got terribly drunk a little while ago. I had what I suppose you would call an epiphany.'

'God.'

'Not exactly. Just a face, if that's comprehensible. A feeling. A notion. Very much along the lines of what you have been describing.'

'I see.'

'I feel uncomfortable telling you this,' she said.

'Of course you do.'

'It isn't right to discuss these things.'

'Oh, do try.'

Nina sipped her wine. 'You're right. Why not?'

'Why not indeed?' Lloyd gulped his wine excitedly.

'I'll try.' She looked shyly down at her empty plate. 'It isn't easy, with you.'

'With me?' said Lloyd, with a bashful hand to his chest.

'It just feels . . .'

Please say *incestuous*, thought Lloyd.

'*Incestuous*,' said Nina. 'We've known each other so long.'

'Indeed we have,' said Lloyd, gesturing over Nina's shoulder for more wine.

'All of us,' said Nina.

'All of us?' asked Lloyd, as the wine arrived and was poured.

'You know,' said Nina. 'You, me—'

'Of course—'

'Little Vic—'

139

'Yes—'

'Owen . . .'

Lloyd saw her pause. 'Owen?'

Nina beamed. 'Hilarious, isn't it?'

Lloyd laughed.

'I mean,' she said. '*Owen?*'

Lloyd laughed like someone struck in the thigh by a poisoned arrow.

'I know,' said Nina. 'It's just too funny. I can't help it.'

Lloyd continued to laugh, less like the poisoned-arrow victim now than the wheezing drunk reminded of his wife's long-term infidelity.

'You'll think it's crazy, I know,' Nina said. 'You'll say "*Owen?*" '

'O-ho-*ho*-en?'

'Right, OK. No need for ridicule. These things aren't conscious decisions.'

'No-ho-ho, they're not,' laughed Lloyd.

Sea bass in red pepper sauce had arrived on the one hand, turbot on the other. Lloyd got a grip of himself. He inspected Nina and saw an excited young woman, blonder than he had remembered, her hair drawn back, her lips pursed at one corner in ironic appreciation of the admission she had made.

Lloyd told himself not to panic, not to weep, not to rush out into the night, ignore the chauffeur as he hailed a taxi, track down his former friend and business associate and gouge out his eyes with a pair of scissors. Fair was fair. He told himself to welcome the competition. Did Owen know *Coriolanus* by heart? No, he certainly did not. Did Owen have an almost complete knowledge of the English dictionary through to the letter F? Again, no. Did Owen have even the vaguest conception of who Darius McLeod was? It was a laughable idea that he might.

'All of this reminds me of something Darius McLeod once wrote,' said Lloyd, regaining his confidence.

140

'Who?'

'Old Darius McLeod, the poet and inventor. Born 1876, died 1976, on the day before his hundredth birthday. A particular favourite of my father's.'

'What did he write?'

'He wrote, "Pity the farmer, sopping his stew, Or at least you must say that you do, For it might have been you." '

'Two things,' said Nina.

'Yes?'

'First, that's abysmal. Second, what does it have to do with this conversation?'

Evidently, Lloyd's first attempt to use Tourraine's Syndrome to his advantage had been less than successful. He fought on.

'Don't denigrate Darius McLeod. He was full of wisdom, earthy though it might have been. I was named after the second syllable of his surname. And in this case I believe he is offering us a variant of the "grass-is-always-greener" cliché. At the moment, it cheers you to think that time spent in Owen's company might be well spent, or you fear that you might later regret not having got to know such a . . . *colourful* figure better, while the objective observer will be wondering why you bother, how long it could possibly last, whether you had lost your mind, et cetera.'

'You sound so strange.'

'Sorry, Nina. I don't mean to. It's been so long since we last met. All this thinking I've been doing . . .' Lloyd was acutely aware of the need not to show his hand. To break down now in a confession of love would serve only to put Nina off – or such was Lloyd's reading of the reputed nature of women. ' . . . It was Darius McLeod again who said—'

'Lloyd, please. You aren't eating your fish. Have some more wine. You look pale.'

'Do I?'

'You've been working too hard.'

'Perhaps,' said Lloyd, mentally adding up the gruelling six

or eight hours of paperwork he had managed over the past four days. 'Must get Owen to contribute more,' he added, reminded bitterly of his capitulation when Owen had asked for a pay rise.

With more wine working its way through his system, the component of love that is sexual had begun to loom large in Lloyd's overactive brain. If he had ever doubted the motivating power of sexual desire – its ability to drive people to murder, or worse – he doubted it no longer. He felt as if his tactile memory had grown as supernaturally sharp as the rest – that he could still feel the powdery-smooth curve of Nina's—

'Lloyd?'

'Sorry, yes?'

'You're miles away. I haven't . . . *distressed* you?'

'Pah!' said Lloyd, drawing the attention of three waiters and four fellow diners.

The visible parts of Nina's body were exerting as much pressure on Lloyd's tender loins as the memory of her invisible ones. His thoughts were indecent. A darker side of his condition had presented itself: he felt lustful and murderous, in that order. Had it been remotely within his power to do so gracefully, Lloyd would have liked to grasp Nina forcefully by the wrist, drag her out to the idling car, instruct the driver to leave the heater on and piss off, then 'take' Nina or 'have' Nina – whatever more brutally seductive nationalities called it – on the back seat. Then, during her inevitable *petit mort*, he would drive to Owen's miserable over-mortgaged flat, and kill him in a novel way that the police would later call the most agonizingly slow death they had seen in all their combined hundred years of service. Nina would awaken shortly afterwards, unaware that the car had moved, and provide him with the alibi that he had seen her through several hours of continuous and unprecedented orgasm.

While Lloyd's mind considered these desperate alternatives to civilized behaviour, Nina spoke of CYSR's tribulations.

142

Most of their projects had been cancelled or postponed indefinitely. There was pressure from the British government on the CYSR Committee to see to it that the Special Relationship was not made to appear *overridingly* special, not with the dreaded United States of Europe blinking like a lighthouse from across the Channel – not that anyone expected too much publicity to be spared on the matter. The US government rarely answered its telephone. All in all, CYSR looked set to fade out of existence around the middle of the year, having done little more than to pay its minuscule salaries to the headquarters team and stipends to the elusive Committee members. Nina said that, although this would appear to reflect badly on her performance as public relations coordinator, she felt that the Special Relationship would be getting what it deserved.

Lloyd listened to Nina's monologue with a fixed smile and several dozen haphazard nods. He loved her so much. His disappointment, his anger, his envy – these were huge. He just had to get through the rest of the evening without betraying these feelings, without losing his temper. If he were going to behave recklessly, he wanted to do so only after careful premeditation.

Already he could feel his crime of passion in his hands – Owen's trachea giving under the pressure of his gloved thumbs, wiping the scene clear of fingerprints, a mad dash through the rain to the bus stop, an anonymous getaway. Then the funeral, one firm arm around Nina's shoulders, the other around Little Vic's. Lloyd and his grieving women. All would be clear to Nina when her mourning ended. Her illusions would necessarily drop away, the memory of Owen would reveal him as an irresponsible parasite, and a true love would rear up to confront her.

Lloyd went through the motions of wrapping up their friendly date – paying the enormous bill, hissing Nina's address to the driver, declining an invitation to come inside that Nina had not quite given, kissing her cheek with monk-like chasteness – all with the disinterested cool of the raving sociopath. Glumly did he slump in the dark back seat, reading his chauffeur's mind: 'So, my friend, even the sleazy *whores*, they will not sleep with you, I am right?' Once home, he tipped the driver so lavishly that, despite himself, the man asked if sir had intended such excess. He dragged his aching skeleton into its home, urinated sitting down with a dead look on his face, thought more seriously than ever in his life about suicide (a mere blink of thought), and brewed himself a cup of tea. He took his cup into his office and stared down at the appointments diary open on the desk. With his free hand he flipped over pages full of dinners, deadlines, travel, lunches, birthdays, holidays, meetings, more travel – almost every entry indicating contact with Owen.

Owen! Owen 'Five Killed, Some Seriously' Hearn! He recalled the first time he had met him, a dry November evening in London when both were boastful Oxford lads in town for the weekend to impress girls. Lloyd had sized up Owen as the sort who would negotiate university in magnificent style, then fade into hopelessness and oblivion – barring a freak success in fiction writing. Owen had regaled this particular party with tales of his cricketing prowess, a poem called 'Owen at the Crease' that included the stanzas,

> The captain never fears a duck,
> Despite the bowler's quick release,
> Nor puts his fortunes down to luck,
> When Owen's at the crease.

> The wicket-keeper takes a nap,
> The third man rubs his knees,
> The slips don't really give a crap—
> When Owen's at the crease.

> Then willow meets ball inevitably,
> As easy as you please,

144

And bounds out irretrievably,
When Owen's at the crease.

The game is slow and the weather's bad,
And England's near decease,
But the ball's still bowled to bat and pad,
When Owen's at the crease . . .

When Lloyd got to know Owen better, he was not surprised to learn that he had never played cricket in his life. He had several other self-congratulatory bits of doggerel shelved away in his social repertoire. He seemed, at first, just the tolerable side of vulgar. Lloyd warmed to him when he discovered how easy it was to find oneself in the company of eager girls when Owen put his mind to such a project. Only now, with Nina's confession still pounding in his ears, did Lloyd admit to himself how attractive Owen had always been. But was it really possible that Nina could ignore Owen's obvious professional failings, his chronic poverty, his – why not say it – his *class*? Women were not supposed to be romantically flexible beyond the parameters of wealth and at least rudimentary hygiene. They did not, in other words, decide to run away with the gardener.

It was with such uncharitable thoughts that Lloyd dozed off in his armchair, waking seconds later when his cup of tea spilled into his lap. Cursing, he stripped off his clothes, padded down the echoing corridor, and threw himself face-down on to his lonely troglodyte's bed.

CHAPTER SIX

'I'm surprised they don't want a full-scale re-creation of the Blitz,' said Little Vic. She had just been on the phone with Washington for the first time – Chad being out of the office, Nina out for lunch – with a CYSR liaison man named Bart Forrest. Bart was a twenty-seven-year-old civil servant, but sounded like a film producer. He asked about budgets and below-the-line costs and production values and, repeatedly, helium balloons.

'Are there *balloons* in England?' he'd asked. 'We're gonna need a billion balloons.'

Little Vic, who was more numerate than Bart, said that a billion balloons was, for all practical purposes, a billion balloons too many. 'Let us take care of the balloons, Bart,' she had said. 'There will be plenty of balloons. Just, oh, *trillions* of them.'

'A trillion red, a trillion white, a trillion blue,' said Bart.

'Give or take,' said Little Vic.

'I'm so excited,' said Bart. 'I'll be there even if I have to pay my own way. Chad Peele around?'

'No, Chad is in Paris, placating the French. Telling them how much you lot owed to Lafayette.'

'Has he got the Germans covered? We really don't want to make the Germans angry.'

'Quite,' said Little Vic. 'Look what happens when you make them angry.' Little Vic had been fantasizing throughout this conversation that she was Prime Minister and Bart was the President.

'I'm concerned', said Bart, all sincerity, 'that the Goodwill Parade might have international repercussions. This is what I am hearing.'

'You are hearing this?' said Little Vic, her feet crossed on her desk, her new cigarette-holder clenched between her teeth at a Rooseveltian attitude.

'If I've learned anything,' Bart confided, 'it's that you don't mess with the international, uhm, status quo.'

'How right you are,' said Little Vic, to a minor representative of a government that had recently sent half a million troops halfway around the world and rained destruction incessantly on a country whose borders had been gerrymandered by foreign powers only two generations ago. 'Mustn't do anything destabilizing.'

'I'm so glad we see eye to eye on this,' said Bart, wildly inflating their respective influences on world events. 'See you on the Fourth of July, I hope. Have a nice day.' Thus did Bart Forrest cheerfully ring off.

In her Prime Minister fantasy, Little Vic saw herself imposing economic sanctions against the United States, allying herself with France – and its handsome intellectuals – against the rest of the world, razing Brighton to the ground, drawing and quartering the Duke of Westminster, moving the capital to Bermuda, banning chocolate, exposing racists to the elements on the slopes of Ben Nevis, closing all-boys prep schools, abolishing bobbies' ludicrous headgear, proclaiming the Lake District off-limits to tourists, reducing television broadcasting output to one station two hours per day, hanging those who would bring back the rope, aborting those who would oppose abortion.

This random chain of thought reminded her of the imprisoned murderer, Claudia Brown. It occurred to her that she was in a position to become *engagé*, where Claudia was concerned. A persuasive word in Chad's ear might prompt him to confront his evil father with modern reason. This course of action was not nearly so dramatic as some of the adventures of Jean-Louis Parent's 'M', but in the absence of twelve-year-old boys to seduce it was the best she thought she could do.

When Chad returned from France in the late afternoon, he was diligent enough to make an appearance at the office. He was understandably unprepared for the outburst he encountered from his most junior member of staff. Interspersed between her routine reports of a conversation with Bart Forrest, of a brand-new Goodwill Parade itinerary, of her lack of success in persuading Kensington Palace to consider releasing the Princess of Wales on the Fourth of July, were calls for his father to address his conscience on the issue of Claudia Brown, for him to show mercy, for him to act for once in a selfless, humanitarian way, for him to bloody well *relent*.

'My father', said Chad, rather smoothly for someone Little Vic had always taken to be a helium-headed golfer, 'answers to the people of his state, and has acted at all times within the law. And might I add', said Chad, with unanswerable poise and authority, 'that I do not consider it polite or professional of you to raise this subject in the office.' Chad had loosened his tie and looked as exhausted as it was possible for a rich, clean-living health-worshipper to look. 'Also, and thank you for asking, I think the French initiative went frightfully well.'

Just like all Americans in London, thought Little Vic. A few months in the country and they said 'frightfully well' in the same breath as 'Have a nice day'.

'Smashing,' said Little Vic. 'Have a nice day.' She collected her belongings and made for the door, writing off another wasted spell at the office.

Lloyd amazed himself with his calm. Since his evening with Nina he had spoken to Owen three times, and not once had he even hinted at the subject that preoccupied him as if he were wrapped in the tentacles of a giant octopus. One of the reasons for his restraint was that he had convinced himself that in no way could Owen be said to be responsible. Even if Lloyd later decided that he had to murder his friend, he would certainly apologize first and explain that there were no hard feelings on his side of the equation. His plan for the moment was to soldier on, to observe the scene, to play his cards only when he could be certain that the odds were in his favour.

One annoying possibility, Lloyd had come to realize, was that he might be completely insane. It was possible, he thought, that Dr Porris had misdiagnosed his Tourraine's Syndrome, when routine nervous exhaustion was a more likely cause of his recent behaviour. It was even possible that Porris had deliberately invented Tourraine's Syndrome in order to spare his friend the news that he had lost, rather than regained, his mind.

Lloyd was no stranger to insanity, but as far as he knew he had never seen it from the inside looking out. Lloyd's mother was psychotic. She was psychotic in a way that allowed her to function – loudly, recklessly, frighteningly – and even to have remarried after her husband was shot by a deer. Her brand of unbalance manifested itself mainly in binges of verbal abuse, which she had heaped upon her husband and children with almost menstrual regularity. One moment she would have been describing an outing with a friend; the next, fulminating at one or another of the closest people in the world to her, absolutely raving. She was a sad woman, a misfit, and society had spent a great deal of effort

149

and money trying to ease her way through life.

The likely answers were that she had suffered as a child, that she was allergic to alcohol, that her rages were mere ventings of invisible pressures. Lloyd simplified these conjectures by telling himself that she was simply *mad*. To say, 'My mother? Oh, she's *mad*,' was both correct and socially acceptable, even among strangers.

Lloyd's mother had always looked mad, especially as a young woman. At thirty she had long grey hair. When Little Vic was old enough to understand, her mother had claimed her hair had turned white during labour. Mad or not, she was a hateful woman. Lloyd considered it one of the triumphs of his life that he no longer communicated with her except by telephone. He felt no sympathy, no love, no pity. It was as if his mother did not exist, except in his maddening genes.

Lloyd consulted a full-length mirror to see if he looked mad. He thought not – clenching and unclenching his fists, reciting Plethicus in the original, steam rising from his scalp. He thought he looked wonderful – a tall, pale Englishman, a man whose name was ever rectitude. A tall, pale Englishman with a good head of steaming brown hair and a strong belief in the glory of his small, damp nation. A man whose first contact with the outside world each morning was the brassy scrape of the *Daily Telegraph* through his letterbox. A man familiar with the burly world of commerce. A property owner. A self-made Englishman. A man who stared clear-eyed and stiff-lipped into a future of inevitable sorrows and compromises, of betrayal and disappointment, of decline and death . . .

'Now hang on one tiny little second,' said Lloyd, aloud. He had caught himself being introspective and, worse, pessimistic. This simply would not do. Tall, pale Englishmen did not address the larger issues: they bought houses in the country; they joined clubs; they snapped open newspapers and drenched themselves in the misfortunes of uncivilized, non-British countries; they married women exactly like Nina and popped on the blinkers in the expectation of sprogs to come; they purchased half-moon glasses so as to stare with good-humoured disdain at those who would doubt the perfection and fundamental *righteousness* of their lives.

Lloyd amazed himself with his calm.

Having worked quite hard for several weeks, Nina suddenly found herself with time on her hands. The few remaining CYSR projects, including *Caesar* itself, were progressing under their own inertia. Chad had flown unexpectedly to Norway, where a functionary of some kind had got wind of the repeated use of the word 'quisling' in a CYSR document having to do with Neville Chamberlain. Evidently chamberlain with a small 'c' had not entered the Norwegian language, and there were those who were resentful. It was a small matter, but Chad had shown himself to be surprisingly thorough. Little Vic had scraped together enough money to escape the May drizzle; she had flown out of Heathrow – that much she had divulged – to a secret, sunny destination, there to exercise her existentialism.

As a practical woman, Nina spent her afternoons at the office trying to plan her short-term future. CYSR would evaporate within months. Public relations had stagnated, along with most other sectors of the London economy. Where her friends and acquaintances in the field had only months ago spoken of nothing but success and ambition, now they were likely to dwell on retrenchment and belt-tightening. Ahead lay the dispiriting routine of CV-broadcasting, of interviews, of choosing a job that might, for all Nina knew, be for life. Nina's pragmatic attitude ensured that she never dwelt on fantasy; she never pretended that life might have more in store for her than a gradual progression of relatively solid employment – interrupted, no doubt, by the dubious joy of offspring. She

151

believed that it was safe and mature to recognize her limitations, and that to indulge dreams – the way Little Vic seemed to do – was a recipe for disappointment. At the same time she found it depressing that, at twenty-five, her most fabulous dreams were of a larger flat, an easier commute, a comfortable reading chair and a washing machine. Only a year ago she would have dreamt of travel, of carnality in the arms of Spanish tennis professionals, of the tantalizing possibilities of *abroad*. Thanks to her upbringing and languages she was worldly enough to be among the few who could successfully emigrate, and a wide-open Europe beckoned; yet to abandon England and her friends was now unthinkable. It occurred to her that if everyone she knew in London who dreamt of leaving were actually to do so, Britain would rise out of the water like an inflatable raft.

With most of the men in her life queuing up to propose to her, Nina had grown accustomed to thinking through the various alternatives they provided. Someone like Chad – who had not yet proposed but could probably be prompted to do so after one brutal set of tennis – would drag her to America and install her as a socialite among people Nina considered philistine barbarians. She would play tennis every day, she would refuse to become pregnant, she would divorce him, she would be rich and she would be ashamed. European men would adore her until the ring was on her finger, then they would beat her and belittle her and betray her. Englishmen, on the whole, would treat her like a nanny until, after she gave birth, she actually *was* a nanny.

It was this general train of thought that had led Nina to consider Owen in a new light. For all his desperation, Owen was an individualist, a spirited *bon viveur*, a man who was not afraid to have fun for fun's sake. The idea of marrying Owen was a joke, of course – no sensible woman would make that mistake. In her conversation with Lloyd she had only meant to suggest that Owen would be a good date, a reasonably exciting boyfriend, fun in bed – and that he had been spending an inordinate amount of time with Little Vic. Why, then, had Lloyd turned pale at the suggestion, why had he begun to quote atrocious poetry, why had he sulked all the way home, why had he not been the same old Lloyd she had known and loved since she was five years old?

Nina was no fool.

Lloyd sat across from Owen in a Mayfair hotel bar, awaiting the arrival of their most prized British customer. Paul Nichols – iconoclast, East-End-boy-made-good, escorter of his betters' daughters – Paul Nichols loved his Sex Balm. His word of mouth alone had accounted for two-thirds of Lloyd's domestic orders.

Paul Nichols was Owen's idol. Built like a bantam-weight, always nervously chewing gum, wearing a working man's annual wages on his back, a voice like barbed wire – Nichols was the acceptable face of *flash*. London had thrown up dozens of these figures during the past decade, but none, in Owen's view, combined the characteristics of class-busting style with such impeccable *élan*. Paul Nichols was said to be worth fifty million pounds.

'Cor,' said Owen, practising his vocabulary for their meeting, 'is he *rich*.'

'That', said Lloyd, 'is undeniable.'

'It could have been me,' said Owen. 'Paul and I, we're the same age.'

'You wasted years on education. Paul hit the streets at sixteen and never had a year in the red.'

'He's sharp as a bloody spear, isn't he?' said Owen. 'Imagine being 'im.'

'Please, Owen. Put your aitches back on. It's unseemly.'

'Imagine being *him*, then,' said Owen. 'You're as jealous as I am. The helicopter. The *houses*. The Christ-almighty bloody *lucre* of the man. My *God. Shit*,' said Owen, who had begun to sweat. 'The man is a *nation state*, Lloyd. Bristling with cash, in *these* times. His Regent's Park home', said

153

Owen, sounding like one of the Sunday magazine features he had disqualified himself from writing, 'is festooned with priceless art.'

'Festooned? As in decorated with a chain of flowers, ribbons, et cetera, suspended in loops or garlands?'

'Bloody *right*,' said Owen. 'Our Paul is a *collector*.'

'Our Paul', said Lloyd, his knuckles white on the leather armrests of his chair, 'is a jumped-up barrow boy in Italian suits. Accidentally cash-rich. An asset to society, perhaps. A one-off, certainly. An "art collector" most definitely. If you want to see some cruddy old Van Gogh sketches, you ought to drop by Paul's place.'

'Van Gogh? My *God*.'

'Yes, hideous. All a pretence, Owen. Pretence of pretences.'

'You quoting again?'

'Only vaguely.'

'The man is stinking, filthy, just *pulsatingly* fucking *loaded*,' Owen exclaimed. 'Jesus *God*, fuck me, *rich*!'

'Owen?'

'Sorry, yes?'

'There are others in the bar.'

Owen looked around.

'I'll keep my voice down. *Fuck*.'

'Shh.'

Owen leaned forward. 'We've discussed this endlessly, I know,' he said. 'I'm sorry to be so repetitive. And I understand that you think it's *déclassé* to go on about this sort of thing, but you would, wouldn't you? I'm not embarrassed. I'm not riddled with class anxiety. I know where I stand. I'd rather have fifty, forty, twenty, ten, two, half a million than anything less. Money, money, money, Lloyd. Just give it to me and I promise I'll shut up.'

'You've been saying that for some time—'

'Of course I have.'

'— while our Paul's been out there *making it*.'

'Oh, you're cruel.'

'He's thirty-five. He's worked seven days a week, twenty hours a day, for twenty years. Let's say realistically he's earned twenty million pounds. That's, hang on—' Lloyd made the calculations on his napkin. 'That's one hundred and thirty-seven pounds per hour if he's *really* made twenty million. Not substantially more than *you* earn, given the laxity of our corporate culture.'

'Balls.'

'If you start now, you'll be as rich as he is when you're fifty-five, having laboured sweatily away the central years of your adult life. Then you could retire to your bloody Van Goghs.'

'You are an élitist, Lloyd. You don't think Nichols knows, appreciates art.'

'I think Nichols knows art appreciates.'

Paul Nichols never appeared unexpectedly; a force-field of heightened expectation always preceded him. Lloyd and Owen fingered their ties and smoothed their hair when the wealth-wind began to blow, signalled by wide-eyed waiters and the bustle of assistant managers. Through the swinging doors he came, tiny and bristling, seeming to wave at an imaginary audience. He had grown a weedy, unattractive moustache. His shoes were as bright as Rolls-Royce mud-guards. His false teeth shone like ice cubes in the dim bar light. With a child's quick steps he approached his suppliers' table.

'And how are my lads?' he said, a hand on each of their shoulders. They had only half-stood before Paul Nichols was upon them. Psychokinetically, he caused them to sit down again. A snap of his fingers later, a bottle of champagne had arrived. Goons took to the corners of the room. Extra waiters had gathered to fawn. Through the bar's curtains, the gleaming side of a gigantic idling car could be seen. 'Don't have long,' said Paul, hopping up on to a farting leather cushion, followed by a great deal of now *faux*

155

Cockney banter designed to put Owen at his ease and Lloyd off his guard.

'So nice to—' Lloyd began.

'All right, mate?' finished Owen, his eye-whites huge.

'Just off the bloody Concorde, aren't I?' asked Paul, rhetorically.

For Lloyd, the conversation had come to an end. He was incapable of mateyness. The possibility that Mr Nichols might soon write him a cheque for thirty thousand pounds kept him glued to his armchair.

'Cor,' said Mr Nichols, sipping his champagne, ratifying Owen's rehearsal of the word. 'Blimey.'

Lloyd felt his face go red, felt his fingers pinching through the leather. He thought he would gag if he drank from his glass.

'Go on, then,' said Paul, gesturing at Lloyd's champagne with a beringed finger. 'Get it down you, my son.'

Lloyd sipped at his glass as if it contained hot tea.

'Last time, right?' said Paul. 'Right, last time? Cor.'

'Bloody 'ell,' agreed Owen, inanely, reaching out to pat Paul fraternally on the shoulder, reconsidering just in time.

'Sex Balm,' said Paul, which he pronounced 'Sex ball 'em.'

Paul Nichols wore a beautiful suit. Paul Nichols sported a fresh manicure. Paul Nichols called women 'Fionas'.

'You lads fancy a piss-up?' asked Paul, expansively. 'I want to order a year's supply. Won't be seeing each other for a while, I expect.'

Owen searched visibly for a streetwise way of saying 'Yes,' and landed on 'Do we look *stupid*? Eh?'

Lloyd tried not to let his exasperation show as the bar tab was mysteriously paid, as he was bundled into a Rolls-Royce next to the most sexual woman he had ever seen, as he was whisked northwards to the Paul Nichols residence. Again he tried to conceal his rage as he was cursorily introduced to Paul's friends, his Fionas, his art. Thirty minutes of revelry

156

had elapsed when he handed Owen the Sex Balm-laden briefcase and announced that he had to leave. He knew he would not be missed.

He walked towards Marble Arch without attempting to hail a taxi. He was almost mugged along the way by a prematurely white-haired individual who wanted Lloyd's watch and wielded a knife.

'Your watch. Hurry, you bastard,' said the individual.

'Right you are,' said Lloyd. 'Not a problem.' He put up his hands in a gesture of surrender. He fixed the robber's gaze hypnotically with his own. He reached over with his right hand towards his left wrist. He placed the nail of his index finger against the clasp of the watchband. With an intake of breath he flung out a fist and caught the robber on the bridge of his nose. Dancing to his right, away from the knife, he struck out again with his left, then his right, then found himself kicking at a supine body. He stepped on the robber's wrist and disabused him of his knife. Laughing, he tossed the knife down the street and kicked the robber in the neck with gratuitous force.

'Sorry,' he said, still laughing. 'I suppose I could have killed you.'

Little Vic stood naked at the edge of the sea. How pleased she was that half a day's journey had seen her to this peaceful spot, alone beneath the aftermath of a North African sunset. How enlivening was the warm sea-breeze on her body. How unique and privileged she felt to stand alone beneath the painted sky, her back proudly arched, her hair swept back in the breeze, her toes lapped by ancient waters, her nipples pointing heavenward, her eyes almost certainly gleaming.

This, surely, was *living*. What could be more different from her ordinary routine than to be exposed to the elements, to be untraceable, to be anonymously, nakedly visible beneath the vaulted—

There was a camel coming down the beach, led by a man.

Little Vic held her pose, strained her eyes to keep tabs on the man and his camel's progress without turning her head from the horizon. The sea made hydraulic noises at her feet. Her shoulders and face felt burned from the hour's sun they had seen. She willed the man and the camel to go away; they came closer. She wondered what language people spoke in this country – something she had forgotten to find out, in her haste to leave 'M'-like footprints on the deserted beach. A prehistoric fishing boat appeared in the distance, its triangle of cloth sail gleaming like a tooth against the blackening sea.

Wishing to remain as 'M'-like as possible, knowing that 'M' would submit to rape rather than allow the world outside her own awareness to interfere with her sipping the drops from the celestial cistern, Little Vic did not move. She stood with her hands just brushing her hip bones, her elbows slightly turned out, her head back. The man and the camel approached. Little Vic did not even allow herself to think that her clothes, bag, passport and cash lay fifty metres behind her on the beach. She forced herself to ignore the camel and the man. If he touched her she would gouge out his eyes with her 'M'-like fingernails. She tensed her body, half closed her eyes, prepared to spring, heard the camel fart – she was almost certain it was the camel.

Statue-like, Little Vic awaited her destiny. If this was not dangerous, if this was not a spit in the face of absurdity, if this was not right out of *L'Amour et la Pitié*, then Little Vic didn't know her Jean-Louis Parent. The breeze had died to a whisper. The sea sucked at her toes. Her breasts, never before exposed to the sun, had turned a different shade of pink from the rest of her English flesh.

She heard man and camel pause. They must have been only a few feet away. She could hear the settling-leather creak of the camel's pack. One of them farted again, which almost broke Little Vic's spell. She heard them move, and, despite not wanting to care one way or the other, she hoped they were going away without stealing her worldly posses-

158

sions. Proud that she had stared down what could have been a ghastly fate, Little Vic glared triumphantly at the horizon. The fishing boat had sailed closer, so that she could see the two bare-chested men on board. She tossed her head and flared a nostril.

Little Vic then heard a splashing sound that could not be explained by the wavelets slopping at her toes. The man had steered his camel into the sea, and had begun to move into her field of vision. It occurred to Little Vic, with a very un-'M'-like twinge of sympathy, that the man might be concerned about her welfare, or at the very least that she had broken a religious code so strict and medieval that man and camel would have to go home and blind themselves with hot pokers.

Man and camel circled round her, the man hunched and fearful, the camel depressed and uninterested. The man had a sun-yellowed sack slung over one shoulder and a moustache above his blackened teeth. His feet were bare. Little Vic caught herself wondering what, in her own world, would constitute as unusual a sight as she did for the camel driver: a seventy-foot robot descending the escalator from his city-sized flying saucer? A tiny Cupid flitting about her bedroom on gossamer wings? Or, simply put, a naked camel driver in Oxford Street.

She began to feel sorry for man and camel. This impoverished camel-driver, no doubt his only friend a flatulent dromedary, his home a sheepskin tent, his sex life as barren as his homeland, his view on existence as simple and tragic as a dumb animal—

'Miss?' said the camel driver. 'Miss? You are OK, miss? *Mademoiselle? Vous êtes française? Mademoiselle? Vous comprenez? Fräulein? Sind Sie Deutsch? Señorita?*'

Before the illiterate camel driver could show off his Russian, Little Vic spoke. 'I am an English girl,' she said, looking the nomad in the eye for the first time. 'Please, go away.'

'You are not ill?' asked the savage.

'No.'

'You are not in need of help?' he asked, in a rather plummy accent.

'Please, go away,' said Little Vic. 'I am an English tourist.'

'I like the English,' said the barbaric desert-roaming Arab. 'Americans, Germans, I hate them.'

'Go along now,' said Little Vic.

The ignorant, black-toothed, Stone Age nomad turned the head of his camel and began to splash away on his aimless course through life. One of them farted explosively.

'I'm worried about Lloyd,' said Nina, sitting on a leather sofa that Owen had borrowed from a journalist friend who had disappeared in Indonesia. Owen stood in his open-plan kitchen, wrestling with the top of a titanium espresso machine that he had never used before. 'His behaviour is awfully odd.'

'You noticed,' said Owen with a grunt, managing to unscrew the contraption, sending several minute metal parts clattering on to the counter.

'He said the strangest things the other night. He's fed up with Sex Balm, fed up with his friends, reminiscing in a maudlin way.'

'Sounds like our Lloyd.'

'Haven't you noticed his speech pattern? His vocabulary? His *non sequiturs*? One moment you begin to understand what he's saying, the next he's spouting the wisdom of Plethicus or Darius McLeod. Aren't you worried about him?'

'To the extent that his behaviour might jeopardize business,' said Owen, giving up on the assembly of his coffee machine, 'yes.'

'I know you don't take this as lightly as you pretend. Something's very wrong with him.'

'I shouldn't say this,' said Owen, abandoning coffee-

160

making and effortlessly uncorking a bottle of white wine, 'but I have an idea what his problem is.'

'Really?' Nina thought she knew what Owen was going to say.

'Yes. Ever since our skiing holiday, he's been under the impression that he has remembered everything he once knew and had forgotten. Information, languages, some rather emotional memories.'

This was not what Nina had expected. 'And you don't believe this? You say he's "under the impression".'

'Of course I don't believe it. He's barmy. He's restless and confused.'

'Lloyd, confused? Not very characteristic.'

'A product', said Owen, with unjustified maturity, 'of loneliness.' He poured them each a glass of wine and sat down next to Nina. He crossed his legs and put an arm along the back of the sofa behind her neck. 'Furthermore,' he said, sounding authoritative, 'he has convinced himself of certain emotional . . . *certainties*. It took me weeks to sort out what he was saying. He has been mulling over his past – all of this is terribly tedious, but I'm a friend, after all. I listen to his ruminations, I absorb them, I try to offer support.'

Nina turned her head sideways and squinted at Owen. 'Go on,' she said. 'But I'm sceptical.'

'As I say,' said Owen, extending an index finger to twirl in Nina's ponytail, 'I'm a loyal friend, and I'm seeing him through his little crisis.' He sipped his wine and arched one eyebrow.

'You haven't told me what the crisis is.'

'There are pop, pseudo-scientific terms for the syndrome, of course, but I believe we are talking about the mid-life one. The one that happens to men like Lloyd. Unmarried men.'

'Men like you, in other words.'

Owen laughed. He made a sound with his lips denoting impatient disagreement. 'I'm still hungry,' he said. 'I have ambitions. I have an agenda. Lloyd is established. He feels . . . *inert.*'

'I find that hard to believe.'

'Let me put it this way,' said Owen. 'I ought not to, really, but . . .'

'Go on.'

'He's fixated on parts of his past. On feelings he had repressed.'

'On?' asked Nina, hoping at last to have her suspicions confirmed.

'On you,' Owen said, nodding his head sadly, as if such an obsession were worse than mere madness.

'I knew it,' said Nina, frowning. 'I knew it.'

'It's been my job during the past weeks', said Owen, with the drooped eyelids of a martyr, 'to guide him back to reality. I've no doubt he'll regain his sanity, with my help.'

'How good of you,' said Nina, not entirely sincerely.

'Yes,' said Owen, with a sigh. 'And I was wondering something.'

'What is that?'

'I was wondering if you didn't think it was a good idea, since I've had the plumbers in, and because it is the first warm day of the year, that you and I popped into the shower together?'

'No, Vincente,' said Lloyd, his telephone pressed to his aching ear. 'Twelve times four ounces is not impossible by Friday week. In fact you shall have them tomorrow, my friend,' he added, in his aphrodisiac-salesman's voice. He quoted a price, he gave reassurances of the product's consistently high quality, he complimented his client on his truly inspiring mode of living, he advised him to take care of himself. '*Ciao*, Vincente,' he said. '*Ciao*, my friend.'

Now he had to call Owen, although it was already evening, to make sure that his promise to Vincente was kept. It was Owen's job literally to deliver the goods, often in

162

person. At the moment the thought of Owen's being exposed to Vincente's glamorous women was an appealing one. Perhaps Owen would stay in Venice for a few months or years, clear the London decks, leave Lloyd alone to confront his destiny in peace.

Lloyd hated his job. Not only did he hate his job, he had a horror, a *dread* of his job. Perhaps that was why, as now, he tended to make his telephone calls in the nude, sitting on the toilet, a towel wrapped around his wet hair, a tennis ball in his free hand. This was a recent development in his approach to business, and he thought he could still think clearly enough to recognize that something about the aphrodisiacs trade disagreed with him.

Just as he was about to dial Owen's number, the telephone rang in his left hand. Dr Porris's cheerful voice greeted him, apologizing for calling after hours, and expressing a casual interest in Lloyd's mental condition.

'Super,' said Lloyd, looking up at the mirror to admire his pink turban, squeezing his tennis ball.

'So good to hear it,' said Porris. 'The reason I ask is that I've unearthed another case. In America. In New York City. Would you like me to go on?'

'Yes.'

'The patient was a fifty-seven-year-old female, married with four grown-up children,' said Porris, apparently reading from notes. 'Her washing machine had clogged. During a thunder storm she found herself elbow-deep in soapy water. Her house was struck by lightning. She was thrown across the room. Her husband, a retired aviation engineer, rushed from his position in front of the television, found her lying unconscious, called an ambulance. Her heart had stopped, but she was revived thanks to the prompt and efficient service of the—'

'Right,' said Lloyd. 'Revived.'

'Tourraine's Syndrome was diagnosed three weeks later, when the bandages came off. The woman was an encyclopaedia of interior decoration. She babbled on about curtains and wallpaper and carpets and plumbing fixtures, about bargains she had known, about painters she had fired, about chintz she had bought at a bargain, about—'

'Interior decoration, yes,' said Lloyd.

'After her doctors released her, she returned to her home. There, to her husband's dismay, she began to demolish the place room by room, ripping at the upholstery, tearing off wallpaper with her bare hands, taking a hammer to the bathroom tiles, unscrewing the—'

'Demolition, yes,' said Lloyd, unwinding his pink turban.

'You can imagine why I'm telling you this, Lloyd.'

'Can I?'

'I'm very concerned now. Two examples of people who reacted badly. Tourraine himself, and the housewife.'

'You haven't finished the story.'

'Her husband tried to have her committed. A psychiatric board of some kind could find nothing strictly wrong with her, except for her amazing memory and her conviction that her house was hideous. They came to look at what remained of her décor, and could only agree with her. They allowed her to finish the demolition job.'

'Then?'

'Then she tried to tear down the house itself, to obliterate any memory she had of a place she had lovingly created over thirty-seven years of marriage. The authorities rethought their diagnosis, and the poor woman was taken away.'

'Result?'

'That's where the case study ends. No doubt she's still clawing at the walls of her room in the Crayhurst Asylum. Just a warning, Lloyd.'

'You are considerate', said Lloyd, 'to keep calling me with horror stories.'

'I don't want to alarm you, really,' said Porris. 'I simply want to alert you to potential dangers.'

'Nothing in the slightest out of the ordinary has happened

to me. My knowledge turns out to be useless. I sleep well. My flat remains intact. I hold only a few grudges.'

'I'm not a psychologist,' said Porris, who might as well have been, 'but you can see, can't you, that the patient in a case such as this might be the last to recognize the danger signs?'

'I understand that. Listen to me. Do I sound unstable?'

'Not in the least,' Porris replied, as Lloyd made a Neanderthal-with-broken-ankle face in his bathroom mirror.

'There, you see?' said Lloyd, standing up, tossing his turban aside, striking a body-builder pose. 'I'll be sure to call you if I have any problems.'

With Porris off the line, Lloyd padded down the corridor of his flat, portable telephone in hand, leaving a trail of wet footprints behind him. He entered the kitchen, stopped, searched the granite counters for the reason he had made the trip from the bathroom. Momentarily emptied of its immediate contents, his brain took the opportunity to brim with annoying memories – public vomitings, prepubescent gropings, outlandish conversational gaffes, cringe-making adolescent episodes with girls clever enough to pierce him with ridicule, and gap after gap when he had failed to act, failed to act. How pitiful he felt, in the face of his regrets. Standing naked in the kitchen, he felt like a caveman suddenly transported into the future. His memory had made a primitive of him. He contemplated the microwave as a chimpanzee would a mirror, maintained a vacant expression, made a motorboat sound with his lips.

The telephone rang in his hand. He raised it to eye level, and drooled. Composing himself, he turned it on and placed the receiver to his ear. He was asked if he would accept reverse charges from his little sister. He indicated that he would.

'Lloyd?' said Little Vic, sounding far away. 'Lloyd?'

'Grr,' said Lloyd, the primitive.

'I'm all right,' said his sister. 'In case you were worried.'

'Grr?' Lloyd asked.

'Well, I did leave the country. Do you know where I am?'

'Grr,' said Lloyd, indicating that he did.

Little Vic told him.

'Grr!' Lloyd exclaimed.

'I know. *Africa!* Can you believe it?'

'*Grr.*'

'I'm perfectly fine. A few dodgy moments. A girl on her own, you know. Unwanted male attention.'

'Grr?'

'Not to worry. I've found a friend.'

'Grr!'

'A Dane, Lloyd. A Danish biologist on holiday, just like me.'

'Grr.' Lloyd, who would never have called himself a racialist, found himself relieved that his little sister's boyfriend hailed from Northern Europe, even if it had to be quasi-Scandinavia.

'Just to say not to worry, Lloyd. I'll be home in a few days. The Caesarians won't even notice. All right?'

'Grr.'

'Bye, now.'

Lloyd held out the phone at arm's length, stared at it as if it were a chunk of meteorite. He was reminded that he needed to ring Owen to organize the delivery of Vincente's Sex Balm order. He dialled Owen's business line unthinkingly, naked in his kitchen. Feeling a chill, he opened the oven, turned it on, and stood with his back to the heat.

'Sex Balm,' Owen answered, rather breathlessly, after several rings. ' "Hard To Do Better!" '

'I hate our slogan,' said Lloyd.

'Why, *hello* there, Lloyd,' said Owen. 'I was just . . . thinking of you.'

Lloyd thought he could hear Owen muffling the receiver,

166

as if to speak to someone else in the room.

'I've finally got Vincente's order,' said Lloyd, who tried at all times to be businesslike, scratching himself. 'I need you to deliver immediately. Twelve times four, this time to his Venice place. I can't go with you.'

'What a shame,' said Owen. 'Under the weather?'

'I want to get the cash-book off my back. This *bloody* business. We're assumed to be criminals from the start. Luckily I remember every transaction, every expense, every—'

'Lloyd?'

'Yes?'

'Do try to relax, old boy. Everything's going beautifully. I'll do the Italy drop in the morning. Stock is in good shape.'

Stocks of Sex Balm depended on only one factor: Lloyd and Owen's respective laziness. They prepared the substance themselves in Owen's flat. Early, tentative efforts had produced a Sex Balm that was too smelly, or too viscous, or too grainy. They were not scientists, after all, and an alarmed Dr Porris vetoed their every attempt before generously suggesting an ingredients list of his own. Lloyd and Owen poured the Sex Balm into perfume vials, labelled it with their black-and-red, swastika-evoking logo, and packaged it by fours in red-leather jewellery boxes, like rifle cartridges. It was, they agreed, just about the tackiest product in the world.

'Good of you, Owen. I still believe in the personal touch. Sex Balm by post would be . . . even more degrading than normal.'

'A pleasure. Now, Lloyd – why so blue?'

It was obvious to Lloyd that Owen was speaking with misplaced good cheer for the benefit of another person.

'Sounds as if you have company. Sorry to interrupt.'

'Company? Not at all. Strictly business here, *chez* Hearn.'

Lloyd thought he detected a faint giggle in the background, and further phone mufflings. Owen really did suffer from satyriasis. He was the only man Lloyd knew who could

167

approach women in the street, in theatre queues, in Continental cafés, without offence ever being taken. Not once, not ever, had he been rebuffed in anything but the most humorous, harmless way. Whoever was in Owen's flat at the moment, he had probably known her for less than a day, and showered with her twice. He was greatly in favour of showers.

'Anyone I know?' Lloyd asked.

'I beg your pardon?'

'I can hear her in the background. What a lad.'

'Sorry, what?' said Owen, suddenly sounding panicked. Lloyd, hypersensitive as he was, his buttocks slowly browning in the oven, did not have difficulty deducing the giggler's identity.

'May I have a word with her?' Lloyd said.

'What? With her? With whom?'

'Let me speak to her,' Lloyd commanded, hedging his bets by naming no names. He could tell by the subsequent pause that he had guessed correctly. Involuntarily, he curled his upper lip like a cowboy catching out a poker cheat. He thought he could hear a shower being turned off in the background. He remembered with painful clarity a scene in his parents' house, ten years ago, when Nina had come to stay with Little Vic. Lloyd, in his aloof post-Oxonian stage, patrolled the corridors with unread copies of random classics in his hands. He heard the rushing of water and paused at a bathroom door. When fifteen-year-old Nina emerged, one towel over her shoulders and another around her waist, Lloyd's mouth filled with saliva, he dropped his book, he felt disturbing palpitations in his chest. Nina excused herself adorably, hurried away towards her room, left Lloyd leaning against an oil painting of his great aunt, a hand splayed against his beating breast. He had not remembered that moment until now.

'Lloyd?' said Nina, as breathlessly as Owen.

'Yes,' Lloyd replied. He had not lied in weeks.

'What did you want to say to me?'

Lloyd imagined Nina clutching a white towel to her bosom, Owen standing behind her, a pool of water fresh from her skin gathering at her feet; her hair wet against her scalp, steam rising, clear drops on the tips of her perfect nose and chin . . .

'I wanted to say hello,' Lloyd said. 'Hello.'

'Hello to you, too. Owen and I were just . . . thinking of you.'

. . . bodies clenched together in Owen's American-style steam-power shower, her ankles around his neck, his head arched back into the stream . . .

'Were you?'

'I believe we were.'

. . . soapy film viscous between their firm stomachs, suds between her breasts, a long-nailed finger . . .

'How nice,' Lloyd said, naked in his kitchen.

'We were wondering,' Nina said, searching for something to say, it seemed to Lloyd, like a blind man for a dropped cane. 'We were wondering where Little Vic was.'

. . . their ecstatic cries muffled by hiss of steam and rush of water, his hooligan-skier's thighs tensed and red, her racket hand clutching a fistful of hair on the back of his head . . .

'Just heard from her, as it happens.' Lloyd told Nina where Little Vic had said she was.

'How marvellous. Just imagine – *Africa*.'

. . . Owen would be stroking her heat-tautened buttocks now, kissing her neck, reaching inside the draped towel to stroke her hip bones, the heartbreaking slope of her belly, her waterlogged navel, her athlete's slender ribcage . . .

'Yes, marvellous. Ought to do her some good.'

'And you, Lloyd? You're well, I trust?'

. . . reaching behind her to discover Owen's almost permanently . . .

'Very well indeed. I was just informing Owen of a rather

huge order from our man Vincente, in Italy. I'm sending him out to Venice tomorrow.'

'That's wonderful news. I understand these are dreadfully tough times.'

. . . leaning over the sofa with the telephone to her ear, guiding him between her . . .

'Rotten,' said Lloyd. 'These are rotten times.'

'Ghastly,' Owen said. 'Sorry, I've picked up the other line. Listen, must go. Bundling Nina into a taxi. Hot date for Owen tonight, if no one minds.'

Ah, thought Lloyd, what a privilege to be able to lie at will. *Je mens tu mens il ment nous mentons vous mentez ils mentent* . . . Owen winking at Nina across the room, gathering a handful of his hair and arching his back, mimicking a barmy, pathetically earnest Lloyd – Lloyd, figure of ridicule.

'Right,' said Lloyd. 'Must go. Goodbye, my friends.'

'Goodbye,' said the lovers in unison, ringing off, no doubt falling on to the floor before the simulated-wood gas fire, tossing towels aside, shrieking with rapturous laughter, intromission occurring within seconds, even as they repeated to one another their hopeless friend's most desperately innocent remarks. ' "A rather huge order from our man in Italy"! What a laugh! What a fool!' Rolling about, locked together on an expanse of parquet floor in a flat Owen had spent two years begging his bank not to repossess . . .

'How do you think he sounded?' Owen asked.

'I suppose you were right. Very odd. So formal, so distant.'

The couple still sat on the sofa, their second bottle of wine opened on the knee-high table before them.

'I knew he would call. I wanted you to hear his voice.'

'What is it, Owen?'

'I beg your pardon?'

'It seems to me that there is something more you want to tell me. What is it you know?'

170

'I know it is the first hot day of the year. *Surely* we ought to pop into the shower together. You *really* ought to see it, Nina. The water pressure practically knocks you down. It will kill you if the steam doesn't get you first.'

Nina, sitting with her stockinged feet folded beneath her, returned Owen's smile. He had a two-day growth of light beard. His hair was longer than usual. His lips formed an expression of challenging good humour.

'It is awfully hot,' Nina said.

'Must be over fifty degrees.'

'A scorcher.'

'Shall I fire up the steam pump?'

'I believe you ought to,' said Nina, arching her back and pretending to yawn. 'Wash off a day's urban grime?'

'Join me?'

'Sorry,' said Nina, rising to go. 'Caesar calls.'

CHAPTER SEVEN

Lesbianism, thought Little Vic: the perfect answer. Something even Jean-Louis Parent could not possibly have experienced – though God knows 'M' had enjoyed her share. In *L'Amour et la Pitié*, just when the reader had begun to believe that only suicide could follow the depravity 'M' had so far courted, she had leapt into a Caribbean hammock with the girlfriend of a well-known singer. Head to toe, they introduced themselves, and much was found in common. Caught in the act by the spliff-addled musician, 'M' had made good her escape – though not without having developed a taste for Sapphism that effectively doubled her pool of potential partners in existential love.

Little Vic had met her Danish biologist on the night of her arrival, only an hour after her unsuccessful attempt to commune with the North African sunset. Looking for as seedy an hotel as possible, Little Vic had spotted a blonde woman sitting at the single outdoor table of a dingy café. The woman might as well have *been* 'M', so aloof was her expression, so nicotine-stained her fingertips. Short-cropped hair, the face of someone just dissipated enough to live on the edge while still holding down a job, this woman looked as if she might know the best place for a Parent fan to stay. With what amounted – for an English woman brought up as Lloyd's sister – to an act of insane recklessness, Little Vic walked straight up to the blonde woman and introduced herself.

'Please,' said the woman. 'Sit. My name is Lise.'

The lesbian fantasy struck Little Vic almost at once. Part of the beauty of this novel plan was that it was almost certain not to succeed. Little Vic could carry on through life with the knowledge that she had tried, and regrettably failed, to sleep with another woman.

'You are English,' said Lise. 'I am lonely.'

Little Vic noticed that the woman had a diamond stud in her nose, and green eyeliner that curved nearly to her temples. She had a hard face, but was beautiful in the creepy, overly hygienic way Scandinavians had.

'I've only just arrived. It was the most boring journey. I spent the early evening naked on the beach. I had to fight off a man and his camel. Had to run for my—'

'How very exciting for you,' said Lise. 'I am a Danish biologist.'

'What are you drinking?' asked Little Vic, pointing at a urine-coloured beverage in the woman's glass.

'This', said Lise, taking a manly gulp and wiping her lips, 'is called "beer".'

Lise wore a man's denim shirt and, for that matter, a man's denim trousers. She was barefoot, her toenails were painted brown. The ashtray was piled deep with twisted fag ends.

'Anyway,' said Little Vic, wishing to ensure proper lodgings before embarking on a thrilling but fruitless seduction, 'I need a place to stay.'

'Of course,' said Lise. 'You will stay with me.' With her non-smoking hand she gestured upstairs in the grubby building that contained the seedy café.

Little Vic caught herself before declining. Of *course* she would stay with Lise. She was abroad. She had left behind her inhibitions. A waiter appeared, gaunt and nearly toothless. Little Vic asked for vodka and was given an uncomprehending look. 'Beer?' she asked, and the waiter turned on his heel. Little Vic felt good now. Only hours into her stay, and she had survived what might as well have been an attempted rape, and found herself seated across from someone who looked as if she might know a thing or two about the world of Jean-Louis Parent. She dug into the authentic leather-strapped wicker bag she had bought at the airport, and withdrew her battered copy of *L'Amour et la Pitié*. She held it up for Lise to see.

'Do you know this book?' Little Vic asked, like a spy making coded contact.

'Do I know this book?' said Lise scoffingly, drawing on her cigarette and inhaling with an audible pop. She exhaled the smoke noisily and looked up at the stars. 'I knew *Parent*, you know.'

Little Vic gulped.

'I sat with him here.' Lise indicated their table. 'Sixteen years ago,' she added.

'You sat with him here? Sixteen years ago?' Little Vic waved a hand in the air in an effort to erase her inane repetitions. She searched Lise's upturned face and decided that she could not be older than thirty.

'I was thirteen,' said Lise, helpfully.

'You lived here?'

'I had run away from home,' said Lise. 'With my boyfriend.'

Christ, thought Little Vic – these Europeans. She remembered herself at thirteen. She had looked like a mosquito, and considered boys useful mainly for running to ground, like foxes.

'I have to know everything,' said Little Vic, regretting

immediately that she sounded so eager, so immature. She could not stop herself. 'Was he beautiful?'

Lise levelled her starlit gaze on the English innocent who seemed to have dropped out of the sky. 'You will never know', she said, 'how beautiful he was.' She reached into a Third World handbag of her own, and extracted a laminated photograph. 'It is', she said, 'priceless. There is no negative.'

She handed the photograph to Little Vic, who held it gingerly by its edges. In the light of the Milky Way, she inspected the image. Unmistakably, it was Jean-Louis Parent, with a blonde girl on his knee. He sat at a table with a beach in the background, deeply tanned, wearing his oval dark glasses, a bottle of some lethal drink before him, one hand on the girl's hip, the other outstretched, holding a cigarette. His expression, despite his surroundings, was eerily sombre. He wore what might as well have been the same white cotton shirt as he had in the portrait Little Vic kept above her bath. Little Vic knew she was meant to infer that the little girl in his lap was Lise.

'I don't know what to say,' said Little Vic, drawing the picture closer, drinking in its every detail. Lise's younger self smiled hugely back at her, her blue eyes squinting in the sunlight. Her little dimpled chin, her blond fringe, her child's body, her blue bikini – none of these could have been more in contrast with the great man's brooding stare, his black stubble, his sweaty chest, his wrinkled shirt. 'Sixteen years ago?'

'Yes.'

Little Vic made a quick calculation and realized the photograph had been taken in the last year of Parent's life.

'One year before he died,' Lise said, confirming Little Vic's arithmetic. 'My God. *Putain*,' she said. '*Merde*.'

'Do you want to speak French?' Little Vic volunteered.

'No thank you.'

'Do you know where I could find a telephone?'

Lise pointed her cigarette at the door of the café. Little Vic excused herself and made her dutiful call to Lloyd, reversing charges as always. When she returned, it was with cigarettes and beer. Her 'M'-like seduction could begin.

At CYSR headquarters the following morning, Nina found it difficult to concentrate on her work. It worried her that the previous evening in Owen's company – which had sensibly ended just before fondling one another playfully at the front door – might have set the scene for a wearing and ultimately pointless summer romance. A man like Owen was good for a laugh; he was probably useful in the shower. Still, *Owen*? If it weren't for the increasingly noticeable and shocking Dearth of Men in London, the idea would be preposterous. It would be like having an affair with *Lloyd*, for heaven's sake: incestuous, laughable, embarrassing.

The work that Nina could not concentrate on pertained to police protection for dignitaries; the hiring of a speech writer to help Sir Ian explain once and for all what the CYSR fuss was about; answering yet another pleading note from Hamish Frederick asking to be spared the humiliation of attending the opening night of his American theatrical company's *Caesar* – now only days away; and a long list of perfectionist errands from the desk of Chad Peele. The American had begun to work his people like galley slaves. Despite Nina's success in getting Chad interviewed and profiled in the London media, the publicity surrounding the Governor had cast an ugly pall on some of the more frivolous aspects of his work for the Committee. And yet, against what Nina considered to be high odds, Chad had shown himself to be winning enough to deflect this unpleasant association, and to make CYSR appear practically indispensable to the continuation of rational world affairs.

The swift completion of the war had not helped. Britain, far more experienced in the field of far-flung military bullying and its long-term consequences, showed some

176

reluctance to dance around the corpse of its fallen enemy, childishly whooping, 'We won! We won!' That was left to the wide-eyed Americans, who paraded up and down their verdant Main Streets in desert camouflage as if the campaign had lasted years, not days. Their self-congratulatory strutting looked, to more civilized countries, like bad sportsmanship. The British kept their frenzied revelry to a twelve-minute parade in the City of London, unarmed troops looking like traffic wardens in the drizzle, the fly-past curtailed by low cloud.

Among the papers on Nina's desk was a newspaper article about Chad, accompanied by a flattering photograph of the American looking busy and decisive – tie loosened, finger pointing, hair perfect. It turned out that Chad was the rare sort of person who, even if he had chosen professional golf as a career, could count on being asked when he would deign to lead his nation into the twenty-first century. 'Nice birdie at the sixteenth, Chad. When are you running for president?' The author of the article had tried his best to belittle this thrusting young American from indescribably rich and right-wing roots, but by the end found himself describing a 'personable and dedicated trainee-president', compared to whom young British men of commensurate backgrounds were a flock of contemptible losers. At least, the journalist seemed to have concluded, it was not beneath him to have an honest job.

Nina looked up from the article and photograph to see Chad, in the flesh, leaning back in his chair, talking on the telephone, his hand gestures suggesting that the person on the other end didn't have the faintest idea how much things *cost* nowadays. It amazed Nina the way her opinion of Chad had vacillated in a few short months – from fear, to disdain, to grudging respect, to sincere admiration, and back to a kind of benign contempt. She had seen how her compatriots ridiculed Chad behind his back. She decided that, inasmuch as Chad was America in microcosm – strong, rich, good-looking and lacking in historical perspective – she ought not to take the United States too lightly.

With the deep sigh of a wage slave, Nina picked up the telephone and started her day.

'Lloyd here, Mother . . .

'Yes, Mother. No, Mother. No need to worry, Mother. By the way, how on earth did you find out she was away? . . .

'You *guessed*, did you? You frighten me sometimes . . .

'Islamic, I would have thought . . .

'No, I don't think she will be murdered . . .

'No, not exactly like Saudi Arabia. More like Greece, with mosques and deserts instead of amphitheatre and olive groves . . .

'Of course not, Mother . . .

'*No*, I don't think I ought to "go get her". She's twenty-five years old, for heaven's sake . . .

'I beg your pardon? . . .

'Oh, very well, thank you for asking. Bloody marvellous. You can just imagine how well my business does during the most severe economic downturn in living memory. Hadn't you heard? Oh yes, frivolous, overpriced luxury goods just fly out of the storeroom . . .

'Aphrodisiacs, Mother . . .

'Oh, several years now . . .

'Yes, "*really*" . . .

'No, Vic never worked for me. She works for a—

'Why, certainly I would, if it came to that, but that's entirely unnecessary. She works with Nina Corrant over at— Oh, it's hard to explain. She's one of the Caesarians . . .

'No! Relax. Let me explain . . .

'*You are not the grandmother of a bastard* . . .

'OK, yes, technically, you *could* be, and *of course* you adore your step-grandchildren. How is the old – the old *step-dad*, then . . .

178

'Oh *is* he? How frightfully smart. I didn't even know he rode . . .

'No, very wise of you to stay away . . .

'Seventy-five, is he, already? Amazing that his birthday should have completely slipped my mind . . .

'A week Friday? Let me just check. Oh, bother, I'm afraid not. One of those ghastly international businessman-of-the-year awards-ceremony banquets . . .

'Saturday? I *don't* think so, Mother – dinner with friends. *Damn* . . .

'Yes, of course, and if you ever come up to London *do* call first and find out if I'm available. *Such* a busy, *urban* life . . .

'Well, probably, since you ask, and if the Opposition get in I've got my eye on a little place in the hills around Lake Como . . .

'But you mustn't worry about *politics*, Mother . . .

'Exactly. Beneath you . . .

'Yes, aren't they *wicked* . . .

'Owen is just fine. Thriving, in fact. I'll certainly pass on your regards, if I ever speak to him again . . .

'Editor of the *Daily Telegraph*? Owen? I *don't* think so, Mother, unless he is a very clever leader of the double life. Owen works for me, Mother . . .

'Aphrodisiacs . . .

'Yes, "really".'

There was salt on the air, and diesel fumes. Bare-legged boys in plastic sandals played tag beneath a buzzing streetlight. Ululant singing slithered through the fly-sheet beads over the café door. An old man shuffled by, bearded and leathery, carrying a half-dead lamb in his arms. Women, shrouded in the mysterious folds of the local *khotsanam*, floated silently by, blacker than the night.

Little Vic felt completely in her element. She had changed into a white tennis dress, had applied insect repellent and sunburn cream to her arms, legs and chest, had exchanged life stories with Lise, had filled up her slender body with beer. There was heat and danger – along with salt and diesel fumes – on the air.

Old men played *khotsanam* at an outdoor table diagonally opposite, the click of their dice deadened by a sand drift piled against the adjacent modern apartment block. Two young women in Western dress chatted together, leaning on a ground-floor window sill – compared fingernails, covered their mouths to giggle, greeted occasional passers-by with smiles and waves. Languidly did Little Vic savour this exotic atmosphere, as the day's last prayer of *khotsanam* was broadcast from the summit of a distant minaret.

Lise claimed to be waiting for her boyfriend, but did not seem to care if he appeared or not. In another setting – at home, in a pub, for example – Little Vic would have said that Lise was pissed as a kidney in formaldehyde. Here, in her element, sitting with her long, tanned legs crossed, a pipe full of *khotsanam* smouldering between her fingers, she looked merely decorative. She had known Parent, after all.

It was an American, of course, who broke the spell. Little Vic saw him coming from fifty metres. The man *walked* naïvely. He wore khaki shorts, leather sandals, a Hawaiian shirt and a great canvas hip pouch clearly containing thousands of dollars in cash. He had sat down at their table before they could say a word, loudly introducing himself and shaking their limp, existential hands. He wore a white *khotsanam* on his left wrist, trying perhaps to pass himself off as a native. His thinning blond hair stood on end in the salty breeze. He wore oversized, light-blue plastic glasses.

'You guys from the States?' he asked, opening his pouch like a marsupial to reveal not only the expected thousands of dollars in cash, but his passport, his watch, a short-wave radio, several maps, a gold chain, coins in various denominations, a tape recorder, a platinum fountain pen and a German camera.

Lise and Little Vic raised their gazes to the intruder, their eyelids heavy and disdainful.

'*Khotsanam*,' said Lise, waving at him with her nicotine-stained fingers. 'Go away.'

'You heard her,' said Little Vic, snapping her fingers to attract the waiter's attention. '*Khotsanam*.'

'Wow,' said the American. 'Can I take your picture?' He had his camera out of the pouch before the women could protest. His flash caught them in aggressive poses, hands outstretched towards the lens, simultaneously mouthing the expletive '*Khotsanam!*'

When in London, Lloyd ate lunch alone at least once a week at his local Vietnamese restaurant; it was one of his missions in life to make the proprietress like him. More than that, Lloyd wanted her to consider him her best friend. For years now he had politely reserved a corner table, politely arrived at exactly the designated hour, politely ordered the lunch special and a bottle of mineral water, politely eaten, politely paid, politely tipped 20 per cent and politely left, clearing the decks for the proper lunchtime crowd. The proprietress, a minuscule woman with a severe haircut and a large mole on her left cheek, greeted him every week as if she had never seen him before, or, if she had, as if she had caught him urinating in her cash register. It bothered Lloyd that she did not seem so overtly angry with her other customers. He had seen her smile, once, at a pair of businessmen who were by no means regulars.

Lloyd wondered if the proprietress, whose name he had not dared ask, considered it rude or perverted of him to lunch alone so often. Had he breached some religious or social taboo? Was his supposedly polite English behaviour a hideous offence to any well-bred Vietnamese? Did he perhaps bear a striking resemblance to a criminal American soldier? Lloyd wondered these things, and he wanted the proprietress to love him. It would have been easier to leave the Vietnamese restaurant alone, to make one of the fifty nearby establishments his local, but no. Lloyd was mono-maniacal in this regard. He would wear down the propri-etress, just as her compatriots had worn down successive waves of imperialist intrusion.

'Good morning,' he said, at one minute before noon.

'Good afternoon,' said the proprietress, testily, glancing at the clock on the wall. She did not make eye contact.

'Rain,' said Lloyd. 'Awful.'

The proprietress, in her starched white shirt, made no reply. It occurred to Lloyd that she might have seen worse things than rain in June.

'Well,' he said, as he took his usual seat. 'A good early crowd. Like me, they must all be looking forward to *yet another delicious lunch*. Here. In your restaurant.'

A menu was snapped open before him, though even in the absence of Tourraine's Syndrome he would have known it by heart. With a gigantic smile and a helpful index finger pointed at the top of the menu, Lloyd indicated that he wished to order what he always, week in, week out, unfailingly ordered. 'And a bottle of mineral water,' he added, enunciating, smiling, making question-marks with his eyebrows, 'if you would be so kind?'

The menu was snatched from his hands. The proprietress turned away, opened the restaurant door for a couple she greeted with the words, 'So very nice to see you.' Lloyd lived only for the day when such an adulatory greeting would be his.

Lloyd took a closer look at the couple, and quickly began to study the small vase of fresh daisies on his table. It was Chad. It had to be Chad, even though there were tens of thousands of Americans living in London and – frankly, well, one had to be honest – they all looked alike. Lloyd knew it was Chad and not some other American for two reasons: his companion, an American-looking young woman, had said, 'Oh, Chad!' in reply to a remark the man had made; and the man wore a card clipped to his lapel that read, even from ten feet away. 'CHAD PEELE. CYSR'. The latter evidence, along with a Union Jack/Stars and Stripes pin, had settled the matter in Lloyd's mind.

Remembering that on their first encounter it had been impossible for Chad to make out Lloyd's face, that he could not possibly recognize him – unless the proprietress for no reason shouted his name across the restaurant – Lloyd looked up from the daisies just in time to see Chad and his companion seated one table away. Chad held the back of the chair for the young woman. The man appeared to have good manners. He wore a summer grey-flannel suit of obvious quality, a blue-and-white striped shirt and a burgundy tie. He wore lensless spectacles. He possessed the hair of three normal men. There was nothing about him that could give Lloyd immediate cause for feeling superior, though he had not yet spoken.

Lloyd wished he had a book or a magazine to read, or a wide-brimmed hat to wear, or that a diversionary fire would break out in the kitchen. Lloyd rearranged his napkin, his glass of water, the daisies, his chopsticks. He sighed and stared at the ceiling and made his face express the sentence, 'I have never eaten alone before; I am not interested in the conversation of my fellow diners.'

Chad's young woman was good-looking, in a tasteless way. Her over-abundant, rust-coloured hair was sprinkled with raindrops. Her fresh, freckled face had not been in London long. She looked at Chad with palpable adoration, her hands folded on the table, sitting up straight, even white teeth poised expectantly on her lower lip.

'Jean,' said Chad. The young woman's name was Jean, apparently. 'I have so much to tell you. So much. So much has happened.'

Touching, Lloyd thought. Jean might very well be this hopeless Yank's high-school sweetheart. Chad's voice was surprisingly high-pitched, out of all proportion to his tall, broad frame.

'Oh, Chad,' said Jean, lashes aflutter. Lloyd reminded himself that Chad was cruelly, heartbreakingly wealthy. 'Chad.'

'Jean,' said Chad. 'Jean.' Lloyd felt himself on the verge of interrupting this conversation and steering it in the direction of information exchange.

'Tell me everything. It's so exciting.'

'I'm having a ball,' said Chad. 'Got the greatest crew. You probably never thought I could handle this, am I right?'

'Well.'

'Sure, at the beginning, a little rough. Obstacles, and all. But you keep pushing.'

'Yes?'

'You should have seen some of these old guys I had to work with. The Committee is made up of all these . . . these old *English* guys with titles, so you never know if you're talking to the Queen's brother.'

'The Queen has a *brother*?'

'That's not what I meant.'

Jean was showing herself to be rather dim. Lloyd pretended to be engrossed in his fingernails, and leaned closer.

'Anyway, I've got these two English gals working for me. You spoke to Nina on the phone, I guess.'

'That's right.'

'Outstanding. Dedicated. She's got me out of a few jams, I'll tell you. A super girl.'

'You sound so British, Chad.'

Lloyd winced into his daisies.

'Aw, come on. Anyway, Nina's the right-hand man. She got me to hire this friend of hers.'

Lloyd felt his pulse racing, his elbow lifting slightly off the table, preparing to lash out.

'She's worked out well. An iddy-biddy thing, you should see her. Cute as a button, and good at French. I put her on the line with the French guys – you just can't believe how

184

difficult the French guys are – and she charms the pants off them.'

Lloyd lowered his elbow.

'I think she's got a little thing for me, Jean,' Chad said.

Lloyd raised his elbow again. If he struck quickly, he might incapacitate the American sufficiently to be in a position to use his knife on the fellow's jugular.

'It was adorable, really,' said Chad. 'She got all gussied up one day and when everyone had gone home she asked me out for a drink. I said OK, just to be a nice guy, and the next thing I know she's drinking Martinis and draping herself all over me and saying "Take me to your place". Can you believe it? I mean, an *English* girl?'

'You loved it,' said Jean. 'Did you take her home?'

Lloyd asked himself if this was the way high-school sweethearts spoke to each other.

'I *drove* her home,' said Chad. 'The girl was smashed. Blotto. Just stinking, violently—'

All right, all right, thought Lloyd.

'—*drunk*,' Chad concluded.

Lloyd had never seen his little sister drunk in his life. What Chad was saying seemed impossible – and besides, how *dare* he? Was this the way American gentlemen behaved? Talking about the indiscretions of young ladies behind their backs, to other young ladies?

'Swine!' said Lloyd.

The American couple stopped talking and turned to look at him.

'Sorry,' Lloyd said. 'The Middle East,' he added. '*Bastards.*'

The couple exchanged a look, and went back to their conversation. Chad continued to describe Nina's verve and efficiency, CYSR's supposed triumphs, the ghastliness of the meddlesome French, his meeting with the President, his troubleshooting forays into Europe, the 'really great' all-American cast of *Caesar*, the lamentable lack of British

185

government cooperation, and his firmly held belief that the Hands Across the Water Fourth of July Goodwill Parade would be a roaring success.

'Royalty,' said Chad. 'That's the key. If you have royalty on your side, you can do anything. The PR is unbelievable.'

'Chad. Are you saying you've been talking to *royalty*?'

Chad made a self-deprecating gesture with his hands. 'A little bit,' he confessed. 'I'm really not supposed to talk about it until we've firmed things up, commitment-wise.'

'You've got to tell me everything.'

'It's all done through these kind of faggy aides,' said Chad, with a limp flick of his wrist. 'The tricky question is, who needs whom more these days?' Chad continued, amazing Lloyd with his correct use of the objective pronoun. 'Do the Brits really want to appear to be siding with the States on *everything*, what with Europe waiting, you know, to . . . to *absorb* them?'

Lloyd shivered.

'It's all very delicate. I shouldn't say too much, but the fact is I do get instructions—' he looked left and right, did not seem to care that Lloyd could hear every word he said, '— I get instructions from Stateside. The thinking at the moment seems to be that something like the Goodwill Parade reflects well on the Special Relationship in a military sense. That's why all the soldiers. It's like another victory parade. Allies. Good against evil.'

Jean found this fascinating.

'I mean,' said Chad, suddenly expansive, 'this country isn't as pathetic as it seems. It's a nuclear power, which is more than you can say for Germany.'

'Thank God.'

'Right. They're really strong at war, and a lot closer to most of the trouble spots. It's like having a whole extra army, and not having to pay for it. So all this Caesar stuff makes them feel important, involved in world events.'

'Who are we going to go to war with?' Jean wanted to know.

'That', said Chad, self-importantly, 'is a secret.'

Lloyd's first course had arrived. Chad and Jean ordered their meal; the proprietress thanked them for their custom and wished them *bon appétit* in a way she had never done with Lloyd.

Chad continued for several minutes in his Secretary-of-State mode, in his loud, high-pitched voice, in his lensless spectacles. Lloyd felt gloom descending upon him. He felt that he was hearing the future – a future of Chad-like specimens telling him and his beautiful old country what to do. Great Britain, swept between the Scylla of America and the Charybdis of Europe. How had this come to pass? What did it mean for aphrodisiacs? In which direction should Britain – cõme now, *England* – lash out first?

Lloyd's mind was suddenly full of hard information about Chad's roots. The facts had been reported occasionally over the years in the fine print of the newspapers and magazines Lloyd had read. The Peele family fortune was usually described as 'awesome'. Great-grandfather Peele had invented something fundamental – it struck Lloyd that he could not remember precisely what it was; could this be the first sign of the decay of his Tourraine's Syndrome? – something everyone in the world needed to buy several of, on a weekly basis. Great-grandfather Peele had patented cigarettes, or stainless-steel, or vinyl, or styrofoam. It was a far cry from Sex Balm, whatever it was. Latex? Polyester? *Plastic?* Great-grandfather Peele had changed the world. Grandfather Peele had bought oil fields and aeronautic concerns. Chad's father, sensing perhaps that enough was enough, had entered politics. Lloyd suddenly found it touching that Chad should have wished to take on so trivial an enterprise as CYSR, when he could have spent his life blowing the family fortune on hedonism of unprecedented intensity.

Lloyd also had to admit that there was no way in which amassing a legitimate fortune of that size could be called 'vulgar' or 'nouveau'. Britain's wealthiest families were stagnant, even parasitical, by comparison to the Peeles. This mature realization in no way mitigated Lloyd's ingrained feeling of condescension towards his affluent cousins; that was only natural. Lloyd had been born in the year of Suez, and yet there was still a part of him that saw the map of the world awash in pink. To have become puny, to have become a mere revolver in the hand of a cowboy-suited superpower – that was shameful.

'Mainly,' said Chad, as Lloyd slurped his soup, 'I've had to deflect a lot of media interest in the Claudia Brown thing. As if I had anything to do with it.'

'It's been tough on me, too,' said Jean.

Were they married? Lloyd wondered, sneaking a look at her ringless left hand. Engaged? This *was* good news.

'How's the Governor holding up?' Chad asked, referring to his father.

'I think this is killing him,' said Jean. 'I'm sure he wishes he could just wash his hands of the issue. But the election, you know . . .'

'I feel bad, being away during this mess. On the other hand, I'd have to rally around the family if I were at home. Embarrassing. Better to have been in exile. They don't press me all that hard here. They just have a horrified fascination. There's no capital punishment here. They abort teenagers.'

'Claudia dies next week,' said Jean, chillingly.

'Have you said anything to him, Sis?'

Jean was Chad's sister.

'Yeah, I have. I told him the election is a year and a half away. People will forget if he does an about-face. The whole thing gives me the creeps.'

What a charming young woman, Lloyd thought. She looked prettier, when she made sense.

'That settles it, then,' said Chad. 'I'm going to put my two

188

cents in. I'll call him this evening. He's making a fool of himself, of the family. That crazy woman – it's just too unpleasant. Will he listen to me at all, do you think?'

'Worth a try. It might take a little of the pressure off. The whole thing is a macho pose he talked himself into. He thought he was responding to the electorate, but they, as *individuals*, don't have to off Claudia.'

What a pleasant young woman, Lloyd thought to himself. How he loved Americans.

Lloyd's second course arrived, delivered by a more than usually gruff proprietress. Chad and his sister discussed family matters, the ill health of a particularly prized race-horse, the ambiguous outcome of the war, the genuine decency of their friend the President, the hilarious second-rateness of Britain, Jean's architect fiancé, and, rather suddenly, Lloyd himself.

'Yeah,' said Chad, munching on an egg roll, 'a total basket case. His friends are worried. His little sister is worried. The guy sells whatcha callits? Aphrodisiacs.'

'What're they?'

'Stuff that makes you horny, I guess. Or, you know, stuff that makes you *virile*, to boot.'

'Do they work?'

'I suppose they must,' said Chad. 'If there's money in them.'

'Have you met him?'

'Ran into him for a moment once. Didn't say two words to me. Sounds like a character. Nina has known him all her life. She says he's going through a mid-life crisis.'

Oh, that's it, is it? thought Lloyd. A mid-life crisis? It was almost thrillingly humiliating to be talked about by strangers. He knew that he would probably never have this opportunity again, unless he resorted to electronic surveillance. He didn't know whether to be offended, or flattered *and* offended, that Nina and Little Vic had betrayed such personal information to their American boss.

189

'His sister isn't exactly stable, either,' said Chad. 'My contacts tell me she just split to North Africa, on the spur of the moment. Kind of funny. She started smoking cigarettes and wearing outrageous clothes and using foul language around the office. Nina says—'

'A mid-life crisis?'

'Too young. No, more like a spiritual thing, I guess. She feels lost. She's in love with a dead French philosopher.'

Lloyd knew he had heard this somewhere before.

'How creepy.'

'She'll grow out of it. She's a neat gal. You'd like her. Spunky. Real bright. Just a little misdirected. Off centre. She needs to be channelled. I'm going to try to help.'

How very kind of you, Chad, Lloyd said to himself. God, these Americans. He felt on the verge of declaring his identity aloud, but suspected that it wouldn't faze a man of such positive outlook. 'Hey, nice to *see* you, man,' Chad would probably say. 'We were just *talking* about you. Talk about a *coincidence*.' Despite feeling violated, Lloyd was determined to hold his tongue.

'I know a guy in the embassy there,' said Chad, referring to the country Little Vic had chosen to visit. 'He's going to keep an eye on her. I was a little worried. That's one shitty country.'

The world's policeman, Lloyd thought, momentarily awestruck by Chad's chivalry. A minor employee had gone on holiday, and Chad had taken the trouble not only to worry about her welfare, but to enlist the services of the State Department in order to ensure her safety. Lloyd thought he would weep.

'Good idea,' said Jean seriously, as if this sort of thing happened all the time. 'That's pretty crazy of her to go there alone.'

'That's what I thought. You hear stories.'

Were they deliberately trying to make Lloyd feel guilty – Lloyd, who had taken the cause of Little Vic's security,

190

physical and financial, and made it the primary mission in his life?

'You really like this girl, don't you?' Jean said, eyes twinkling.

'Naw, it's not like that,' said Chad. 'She's like a little sister, you know?'

The American tourist in the khaki shorts and Hawaiian shirt had gone away, but not far. He was seated diagonally opposite Little Vic and Lise, next to the men playing *khotsanam*. Little Vic and Lise held hands under the table. Somewhat to Little Vic's surprise, Lise had reciprocated every hint, verbal and physical, of the sexual liaison she had hoped was not actually going to materialize. Still, having met someone who had probably slept with a dying Jean-Louis Parent, Little Vic felt compelled to play out her fantasy. Pleasantly drunk and sunburnt, she played with Lise's fingers and gazed into her glittering eyes. Lise had twice mentioned a boyfriend but, in his absence, seemed eager to see through whatever her new acquaintance had in mind. One could expect no less from an adept of the great man.

Drink upon drink was ferried to their table by the nearly toothless waiter. An orange moon rose over crumbly rooftops.

'Oh my God,' said Lise, polishing off a drink. 'How are we going to pay for all of this?'

'I have plenty of money,' said Little Vic, indicating her authentic handbag. 'I brought everything I have in the world, just in case, you know. In case I decided to stay here for ever.' Little Vic said this in a way meant to suggest that this possibility was still not out of the question. 'That's another reason I was worried, on the beach. It's all cash.'

'Keep your voice down,' said Lise, in her American-accented English. 'There are thieves everywhere.'

'I don't mind. What's the worst that could happen?'

Little Vic felt Lise's fingers travelling up her arm to her shoulder, to her neck, to her *engagé* haircut, to her cheek. This was nice enough, as long as . . . Lise traced Little Vic's upper lip with a nicotine-scented index finger.

'Don't you think', said Lise, 'that we should take some beer to my room? To *our* room?'

'Of course, that's exactly right,' said Little Vic, suppressing her instinctive horror. 'That is exactly what ought to happen.'

Before she knew it, Little Vic had paid the waiter almost all of the money she had exchanged at the airport, and found herself climbing a flight of steeply canted stairs, a plastic bag of beer bottles clanking in her hand. A door was opened for her. She saw drab floral wallpaper, a small double bed. There was a musty smell, open windows, a balcony. Now Little Vic stood on the balcony, surveying the outskirts of town, the silver line of moonlit sea, drink in one hand, harsh tobacco in the other. Lise joined her. The women leaned their heads together and drank in the scene. Forcing herself not to cringe, Little Vic allowed Lise to kiss her hair, her temple, her cheek. This was getting perilously close to the real thing.

'Look,' said Little Vic, pointing up at the star-washed sky. 'An asteroid.'

'You mean', said the Danish biologist, 'a meteorite.'

'A shooting star, then,' said Little Vic, who hated to be corrected.

'Kiss me,' said Lise.

Beerily, Little Vic did so. She had not kissed anyone except Owen in five months, not since she had kissed Alan Forsythe, an impoverished lush. She preferred kissing Lise, but only just. She told herself to taste the residue of Parent on Lise's lips.

'Did you make love to him?' Little Vic asked, pulling away.

192

Lise sighed theatrically, looked up at the stars, took a drag on her pipe of *khotsanam*.

'I did,' she replied weightily, exhaling smoke.

'When you were thirteen?'

'Nearly fourteen.'

'Magical, I'd imagine.'

'I had told him I was a virgin. He responded greatly to that.'

'And your boyfriend?'

'He was older. He was seventeen. He watched through the curtains.' Lise nodded towards the interior of their filthy room.

'Here? Here in this room?'

'Yes. It is sixteen years ago.'

'Indeed it is,' said Little Vic, elated and terrified.

'It was beautiful and it was sad,' said Lise, probably not for the first time.

There was lamb on the cooling air, and wood smoke. Lise stroked Little Vic's neck.

'Did you hear that?' asked Little Vic.

'Hear what?' Lise kissed Little Vic's ear.

'In the room. Did you hear it?'

'Nothing.'

'It sounded like, sorry—' Little Vic had to do some kissing before she could continue. 'Sorry, it sounded like someone in your room. In our room.'

'Let me look.' Lise leaned through the peeling French windows, then back again. 'It is nothing. Kiss me.'

They kissed, rather more fervently than before. Tipsy, disoriented, abroad alone, possessed by the spirit of Jean-Louis Parent, Little Vic tried to throw herself into this activity. She thought that she might be enjoying herself. She felt Lise's fingers raking through her hair, and thought it felt awfully good. It would require a drastic change of attitude to become a lesbian, but Little Vic's mind was determinedly open. She knew that by her own behaviour she had locked herself into several hours of progressively more intimate contact with the Danish biologist. She didn't mind. She was drunk. She was alone abroad. No one knew exactly where she was. Her senses would open like blossoms to a new season of life. She still thought she had heard something in the bedroom, but she could not concentrate on that at the same time as she kissed another woman for the first time.

Not for the first time. There had been that hugely embarrassing bank-holiday weekend in the country. Little Vic had come running in from the tennis court to find Nina apoplectic with shame and claiming to have lost control of herself with Lloyd. Nina had leapt into the bath, thrashed around in the water, and recounted details of her kiss. Her embarrassment proved contagious, causing Little Vic to crawl into bed and cower under the covers. Nina soon joined her there, so that they could giggle in horror at what had transpired.

Nina was not only Little Vic's best friend – she was her idol. Little Vic felt privileged to be in a position to offer comfort. She had asked Nina what it had been like to kiss Lloyd, much as the thought tended to revolt her. Nina had tried to explain, but demonstration had seemed in order. They had appeared at the dinner table one hour later feeling very strange indeed. Lloyd had long since fled.

On the balcony, in Lise's arms, Little Vic decided that while she was not altogether comfortable kissing a strange woman and having her back and shoulders and chest massaged by her, it was a hell of a lot better than a similar situation in the arms of a strange man. In fact, Little Vic was profoundly aroused, though not yet committed to the great unknown that awaited her indoors. Had her years of reading been in vain? Had she not learned that the restless pursuit of gross sensation was the only answer to the miserable burden of human existence? Bearing in mind, of course, that such a life led inexorably to hell; the voluptuary fell into a jaded torpor, dazed by his need for ever more intense satisfactions, until at last the only stimulant left was *suicide*. She kissed

194

harder. She licked a sheen of sweat from Lise's shoulder. Had she not learned that action defined existence? That each drop from the celestial cistern was infinitely grand? Lise's tongue was a mindless creature of lust. There was a more obvious noise in the bedroom, but never mind, never mind. How much time had passed, on the balcony? A Parentian eternity. Her tennis costume had been removed. Lise stood splendidly naked before her. This was wonderful. This was new. Pregnancy was inconceivable. Sexually transmitted disease, the remotest of possibilities.

Action, thought Little Vic, one of Lise's nipples between her lips. *Volo ergo sum*. She knelt before the Danish biologist. The rusty moon coloured Lise's skin. She felt two hands pressed behind her head. She kissed a navel for the first time. She clutched a woman's hips for the first time – in this case, Scandinavian hips. Her mind was almost free of intellectual thought. The celestial cistern dripped before her. *L'Amour et la Pitié*? Little Vic thought. *'M' c'est moi!*

This was truly excellent. The encouraging sounds and motions Lise made. The taste, the odour of her new life. The slender Danish fingers working her scalp. Out of the corner of her eye, Lise's fingers grasping the iron railing. A hip bone to be kissed. The chance of neighbouring *voyeurs*. The scent of the sea. Little Vic pressed on into the unknown. Little Vic felt superhuman. Little Vic felt attuned to the rhythms she thought only existed on the printed page, in the imagination. Little Vic felt like a woman. Little Vic felt . . . Little Vic felt . . . Little Vic felt *silly*.

CHAPTER EIGHT

Little Vic froze, a quasi-Scandinavian buttock in each hand. How to extricate herself? She found it hard to believe that she could simply stand up, naked under a Moslem sky, and protest that she had erred. This was sex, after all. It wasn't like returning a bad bottle of wine. There were feelings involved here, as well as her duty to Jean-Louis Parent's hedonistic creed.

Her hesitation had not gone unnoticed. Lise knelt down and kissed her wetly, then lay down on the dusty balcony. Little Vic felt on the verge of panic as she was pulled on top of the Danish biologist. She knew she had asked for this, that it would be unladylike to alter her course. She tried to focus on the idea that one useful fact had been proved to her, something that would come in handy whenever she decided to court abandon: she did not have hidden homosexual leanings. She liked men, exclusively, hard as that was to believe. Meanwhile, she was locked in passionate embrace with a blonde woman on a hotel balcony: such was travel.

There was another noise in the bedroom. Sensing an

opportunity for escape, and suddenly preferring the idea of being robbed to what lay before her, Little Vic sat up on her haunches and pressed a finger to her lips.

'Shh,' she shushed. 'Listen.'

'It is nothing. Come.'

'I'm going to look.'

'Don't leave me.'

'I have to look. I'll be right back.'

Though she understood Lise's disappointment, it surprised Little Vic when the woman held her by the wrists, preventing her from standing. She had to wrest herself free. She poked her head into the dark bedroom. There was someone there. She searched along the wall for a light switch. Finding none, she called out to the shadowy form on the other side of the bed.

'*Khotsanam!*'

There was a bang and a male grunt. The intruder had apparently barked his shin against a bedpost.

'Lise,' she said, turning towards her ex-potential-lesbian lover. 'There's someone in the room. Lise?'

In the starlight she made out Lise's form, standing, approaching. Little Vic felt herself being pushed roughly into the bedroom. She fell on to her hands and knees. She was picked up by the hair and thrown on to the bed. She kicked and punched at the darkness, then felt her hands and ankles pinned down. She was being tied to the bed. She struggled, heard a man's guttural voice, heard Danish spoken. The boyfriend? A pair of Danish con-artists? It had seemed odd that a woman who had known Parent and run away from home at thirteen should have managed to become a biologist. Her eyes grew accustomed to the darkness, so that she could make out the shapes of the man and Lise as they tied her down. If this wasn't 'M'-like, Little Vic thought, nothing was. She relaxed and allowed the pair of Scandinavian scoundrels to finish their work, and to gag her. The bumbling man had located her bag, and emptied it of its contents.

Lise put on her clothes. Without another word, the pair departed, slamming the door behind them.

Suddenly sober, Little Vic reflected on her evening of excitement and novelty. Not bad, really, by existentialist standards. Nearly raped by a camel driver on the beach, seduced into her first lesbian affair, tricked and battered and robbed, left helpless, penniless, naked, gagged, tied to a bed. Would she die now, too, just to make her trip a complete success?

The moon rose higher in the sky, illuminating the filthy bedroom. Little Vic examined her bonds: a camera strap on one ankle, a length of torn sheet on the other, handkerchiefs on each wrist. She could escape, given time. She had lost six hundred pounds, nearly all her savings. A visit to the embassy or consulate would be necessary. The police would want to interrogate her. There would be residue of *khotsanam* in her room. She might languish for ever in a North African gaol.

She thought she ought to fall asleep, and free herself in the morning. Her extensive reading had taught her that she ought to revel in her circumstances. She might never be tied to a bed in a North African hotel again. This was a unique predicament. She would learn from this. She would know an extreme of human experience, as close as she might ever come to joining a resistance movement, to being incarcerated in a Guatemalan prison, to being a kidnapped princess. Yes, this was going to be fine. Daylight was only hours away. She could sleep through most of her ordeal. For amusement, she could fantasize about tracking down Lise and the boyfriend, and exacting her cruel and satisfying revenge.

There came a knock on the door. Little Vic at first hesitated to answer, but was overcome by her ingrained good manners.

'Yeth?' she tried to say through her gag. 'Who ith it?'

'Victoria?' came a man's voice. An American man. An American man who knew her name.

'Yeth?'

'Are you OK? Can I come in?'

Now, there was an interesting question. She was, after all, spread-eagled naked on a bed. The man was, after all, a stranger.

'Yeth,' said Little Vic.

The door opened. The overhead light, a single bare bulb, was switched on. Little Vic blinked and squinted.

'Oh, God,' said the man. It was the man in the khaki shorts and Hawaiian shirt. He rushed to the bed and untied Little Vic's gag and the handkerchiefs at her wrists. He covered her in a sheet. He untied her ankles.

'You're OK,' said the man.

'Who are you?'

'My name is Sam,' he replied. 'Chad sent me.'

Little Vic thought about this. 'How did Chad know where I—'

'Easy to find out. He just wanted me to keep an eye on you. This is a really shitty country.'

'Well, the Danes don't add a great deal.'

'Here,' said Sam, holding up a plastic bag. 'Your stuff. I got your stuff back.'

'My stuff? My money?'

'Yeah. And about a thousand dollars extra they had on them. Good idea to confiscate it, don't you think?'

'What did you do to them?' said Little Vic, imagining headless corpses washing up on the coast.

'Next flight to Copenhagen,' said Sam. 'Too much trouble dealing with the authorities. A friend's going to make sure they're on the morning flight. Real shits, those people.'

Sam sat on the room's only chair, swept back what remained of his blond hair, adjusted his blue glasses.

'I kept an eye on you from across the street,' he said, pulling a pair of binoculars from his cash-laden pouch. 'Sorry about that.'

'How embarrassing,' said Little Vic. 'I've never . . . I'm

not a . . . she seemed to . . .' There were no excuses. Little Vic was a lesbian in Sam's eyes.

'It's OK,' said Sam. 'You're fine now. I've got your clothes.'

Little Vic felt a powerful Parentian urge to seduce Sam, her spy saviour, but quickly decided not to push her luck. She thanked him with almost unbecoming profuseness. He gave her a plane ticket, he shook her hand like the presenter of an award, and he left. Little Vic reclined on the bed, one thousand dollars and one lesbian encounter to the good, faintly in awe of Chad's foresight. American can-do spirit had done it again. How *galling*.

Lloyd thought he might have begun to lose the parts of his memory that Tourraine's Syndrome had reinstated. The problem with memory was that he could not be sure: he could not remember what he had forgotten. There was no way to tell, for example, if he had ever truly known the dates of the Pleistocene epoch; he certainly did not know them now. The inside of his head was still a landscape dotted with facts, but they were looking decidedly sparse compared to a few days ago.

The inability to lie had crippled Lloyd socially, made him boring and pedantic, made his business almost impossible to run. He tested it now, gripping the arms of his swivelling chair in anticipation of agony: 'I am the Duke of Westminster,' he said, and felt only the vaguest tug at his innards. 'How do you do, young lady,' he said, extending a hand in mid air. 'My name is John Paul. I am the Pope.' A minor stab in his bowels. 'Would you like to come to my concert tonight, my dear?' he asked the woman in his painting. 'I am a Chilean violinist.' At last, thought Lloyd, he could carry on as a normal person, exaggerating, embellishing, covering up. His conversation could be colourful and entertaining. His business could operate smoothly. He could flatter and seduce. He could file tax returns in peace. 'I'm not allowed to talk about it,' he said, 'but the Prime Minister does nothing without asking my permission. I have photographs of him with a Blackpool whore.'

While it was possible that some of Lloyd's memory had disappeared into the folds and creases of his brain, and while it was now certain that he had regained a normal ability to lie, there remained one powerful side-effect to be reckoned with. He loved Nina. This was incontrovertible. His memories of her were as clear and powerful as ever. He saw her across dozens of rooms, dozens of dinner tables, dozens of lawns, a tennis court or two.

Love terrified him. He had seen the past with awesome clarity during the past few weeks, but now he began to focus on the future. Love of this intensity meant inevitable misery. If he understood love correctly, it meant loss and betrayal and a staggering potential for emotional pain. He thought of Nina dying in his arms of a wasting disease. He visualized this scene with the same realism as he saw the past. He saw Nina holding their dying child in her arms. He saw Nina at his own funeral, after he had died of gunshot wounds incurred on a fateful business trip to New York. He saw himself and Nina together, retired to a damp and draughty cottage, wondering who would die first. He saw himself confessing – in a whisper, because the children were asleep – that he had been unfaithful to her. He saw her brushing away tears – or, on the other hand, confessing to her own far more serious and long-term infidelity. He saw her face as she broke the news that their youngest child – a perfect girl of fifteen – had been decapitated in a road accident. One had to be awfully brave, to fall in love.

Lloyd had learned that to know the past, to be haunted and nagged by the past, was unpleasant and disconcerting; to know the future would be *hell*. It would be enough to drive an otherwise sane man to religion – or worse. Who in his right mind would carry on if he knew even one of the dozens of disasters and heartbreaks that awaited him, as surely as the earth would one day be consumed by the sun? Who would carry on, and how, knowing the precise date of his demise? The future, always a heartbeat away, was dark as death.

Lloyd inhaled. Lloyd exhaled. He knew that self-pity was unbecoming in the young and privileged; but, really, what a *disaster* it was to be alive. In the grip of his inconveniently heightened memory, he had felt groggily sympathetic to misfits and drunks and spinsters on park benches. He had walked past a nun, and had to steady himself against a lamp-post under a wave of pity. Love and pity, he thought to himself – that French bastard. He felt a great deal of love, and a great deal of pity, and he did not know what to do with himself.

Control. Control was Lloyd's *métier*. He owned his flat, his shelter, did he not? He would probably not die for forty years. If actuarial tables were to be believed, he would die on 27 August 2033. Lloyd thought he ought to keep that date in mind. He would try to wait until then, or nearly then, to go completely insane. He would hope that hormonal activity would soften his decline. He would express no firm opinion, he would harm no man. He would strike a balance between self-gratification and charity. He would make Nina happy, in lieu of himself. He would never, ever complain in public. He would keep his tragedies to himself. He would read the autobiographies of people who had *really* suffered. He would consider himself pathetic by virtue merely of being alive. He would take up golf. He would drink more and think less. He would hold the trump card of suicide.

Meanwhile, Nina. He dialled her office number. He held the receiver to his ear, and sniffled manfully.

'Chad Peele,' said Chad Peele. 'Caesar.'

' "Chad", how nice to hear you. Lloyd James here.'

'Lloyd? Hey, great. How are you?'

' "Chad", I'm fine. You?'

'Outstanding. I have news. This is the most amazing coincidence. I had my hand on the phone about to try to track you down when you called.'

'Is that so?' Lloyd operated under the first-hand knowledge that Chad believed he was insane.

'Yeah. It's your sister. Got into a scrape in—'

'A *scrape*?' Lloyd stood up.

'Let me just say right away that she's OK, she's absolutely fine. She can tell you the story. She arrives in London tonight. Something about a couple of drug-addict hippie thieves. They robbed her. I hope you don't mind, but I had a guy down there keeping an eye on her. It's a really *shitty* country, Lloyd.'

'So I hear.'

'Anyway, my pal did fine. Got her on the next plane out.'

'*Did* he?'

'Yeah, everything's cool.'

'*Is* it?'

'Sure. Say, want to come to the airport? I thought I'd meet her. Poor thing.'

Lloyd gave Chad his address, and put down the telephone. He had forgotten to ask for Nina.

He had also forgotten that Chad was likely to recognize him from the Vietnamese restaurant. When Lloyd met Chad at the door, therefore, it was with the realization that the American would have all the rumours of Lloyd's mental instability confirmed: despite the drizzle, Lloyd wore a Panama hat and dark glasses, his loudest and most outdated jacket, white cricket trousers and a pair of red loafers Owen had once left behind after a party and had preferred not to retrieve. Lloyd had believed, correctly as it turned out, that dressing this way might reduce the odds of Chad's recognizing him.

They drove to Heathrow in Chad's magnificent motor, Lloyd sulking in the passenger seat, Chad talking excitedly about CYSR and about Little Vic's escape from the clutches of thieves. Lloyd found Chad to be almost annoyingly

203

friendly and considerate. He spoke well and even humorously. He drove terribly fast, often making eye-contact with his passenger. It pained Lloyd to realize that, of the two men, Lloyd was the more likely to tell his grandchildren that he had once shared a ride to Heathrow with the other.

'I can't thank you enough for what you've done,' Lloyd managed to say. 'Silly of her to dash off alone.'

'She's young,' said Chad. 'She'll learn from this experience. We can't say we didn't do foolish things at her age, can we, Lloyd?'

'I suppose not.' Lloyd wished he had done *more* foolish things.

Chad wanted to know about Lloyd's business. 'Do they work?' he asked, meaning aphrodisiacs.

'Yes,' Lloyd replied, revelling in his recovered ability to lie.

Chad did not go on to say that he might want to give Sex Balm a try, which was a first. He probably thought aphrodisiacs were immoral. Chad was nothing if not an upright citizen. Lloyd found that he wished to impress Chad somehow, and not to appear insane in doing so. His past attempts to use Tourraine's Syndrome to his advantage had left him sounding like a train-spotter on amphetamines, reeling off lists of historical dates, describing the weather on any day during his conscious lifetime, reciting the verse of Darius McLeod, begging his interlocutor to ask him anything, anything at all.

'Are you feeling OK, Lloyd?' asked Chad, with chilling directness. 'I hope you don't mind my asking. Just that Nina said—'

'What *did* Nina say?' Lloyd asked sharply. Just who, he wanted to know, did Chad think he was? Why did he think he could invade people's lives? It was one thing to send American spies off into the desert to retrieve a missing employee, but to pry into the private concerns of employees' relatives, surely this was too much?

'None of my business,' Chad said.

'Quite.'

'Just that she said you didn't seem like your old self. I wondered if there was something I could do to help.'

Bloody *hell*, thought Lloyd. The man was a relentless doer of good.

'Never mind,' said Chad, actually reaching over and patting Lloyd on the knee. Lloyd gagged and flinched. 'You look perfectly fine to me, Lloyd.'

Lloyd wasn't even sure they ought to be talking to each other on a first-name basis.

'Thanks for saying so, "*Chad*".'

'It's just that—'

'*Please.*'

'Well, listen. I figure if you can't help your friends, you know? I thought it might be your business – pressure, stress, that kind of thing. Times are tough, aren't they. The entrepreneur, well, it's just plain *heart disease* for him. Am I right?'

'*Heart disease?*'

'Work, work, work, go, go, go. The spirit of the age. It gets to us all, Lloyd.'

Lloyd tried to remember a day in his life when he had worked, worked, worked, gone, gone, gone.

'I really admire guys like you. The businessman. The go-getter. Be your own boss, I say.'

This, thought Lloyd, from one of the heirs to the Peele fortune? He had just begun to take offence when, with a quick glance at Chad's open, honest face just to be sure, he understood that Chad was simply being as friendly and conversational as one can be with complete strangers trying to be pleasant, making small talk. His familiarity was only annoying because it was American familiarity; Nigerian familiarity, for example, Lloyd would probably have taken as exotic and charming.

Anyway, it was bloody annoying, and Lloyd decided to beat the man at his own game.

'By the way,' he said, 'how are *you* holding up?'

'I beg your pardon?'

'These last months must have been terribly difficult. Ghastly. I say, when *is* the execution by lethal injection of the pregnant murderer, "Chad"?' Lloyd thought he might enjoy watching Chad squirm.

'Good news,' said Chad.

'Oh, really?' said Lloyd, looking at Chad under the rim of his Panama, over the rims of his dark glasses. 'They've killed her already?'

'No, no. The Governor has changed his mind,' said Chad, winningly. 'He's decided on a stay.'

'You're joking. But he sounded such a . . . *firm* individual.'

'That he is,' said Chad. 'In this case he is firmly in favour of clemency.'

'How astonishing.'

'I'd appreciate it if you'd keep it under your hat for the time being, Lloyd. He won't make the announcement until late tonight, UK time. After the evening news, if you follow.'

'So the poor woman doesn't know she will be spared?'

Chad gave Lloyd a superior squint. 'She won't exactly be relieved,' he said.

'Then you've spoken to your father about this, in private?' Lloyd asked, remembering what he had overheard in the Vietnamese restaurant.

'Well, sure.'

'Did you perhaps have something to do with his change of heart?'

'The Governor is his own man.'

Modesty? From an *American*? How casually Chad saved a human life or two.

Lloyd briefly considered leaking this scoop to Owen, who still claimed his journalistic career was not in tatters, that if he chose to he could work for the sleazier end of the popular press. The Claudia Brown story would be just the boost he needed. Lloyd rejected this spiteful course of action on the grounds that he did not owe Owen any more favours.

'Say, Lloyd?'

'Yes, "Chad"?'

'I was wondering if you'd like to come along to Caesar's *Caesar* tomorrow night. You could join Nina, your sister and me in the royal box.'

'How simply unbelievably kind of you, "Chad". I should be delighted. Are we to be joined by royalty?'

'I'm afraid not, Lloyd. That's why the spare tickets. The royals are all real busy, or injured. I'm still optimistic about the crowd, though. We haven't spread the word that the royals cancelled. Plenty of VIPs. Also some big Hollywood names.'

'I'm so glad.'

'It's a great show.'

'So I've heard,' said Lloyd.

'You know, Lloyd,' said the talkative Chad, 'I think Nina is a terrific girl.'

'Grr,' said Lloyd.

'You keep in touch, don't you? You and Nina?'

'I haven't seen much of her this year. Busy. Go, go, go, work, work, work.'

'I know what you mean, Lloyd.'

'I've known her since she was a little girl.'

'So she tells me.'

'Our parents were great friends. Is that your information as well?'

'Yep. You ever – you know, go out with her?'

'Me? Me? Heavens no.'

'She says you were the one who pointed her towards Sir Ian and Caesar. I owe you big there, Lloyd.'

'I do what I can.' Lloyd wondered how long it would take Chad to describe what Nina was like in bed. Despite the

207

fading of his Tourraine's Syndrome, he thought he might still fairly readily be reduced to tears. This was truly awful news. Lloyd had been on the verge of deciding that Chad ought to marry Little Vic. Chad was stable, wealthy, considerate, he would watch out for his young wife; divorce was said to be extremely common and profitable in the United States. Little Vic would make a wonderful First Lady, if the marriage lasted.

'My sister was just in town,' said Chad. 'I really wish she'd had a chance to meet Nina. They have a lot in common.'

Chad was pure optimism.

'She has a real talent,' said Chad.

Here we go, thought Lloyd. He would be spared no detail.

'She's extraordinary,' Chad added, grinning behind the wheel. 'Who-ee, shit. You should see her.'

Go ahead, thought Lloyd. Make me strangle you at ninety miles per hour.

'She's a very special girl.'

Thanks, Chad, for telling me.

'She likes you a lot, too.'

Oh really? Will I be invited to the wedding?

'Speaks very highly of you.'

But worried, of course.

'You should see her.'

Please don't tell me.

'The way she . . . the way she . . .'

'Yes? The way she?'

'Just the way she . . . *handles* people.'

'Handles them?'

'The best woman I've ever worked with, people-wise.'

'People-wise?'

'Here's our exit. Still weird, driving on the left. Creepy. Unnatural.'

Chad did not have an opportunity to expand on Nina's special qualities. Little Vic's flight was on time. She emerged from customs beaming, wearing an authentic-looking *khot-*

208

sanam, falling into Lloyd's arms – and Chad's, for that matter – with giggles of relief.

'You wouldn't have believed it,' she said, sounding a little more like her old self. 'It was a nightmare, a scream. Less than twenty-four hours in the country, and we had an international incident on our hands. Am I hungover? Ask me if I'm hungover. Do you realize? Do you realize that I came within an inch of —'

They were halfway back to London on the motorway before Little Vic even paused for breath.

'Have you thanked "Chad"?' Lloyd interrupted.

'Oh, thank you, Chad. Thank you. Your . . . *friend* was ever so gentlemanly. Sam, is it?'

'Uhm, yeah. That's it. Sam,' said Chad, unconvincingly. 'By the way, your brother's coming to the theatre with us tomorrow night. He can be your date, if you'd like to come. A lot of royal no-shows. I've asked Nina along.'

'Super,' said Little Vic. 'Great to be back in civilization. I feel as if I've been away ten years. Do you know that the woman who helped rob me and tie me to the bed' – Little Vic had censored from her report any mention of her near one-night stand with Lise – 'had *met* Jean-Louis Parent? Probably *slept* with him when she was only thirteen?'

'How moving,' said Lloyd.

'How gross,' said Chad. 'I picked up his book, you know. The one you're always reading?'

'*L'Amour et la Pitié*?' asked Little Vic, from the back seat.

'Right. I can't read French, so I got a translation. You know, I really think it's a terrific story.'

'I'm impressed, Chad,' said Little Vic.

'I'm *amazed*, "Chad",' said Lloyd. 'Didn't you find it slightly – I don't know – pornographic?'

'I haven't got that far into it. That sort of stuff doesn't bother me. It's just exciting as hell. To think, someone just says to *hell* with the rules, lives her life on her own terms, has all those adventures, goes and finds what she wants, and *gets* it.'

Lloyd was beginning to glimpse a human being inside the grey suit and behind lensless spectacles.

'It really made me think,' Chad added seriously, furrowing his brow. 'Know what I mean?'

Lloyd wondered if Chad had decided that he wanted Nina, and was going to *get* her. That maniac Frenchman had a lot to answer for. He was affecting people's lives from the grave, sending them off on dangerous holidays, causing them to reassess their love-lives or careers. He wished Little Vic would find another, healthier enthusiasm. Even Chad. They now appeared to have one irresponsible philosopher-novelist in common, and she might be able to distract him from Nina. It said a lot for Lloyd's own preoccupation with Nina that he was willing to sacrifice his only sister to the clutches of an American. Still, she could do – and had done – far worse in the boyfriend department. With Chad out of the picture, only that bastard Owen remained in his way; Owen, and two or three thousand other eligible men who might cross Nina's path during the next few critical years.

'I still say it was terrific,' Little Vic was saying, in the back seat, referring to her day and night in a hot country. 'A learning experience. A builder of character. Nothing ventured. A happy ending. It was so beautiful, on the beach. I thought I might be on the verge of discovery.'

Chad had pulled his car to a stop in traffic. Little Vic had gone silent. The two men turned around in their seats to see Little Vic dabbing at her eyes.

'I was *really* frightened,' she said, with an adorable, tearful smile.

An audience of luminaries hacked and grumbled in the Varrenwold Theatre, read with disbelief the actors' autobiographies, settled down in a scent of wet hair and perfume. It was a black-tie occasion for men; women wore bizarre or hilarious costumes, as usual. There were famous and important Americans in the audience, most of them film actors; there were famous and important Britons in the audience, most of them not really famous or important, but in fact civil servants or politicians. The stained gold curtain hung heavily over the stage, threatening to rise at any moment. Chad, Nina, Sir Ian and his daughter, Hamish Frederick, Lloyd, Little Vic, the Foreign Secretary and his wife occupied the royal box. No one had mentioned the embarrassing fact that even third-string royals had declared themselves too busy to attend this, one of CYSR's premier events of the year, and that the Foreign Secretary and his wife had been prepared to accept their invitation at two hours' notice.

Shakespeare could be tedious even on the best of nights, but from what Lloyd had heard about this particular performance, it was likely to be good for a laugh or two. The director, who gave off a shimmering aura of evaporating alcohol, was already laughing. He had his arm around Sir Ian's shoulder, and was telling him in a loud voice about his night of violent love-making in the arms of an Italian opera singer. 'Never', said Hamish Frederick, 'did I approach, *approach* an erect state. Hah! Bloody woman didn't know the difference.' Sir Ian smiled like a condemned nationalist revolutionary, and raised his bristling nostrils to the theatre's chandelier. 'Hah! I managed to insert a . . . to insert a . . .' The Foreign Secretary, on Hamish Frederick's other side, remarked that the weather had been jolly poor recently, though it wasn't bad for the water table, didn't everyone agree? '*You've* heard her sing,' said the director, skewering Sir Ian with his index finger, 'but not like *I* have. *Phwoar!* I got my legs tangled in her hair and we had to crawl along the floor together like a pair of—'

The lights dimmed. Lloyd kept an eye on Chad and Nina. In fact, he bored his gaze into the back of Nina's head, still believing in an adolescent fantasy that brain power could alter exterior matter. Every now and then he bored his gaze

211

into the back of Chad's head, for good measure, trying to make it explode. Chad sat with his legs casually crossed. Nina sat upright with her hands on her knees, leaning ever so slightly away from the director and his stench. She wore a black-satin off-the-shoulder dress exactly like Little Vic's, but one size larger. She wore her hair up, and the groove in the back of her neck caused Lloyd to mutter almost aloud that there never had been a love to rival his.

The curtain rose to reveal a minimalist set – Nina's compromise with the Americans and other Blitz London supporters. This comprised a few oddly Greek – and oddly ruined – walls and columns, and a portentous flight of steps. Lloyd thought he was about to fall asleep, which usually did not happen until the second scene of the second act. He tried to cross his legs, and kicked the Foreign Secretary's wife in the shin. He whispered an apology to her. He looked to his other side and saw his sister roll her eyes. The director had been persuaded to stop talking.

Solemnly, the American actors took to the stage. The sarcastic cobbler was actually rather good, or at any rate he gave it his all; a quick glance at the programme showed him technically to be an extra, therefore British. The titters did not begin until Antony accompanied his first line, 'Caesar, my lord,' with a crisp American-style salute. This choked laughter came not from the reserved British section, but from the American quarter. There the multi-millionaire thespians, rightly ashamed of themselves, seemed to laugh more out of nervous empathy than anything else. Those who had been recognizable to Lloyd when the lights were up tended to be known for whispered catch-phrases such as, 'You fuckin' fuck with me, you die, you fuckin' fuck.' Those were the artistic ones. The more commercial actors wore big hair, men and women alike, and were known in Britain for puffing their risible films by proclaiming a love for the West End and invoking the names of ennobled British actors long-since dead.

Cassius' speech about the narrow world and the Colossus provoked raw laughter, this time from the British, who could contain themselves no longer. The American read the speech as a paean to Caesar, rather than as an incendiary tribute to Brutus. An easy mistake, really, and one that Lloyd himself had made at the age of eleven. Hamish Frederick snorted grotesquely, wiped his face, wiped his hands on his trousers, snorted again, rocked forwards and backwards in his seat. The Foreign Secretary and his wife remained impassive. Lloyd pressed on his eyeballs with thumb and forefinger, prayed for a bomb-threat. The actors soldiered on, tugging at their togas. Poor old Shakespeare rolled over for the millionth time, clamped his hands over his ears. Little Vic clutched Lloyd's arm, bowed her head, covered her mouth. The back of Nina's neck remained immobile, but even in the darkness Lloyd thought he could see tiny golden hairs standing on end. The guttural chortles of security guards could be heard in the corridor behind the curtain of the royal box.

Lloyd, who still knew this play by heart, leaned towards his sister and whispered the lines along with the actors, adopting what he thought of as an Appalachian accent: 'Ah'll do so. But, hey, Cassius, the angry spot doth ga-*low* on Caesar's ba-*row*!' He was not in danger of being overheard, now that most members of the audience had begun to laugh openly, even to jeer. The Special Relationship had suffered a blow.

How excruciating the theatre could be. It seemed to Lloyd the most anachronistic of diversions. The Americans had responded to the jeering by defiantly raising their voices. The man interpreting Antony smiled more broadly than ever, like a politician pretending for the sake of tele- vision cameras that the masses weren't throwing rotten fruit.

'Sleeping pills,' Hamish Frederick was heard to say. 'That's how I'll do it.'

Nina reached across Sir Ian and patted Hamish Frederick's thigh.

'You're right. Too private. I will drive my car off the Hammersmith flyover.'

Another pat.

'You're right. I should take the cast with me. Arson at the cast party. Stay away, if you know what's good for you.'

'I don't know what everyone's laughing at,' whispered Little Vic. 'I think it's going beautifully. Call me psychic, but I think those guys have it in for old Julius. God, the suspense.'

Chad handled the débâcle with immaculate poise. He sat stock still, eyes fixed on the stage, hands folded carefully on his crossed knees.

Somehow, intermission arrived. Lloyd duly enjoyed a drink with the Foreign Secretary's wife in a special room cordoned off for that purpose. Hamish Frederick had rushed away to shriek at his cast. Nina and Chad had left to press the flesh in the downstairs bar. The Foreign Secretary was escorted to the men's room, and returned looking chipper. Even the security guards, accustomed to inhuman boredom, had the dead look in their eyes of men who knew that yet another session of live Shakespeare awaited them.

The audience, or some of it, fell back grumpily into their seats. The gold curtain rose. Game as ever, the Americans powered on through what was now a double tragedy. They seemed to be good at the violent bits. Antony's line about having neither wit, nor words, nor worth rang pathetically true. With twenty minutes to go, all thoughts turned to drink and food. A calm came over the audience. Caesar, *Caesar* and CYSR were dead. Chad's plants in the audience tried to lead a standing ovation, clapping loudly in the front rows and watching over their shoulders as the remainder of the crowd filed out on tip-toe. Hamish Frederick wept openly, mostly with relief: now he could flee to Tuscany and his bitter autobiography.

When Lloyd asked the Foreign Secretary if he and his wife wanted to join the gang for a bottle of champagne and canapés, the man looked wistfully at his watch and appeared to take the offer seriously. The idea was vetoed by a member of his entourage, so that he could not reply definitively before he and his wife were swept away. 'All in all', he said to Chad as he departed, 'a very stimulating evening. Well *done*.'

'Onward and upward,' said Chad at the cast party, his glass of champagne raised high. 'Here's to the Goodwill Parade.'

The assembled CYSR staffers and Committee members groaned, then returned Chad's toast with lowered eyes.

Lloyd felt handsome in his evening clothes. He stood next to Nina, thinking to himself what a lovely couple they made. He tried not to consider the gulf that separated his fantasy from reality.

'I have to say something,' said Nina, stepping forward on the carpet of the hotel function room, addressing not only her colleagues but the members of the *Caesar* cast who had felt up to attending the party. 'In the past year or so, many people have contributed to the successes of Caesar and its various projects. I think I should take the opportunity to offer special thanks, from all of us, to the man who has done most to keep us all on an even keel. A tireless job has been performed by the special envoy, a man of such energy and dedication—'

Lloyd felt the champagne rising in his nose.

'—who never once let the pressures of his complicated task interfere with what has been a most . . . *difficult* year. My personal thanks, then, and thanks from all of us to you' – she raised her glass and beamed – 'Chad Peele.'

There were whistles, secondings, and as much applause as champagne-laden revellers could muster. Lloyd heard himself shouting 'Bravo!' even as he scowled at Nina. The look on her face was worshipful. Little Vic rushed through the crowd and gave Chad a hug and a kiss; the crowd sighed.

Lloyd turned and walked away. He pressed his face against a window that looked out over his grand city. The rain had paused to regain its strength. Lloyd exhaled against the pane to give London its authentic foggy look. He wiped away the condensation with his sleeve to bring the lighted landmarks and monuments back into focus. Just over there his new friend, the Foreign Secretary, had regained the dubious safety of his house. And over there Paul Nichols would have begun another working-class-millionaire orgy. And way, *way* over there Owen would be stumbling home with tonight's date, inventing a life story.

'Thank God *that's* over,' said Nina, materializing at Lloyd's side. 'Did I look sincere?'

'Nina. Sorry, just inspecting the city. The play took everything out of me. The splendour of – sincere? Did you look sincere? Of course you did.'

'I meant to be. It was just one of those things I thought might have been expected of me. Still, I'm dying for this to be over. Only a few more weeks.'

There were two things Lloyd wanted to do. He wanted to have a pleasant conversation, and he wanted to put his arm around Nina's shoulders. He knew he was not constitutionally capable of doing both simultaneously.

'What will you do, when Caesar disbands?'

'Oh,' said Nina, pausing to sip and swallow champagne, 'I thought I'd just give you my CV and let you take care of me. As usual.'

'I only mentioned your name, last time.'

'Which was sweet of you, in rotten times like these.'

'Ghastly,' Lloyd agreed, accepting, after Nina, the offer of more champagne and salmon pâté from a passing waitress.

'What are we going to do?' asked Nina, with a direct look that Lloyd could not remember receiving from her before. If there had been one like it, he would have remembered.

'We? Or rather—'

'Don't you feel that we are at an impasse?'

Lloyd decided that it was her cheeks that made her so beautiful.

'I've gone from job to job, just feeling as if I have to stay afloat. It's a terrible bore, having very, very little money.'

No, it was Nina's jaw, definitely her jaw and her mouth and her lips.

'I want to feel self-reliant, and then again I don't, or can't be bothered.'

It was her collar bones.

'There was something about this year – Caesar, the war, the collapse of Eastern Europe, the third year in a row that my boiler had to be repaired – that put me in a contemplative frame of mind. That evening we spent together? I think you were saying the same sort of things.'

It was her hips. It had always been her hips.

'Sorry to go on this way, but it all just fell into place, or apart, tonight. It feels as if *I* put together that horrendous show. I've never worked so hard for so little. I blame Shakespeare partly, of course. Miserable play.'

'Yes, awful.'

'And I blame America.'

'As always.'

'And I blame Chad.'

'Really? Not "Chad", surely? The tireless, dedicated one?'

'The ambitious, calculating one.'

'That surprises me. Last time we talked about this—'

'I haven't said this to anyone. You, I can trust. You don't work for Caesar. They all knew it was a disaster, but Chad carried on the way he did just to humiliate us. Now that I say it aloud, it seems so obvious.'

'"Chad"? But for heaven's sake, Nina. He's—' Lloyd didn't think it was a good idea to say what he was about to say, but he couldn't stop himself. 'He's bloody influential already, you know. Most people would have considered Caesar to be a step down.'

'I have many theories,' said Nina. She spoke confidentially now, glancing over her shoulder, more serious than Lloyd had ever seen her. 'I know that he is not a spy, because that would be beneath him. But it isn't out of the question that Chad might be some sort of informal operative. An envoy sent to undermine, rather than celebrate the Special Relationship. How else do you explain the travesty we all saw this evening? With the Foreign Secretary in attendance? The play was Chad's idea. Hamish was Chad's idea. The cast was Chad's idea.'

'You think he hired a cast of CIA operatives? Seems a lot of effort for such a tiny result.' Lloyd dimly remembered Chad, in the Vietnamese restaurant, telling his sister that he worked under instruction from Stateside.

'Certainly, it *seems* that way. But these insidious superpowers – you know how crafty they can be. They probably look at Shakespeare and think that he's all we have left. If they appropriate Shakespeare – or, better yet, ruin his reputation – what do we have?'

'Jane Austen?' Lloyd asked, entering into the spirit of Nina's paranoid argument. 'You're right, it is truly frightening.'

'Exactly,' said Nina. 'And *then* where would we be?'

'An interesting theory,' said Lloyd. 'That the United States of America might have begun to wage a war of literary attrition. They're attacking the very foundations of our culture.'

'Our language, anyway.'

'Next thing you know,' said Lloyd, 'we'll all be watching only American films, listening only to American music, toeing the American political line—'

'No need to be sarcastic,' said Nina. 'It has already happened, and it isn't funny.'

'Something has to be done.'

'It's too late. We're finished.'

'Why so defeatist?' Lloyd was only going through the

motions of engaging in this conversation. Inwardly, he swooned.

'I want to be Prime Minister,' said Nina. 'Sort things out.'

'You'll have competition from Vic on that front. She wants to merge with France, face up to the Boche.'

'Look at her,' said Nina, nodding her head in Little Vic's direction. 'Such enthusiasm. It makes me want to cry. We're doomed.'

'Listen to you.'

Nina leaned against the window pane, fourteen storeys up. She curled a strand of hair over her ear. The closest member of the party was twenty feet away. Lloyd could lean down a few inches and kiss her cheek without causing a scandal. Lloyd tried to see himself through Nina's eyes: an older man, an old friend, a pillar of society, a relative success, a generous brother, a partial eccentric, a man who looked good in black tie. It amazed him how this exterior view differed from the way he looked through his own eyes: an immature, paranoid, repressed, guilty product of at least one unbalanced parent. He could kiss her now, and everything would be clear. Nina was nothing if not honest. Her reaction would show him the future. The over-examined life . . .

'Hey, guys? Why the whispering?'

'Hello, "Chad",' said Lloyd, who found that he had closed his eyes, that his lips were three inches from Nina's cheek. Chad looked like someone who knew he ought not to drink more than one glass of champagne, but had drunk two bottles anyway. His suit had collapsed. His hair showed signs of mortality.

'Come on, babe,' he said. 'Let's dance.'

'Very kind of you, Chad,' she replied. 'But we have no music.'

Chad swivelled his substantial hips, poked his index fingers into the air, said, 'Wooo.'

'And don't *ever* call me "babe",' Nina added.

'Sorry, babe. Maybe Little Vic will dance with me.'

'Perhaps she will,' Lloyd said. 'And don't *ever* call my sister "Little Vic".'

Chad laughed, and waved a hand perilously close to Lloyd's face. Lloyd remembered the spurt of adrenalin that had caused him to disarm the knife-wielding mugger. He wondered if the Special Relationship would be irreparably tarnished if he delivered a swift elbow to the bridge of Chad's nose. Chad danced clumsily away before Lloyd could make up his mind.

'Does Chad have any friends?' Lloyd asked. 'I mean, apart from far-flung spies?'

'He seems to have a circle of American friends. City types. They go golfing and rafting and jet-ski racing. They run around in the forest and shoot paint pellets at each other.'

'How very *male*.'

'A huge amount of physical exercise. They're like hamsters on bloody treadmills, these characters. Chad's body is a temple, of course. As you can see, drink does not agree with him. Apparently the idea is to live a very long time, even if much of that time is spent in a sweaty gym climbing mechanical mountains.'

'I'd like to see you play tennis with him.'

'I have. On grass, during one of our regional junkets.'

'And?'

'You know how I can be, Lloyd. I let him win two games, just waiting for the first patronizing, patsy serve – waiting for him to say, "Hey, nice *shot*, babe." Then I thrashed him.'

'Was he mortified? Tell me he was mortified.'

'He just kept coming back for more punishment. We played five sets. Admittedly, they were short sets. I don't mean to brag—'

'Go on, Nina, brag away.'

'I think he strained every muscle and ligament in his body, throwing himself around the court the way he did.'

'*God*, I wish I'd been there to see it. You haven't lost your touch, then?'

'It's about the only thing I can really do. I used to be pretty good, didn't I?'

'Inspirational.'

Nina looked happy. 'I was simply ruthless. Brought him to the net, lobbed over his head, left corner, right corner, back to the net, and *bang*, down the line. Over and over again. Fish in a barrel. It was almost pitiful, the way he kept wanting more.'

'What did he say afterwards? Excuses? Graceful in defeat?'

'Oh, sure. "Not bad for a girl," that sort of thing. I don't know if he consciously admitted to himself that I had simply *thrashed* him.'

'You've struck a mighty blow for Britain.'

'I hope so.'

'I don't think I ever dared play against you. At least not after you were about seven or eight years old.' Lloyd remembered the day, the hour, the humiliating score. 'From then on we were strictly a team.'

'Our victims must still wake up screaming.'

'I hope so.'

'I suppose I could always become a tennis instructor. Move to Florida, or somewhere people can actually play.'

'Don't do that, Nina. England needs you.'

The party wasn't going well. The few dignitaries who had allowed themselves to be escorted to the hotel from the Varrenwold Theatre had drifted away. Chad had convinced someone to play the piano, and tried to lead the group in song. No one knew songs any more, not even the piano player.

'Oh my *God*!' Chad said, silencing the guests. 'Oh my *God*!'

People wanted to know what was the matter.

'I have to play St *Andrews* tomorrow morning! I'll miss my flight! Oh my *God*!'

'I think that it is my duty', Nina said, 'to see Chad safely home. It was sweet of you to come along.' She kissed Lloyd ever so casually on the cheek, and followed her lips with a gentle stroke of her palm. Lloyd tried to form words of gratitude for this simple, eloquent gesture, but was paralysed by his Englishness. The noise he ended up making sounded like the underwater exhalation of a scuba diver.

'Lloyd? Are you all right? Lloyd? The party's over.' It was Little Vic. The room, indeed, was nearly empty. 'Sorry I couldn't introduce you to more people. You noticed, I suppose, that the great director made an appearance?'

'I didn't . . . I didn't . . .'

'I know. Insult to injury. The man was raving. I cannot *believe* he spoke to Sir Ian that way. Barmy.'

'I didn't . . .'

'And Chad? People *never* grow up. They were more civilized in North Africa. You're looking a little green, Lloyd. Do you think it was the salmon? Everyone's . . . Lloyd?'

'My brain,' said Lloyd, looking out the window at London, then back down at his sister. 'My brain . . .'

'It's worse than I thought. Do you want to sit down?'

'No, no. I feel fine. I feel wonderful. My brain . . .'

Lloyd's brain felt muddy, imprecise, unimpressive. His brain reacted slowly, with primitive caution. Everything was unfocused, debatable, dimly recalled. He knew practically no French, no Latin at all, he had to struggle even to remember Little Vic's address. His brain, in short, was back to normal.

'Lloyd, come on. You're frightening me. What's wrong with you?'

'Absolutely nothing. Ask me to name the counties of England. Or even how many there are. I couldn't begin to tell you.'

'I'm calling a doctor. This has gone on long enough. We've been so worried.'

'You don't understand. It's over.'

222

'What's over?'

'I've had a brain problem.'

'So we've noticed.'

'Not to worry. All cleared up.'

'You really are frightening me. Have you seen a doctor?'

'Porris, yes. Swore him to secrecy. Shipshape, now.'

'You aren't making any sense. Has everyone gone mad?'

'All right, I feel a little . . . dizzy, if you will.' In fact, Lloyd felt as if all of the blood and other fluids were being drained from his head. He was not accustomed to the sensation of having the vast majority of his memories leak out of his skull. He steadied himself against the window frame. London reeled beneath his feet. He felt Little Vic's hand on his elbow. He caught a fleeting glimpse of ceiling.

CHAPTER NINE

'I did warn you,' said Porris. 'Tricky item, the brain.'
'I was unconscious for all of ten seconds. Not exactly a drama. I fainted. The blood drained from my skull, along with several million useless shards of information. You've looked me over – fit as a fiddle, aren't I?'

Porris removed his oval glasses and cleaned them with his shirt-tail. Like all wearers of spectacles, he looked naked, pale and vulnerable until he put them back on. 'You'll live,' he said, sadly. 'Recite some Herbert for me.'

'Don't know any.'

'Wyatt?'

'Never heard of her.'

'How many chromosomes in the human cell?'

'A million?'

'Capital of Paraguay?'

'Asunción. Sorry, a true memory. One of the things I actually know on my own. I used to have a huge client there. I do remember *some* things, you know.'

'If I could just study you, interview you for a few days, I

224

might be able to discover the ratio between total and "normal" recall. Useful. Ground breaking. Can you estimate it for me?'

'The ratio? I'd say it's off the scale. I forget *everything*, for all practical purposes. All people must. I remember the *shape* of things, not the specifics. Plethicus? It's just a name to me now. It used to be a canon. In a way I prefer only knowing the name, and the *shape*.'

'I think you've handled the syndrome very well. Most of the others—' Porris drew a finger across his throat, waggled another finger in a circular motion around his ear, bulged out his eyes, made a gagging sound. 'Most of the others died of their convictions. That is why I rang you so frequently. I would have intervened, if you'd gone round the bend.'

'Good of you, Porris.'

'It strikes me that one of the things that distinguishes you from the victims I've read about is that you actually had an education to fall back on. Tourraine himself, the Long Island woman, an Egyptian I've learned of since, these people had their memories handed to them on a plate, and could only remember visceral, rather than intellectual things. They weren't quoting Plethicus, they were quoting their fathers, their priests, their public idols. The worst case was a youngish German, who—'

'Please, Porris. It's behind me now.'

'Let's hope so. A frightening organ, the brain. If you would only co-operate, I could publish something on the Tourraine's front. Of the cases I've studied – get this – *only the English victims survived*. Makes you think.'

'I don't want to think any more, if it's all the same. My synapses are sapped.'

'The telling of falsehoods – back to normal?'

'I've swum the English Channel. l fought in the Falklands. My father is a peer. I keep a Parisian mistress. Sex Balm has been scientifically proved effective and safe.'

'Good. Very good.'

'I'll do what I can to help your research, if you'll keep me anonymous.'

'Wonderful.'

'It's too bad, in a way, that it isn't fun, or even healthy, to know it all. How do *you* cope, for example?'

Porris blushed, drew a hand through his greasy hair. 'I don't know all that much. It isn't memory, it's study.' Porris paused, then said, 'I haven't had a terrific amount of sex.'

'Have you thought of asking girls out to dinner? They almost always say yes, it turns out.'

'What a thought.'

'Oh, I'm a genius on that front, Porris. Take it from me. You use the telephone. They say yes. You have a decent meal. They like you.'

'It seems so simple.'

'It's important to act on these impulses. Any girls you like, particularly?'

'Yes, as a matter of fact.' Porris studied his fingernails. 'You don't know her. I met her fifteen years ago. A biochemist, she was then. I spent day after day – God, year after year – thinking how attractive she was. A very pleasant girl. Anyway, never mind.'

'Do you know where she is?'

'Certainly, yes. She's down the street. She's an abortionist, to be frank.'

'Married?'

'No.'

'Let's call her.'

'What?'

'I'll dial.'

'No.'

'Do it, Porris. Trust me. I've learned a few things. You won't regret it.'

Lloyd reached out for Porris's telephone. 'Give me her number.'

He flicked through to the back of his diary. He read out

the number. Lloyd dialled, then handed the receiver to his
doctor. He listened as a zombie-like Porris asked for his
friend, admitted that he missed her, wondered if she might
be free any time during the next forty years for a bite to eat.
He put down the phone.

'Well?'

'Tonight,' said Porris. 'In two hours, in fact.'

'Did I tell you? She'll live with you, marry you, if you
simply ask her. You're a good man, Porris, and just her type.
She already loves you. That's obvious.'

'You're right, Lloyd,' said Porris. 'You *are* a genius.'

His most recent good deed done, Lloyd left Porris's office
and descended into the street. His vacant mind was such a relief
that he floated carelessly on the tide of the throng. The point he
had made with Porris was one he hoped to apply to his own
situation. His brief conversation with Nina at the hotel, her
palm grazing his cheek, the direct look in her eyes, all of these
added up to triumph. There would be no more regrets, only
action. He would avoid emotional procrastination. He would
never lose an opportunity again: he would work out a way to
abandon aphrodisiacs; he would kiss Little Vic extra hard each
time he saw her; he would tell Nina he loved her. He would be
pathetic no longer. He smiled at passers-by, and it amused him
that they thought he looked insane.

'Lloyd's insane,' Owen said, addressing Nina and Little Vic.
They sat at a corner table in a filthy pub near Owen's flat.
Owen had convened this summit meeting with the hushed
telephone messages of a spy organizing a drop.

'Agreed,' said the women.

'I've seen a lot more of him than either of you during the
past couple of years. Frankly, he has been a picture of
decline. It's not just the usual Lloyd-like wetness getting
worse—'

'*Owen*—'

'You know what I mean. Anyway, he's our friend or

brother, and we owe it to him to intervene.'

'In what way?'

'I use the word "intervene" in its American popular psycho-jargon sense. It's what you do to alcoholics or junkies. The family and friends gather round and scare the life out of the poor bugger by announcing that they know he has a problem. The question is how to define Lloyd's specific ailment, then to gather round and surprise him with our knowledge of it. Any suggestions? Is he just so repressed that he has shrunk to the size of a white dwarf? Because I am acting as his analyst, I do not think the ethics of confidentiality allow me to tell you too much of the inside information I possess. Suffice it to say that he feels he is drifting, doesn't want to complain or burden anyone with his problems. The love of a good woman might not be entirely a waste of time,' he said, not looking at Nina. 'Ought we to consider sending away to Thailand for a wife?'

'Owen, I don't like this,' said Little Vic. 'It isn't fair to talk about him that way, behind his back.'

Nina watched this exchange impassively, sipped her tonic water, couldn't help noticing that Owen and Little Vic were *holding hands*. This was the first time she had seen them do so in public.

'What we have been watching', said Owen, 'is a slow-motion breakdown. Let's face it – he spent years concentrating on making *order* for himself, and for all of us. A generous chap, don't we agree? But he must feel that his mission is accomplished, with very little left over for himself. Think of him right now, at this moment. What *can* he be doing? All alone in his vast flat, poring over the books, staring out the window on to a rainy square, doing a few press-ups, brewing yet more tea, watching snooker on the telly? I don't want to put it too starkly, but it's a pathetic, empty life he's fashioned for himself.'

'Faster!' cried the woman, a friend of Jane's.

228

Lloyd obliged.

'Even if what you say is true,' said Little Vic, 'I don't know if it's any of our business. Who are we – who are *you*, in particular – to criticize the choices Lloyd has made? He's had to build everything by himself – no offence – and it hasn't been easy. The business is probably not ideal for him. He's always been embarrassed by it, unlike his unconscionable partner.'

'Employee,' said Owen. 'And aphrodisiacs are my life.'

'My point exactly.'

'He's a businessman. He might as well be selling upholstery. It's the personal side that is a desert.'

Nina listened to this, wondering if Owen thought her a complete fool. It amazed her that two such different men had remained close friends for so long: Owen devious, reckless, emotional; Lloyd straightforward, controlled, repressed. Lloyd would never have subjected someone to so transparent a ploy. Did Owen really believe he was helping Lloyd by making broad hints that she might be the answer to his problems? Nina thought that matters as important as romance and marriage were best left to the mysterious winds of nature, that they could not be orchestrated like mercenary coups.

'Think of him,' said Owen, with despicable obviousness. 'Padding through the rooms of his *fabulous* flat – which he owns outright, girls – wondering if that's *all there is*.'

'Faster!' cried Jane's friend.

Lloyd obliged, with a certain amount of weariness.

'Let's give him a ring,' said Owen. 'Spice up his life. When's the last time we all went out and drank far too much together?'

'New Year's Eve,' said Nina.

'Exactly. Never mind the phone. We'll go straight round to his flat. Intervene. Drag him back into society. Shake

229

some life into him. Bring him out of his shell. What do you say, Vic? Nina?'

'Suits me,' said Little Vic, still *holding Owen's hand*.

'Fine,' said Nina, hating the idea.

'A quick one first, girls,' said Owen, patting his pockets. 'Can one of you lend me a fiver?'

'I'm glad I dropped by,' said Jane's friend.

'Oh, me too.'

'Do you mind if I smoke?'

'Don't be silly,' said Lloyd, who minded terribly. 'You can use the top of the alarm clock as an ashtray. I don't think I can get up.'

Lloyd watched Jane's friend smoke. He wanted her to leave. He wanted her to leap up and announce that she had forgotten all about an important engagement in Bournemouth. He wanted her to dress and depart with mind-boggling swiftness.

Jane's friend had interrupted Lloyd in the process of divesting himself of the hands-on control of Sex Balm. He had drawn up a contract that would see the aphrodisiac business solidly in Owen's hands, if Owen were amenable to the terms. Owen was made for aphrodisiacs. Owen could run the business single-handed. Lloyd could live on the proceeds of his diminished share of the enterprise, and find himself. Enough was enough. Somewhere out there, even in a depressed London, there was a fascinating job waiting to be filled. Gentleman's work.

Jane's friend exhaled a jet of smoke towards the ceiling. She had described herself as an antiques dealer. Lloyd knew that she bought antiques, but never sold them. Like most of Jane's friends over thirty-two years old, she was in a holding pattern, waiting to dive. If Lloyd had said, 'Oh, by the way, we're getting married tomorrow morning,' Jane's friend would have been delighted, and the wedding would have gone ahead.

'Do you ever think about getting married?' Lloyd asked her, with a rush of guilt.

Jane's friend turned her head and exhaled tarry breath into Lloyd's face. 'What makes you ask that?'

'Only that I'm starting to.'

'Oh.'

'Only wondering.' Lloyd marvelled at his own cruelty. He had never behaved this way before. He pitied Jane's friend, and yet he felt an anarchic need to torture her.

'Anyone in particular you want to marry?' asked Jane's friend, rolling on to one elbow.

'Yes,' said Lloyd.

'Why don't you tell me?' said Jane's friend, kissing Lloyd on the tip of his nose, smelling of wine and lipstick and fags.

Lloyd gathered in her gaze, brushed aside a lock of her hair and, feeling ill with the horror of it all, said, 'You don't know her.'

The taxi driver asked Owen, Nina and Little Vic if they knew what he meant when he said that the rain had been unrelenting during the month of June. They replied that they did. He asked them if they didn't agree that it might have been a nicer June without all of that unrelenting rain. They replied that they did. He asked them if they did not join him in hoping for an improvement in the weather, that otherwise it would be winter again without the considerable benefit of a proper summer beforehand. They replied that they hoped for sunny weather as fervently as their driver did. They reached their destination just as the driver had begun to pronounce upon the crippling bite the economic downturn had taken out of his and his colleagues' daily takings, remarking in passing that tips had fallen off drastically and his children were not being sufficiently nourished. Little Vic and Nina split the fare.

The threesome stood before Lloyd's building in a neighbourhood so quiet only the faint fizz of drizzle was to be heard.

'He'll hate this,' said Little Vic. 'He hates to be surprised.'

'We'll pretend to be drunk,' said Owen, who probably was.

'His lights aren't on,' Nina pointed out.

'In the kitchen, then? Taking a nap? A bath? He's home, I'm sure of it. Where else would our Lloyd be? Where would he go?'

'We can't just stand here in the rain. Let's ring the doorbell, get it over with.'

'We are intervening,' said Owen, leading the charge up the steps.

Despite himself, Lloyd was pleased with his virility. The ring of the doorbell caught him in a sea-lion pose, back arched, head raised, arm-tendons straining. The obvious response was to ignore the bell, to attempt manfully to carry on. When the latter proved physically impossible, Lloyd found himself imagining a list of frightening reasons for his doorbell's having rung: robbers casing the joint; Little Vic bearing tragic news; Jane's friend's real boyfriend bent on revenge; Owen battered in the street by a dissatisfied Sex Balm customer; *Nina* . . .

'I have to answer it,' said Lloyd.

'Ouch,' said Jane's friend, as Lloyd rose and moved away. 'What day is this?'

Lloyd did not reply. He put on his robe and tied it carefully. Down the corridor he hobbled.

'He isn't home,' said Nina. 'Let's go.'

'Give him a minute,' said Owen. 'He'll want to be presentable.'

The door opened seconds later, revealing a most unpresentable Lloyd.

'Lloyd!' sang the trio, as if they might have selected a London doorbell at random.

'Oh dear,' said Lloyd, with an involuntary look over his shoulder. 'I was just . . . pruning the viscous.'

'Ficus,' said Little Vic. 'I didn't know you had one.'

'Look, I . . . wonderful. You must come in.' Lloyd did not immediately hold open the door. His mind, back to normal, worked through his options at a deliberate pace. His post-Tourraine's-Syndrome resolutions instructed him to be bold, to be cruel if necessary. 'All a bit embarrassing,' he said, looking directly at Nina. 'A friend, a woman.'

'We were just leaving,' said Little Vic.

'Nonsense,' said Owen. 'What have you got to drink? We're all, all three of us, on a pub crawl. You're a pub, sunshine.'

Lloyd unthinkingly ushered them inside, clapping his robe to his sides, rushing ahead of them down the corridor. 'All a bit embarrassing,' he said again. 'Make yourselves at home.' Chivalry beckoned. Jane's friend, whiter and heavier than Lloyd had remembered or feared, was retrieved from the bedroom and introduced – clumsily, for Lloyd did not know or remember her name. 'Tell . . . all about Caesar,' said Lloyd cheerfully. 'Owen, fetch drinks – you know where everything is. I'll finish dressing. What time is it?'

Lloyd dressed, his mind an empty vessel. He returned to his sitting room and poured himself something like three-quarters of a pint of vodka. Lloyd's sitting room was long, high-ceilinged and seldom used. He had resisted decoration not simply because he did not trust his own taste, but out of habit formed during his property-development days when future buyers had always to be kept in mind. He had not admitted to himself that he was likely to live in this flat for the rest of his life.

Owen and Jane's friend, who knew each other by sight and had probably showered à deux at least once, sat chatting on one of the sofas. Nina and Little Vic sat together in silence on the other, making no effort to conceal their contempt for Jane's friend; in fact, they glared. They knew several of Jane's friends and, with some justification, considered them no better than whores. It had long been one of Little Vic's worries that her brother might accidentally marry one of them, making Little Vic's permanent flight to the Continent a certainty. She did not want a tart for a sister-in-law, her family having been effectively reduced to one. This particular friend of Jane's looked as if she would spend a skiing holiday complaining about all the cold and snow.

Lloyd took courageously to the centre of the room, and proposed a toast to the new arrivals. He gulped his vodka, coughed, put down his glass.

'I'm very pleased that you're all here,' he said. 'I have an announcement to make, and a document-signing to be witnessed. Owen? Prepare to listen carefully.'

Holding up an index finger, Lloyd left the room, returning one minute later with a sheaf of papers. When he described to Owen the transformation of the company that was imminent, he did so not in a spirit of consultation, but as a direct order. There was no conceivable way that Owen could complain, for the terms of this transaction meant that if Owen merely carried on as he had done for the last couple of years, the company would be his in five years' time. Lloyd would immediately be absolved of his day-to-day duties, but would be available to help Owen one afternoon a week. Owen would not be bankrupt. He would keep his flat. The terms of the agreement were so generous to Owen that someone who did not know Lloyd well would have suspected ulterior motives, or a trap.

'Where do I sign?' said Owen, who knew Lloyd well.

Lloyd indicated the spot, then asked Nina and Jane's friend to sign as witnesses. Jane's friend suggested that Owen might have been hasty, that he had not read the fine print, that what she had heard sounded too good to be true. The others told her that it really wasn't any of her business. Lloyd and Owen shook hands. Nina and Little Vic clapped. The agreement was drunk to with appropriate solemnity.

Owen sat down next to Little Vic.

Lloyd thought that he had so far coped quite well with the incongruousness of Jane's friend. His embarrassment, while complete, was something he was used to. Still, it worried him that he could not catch Nina's eye, that she sat so coldly on the sofa, fingers crossed. He was building up to a confession of love – another of his post-Tourraine's-Syndrome resolutions – and even Lloyd was aware that being discovered lowering himself in the arms of Jane's friend was not likely to be helpful in convincing Nina of the purity of his affections.

Lloyd thought hard about this, so hard that he did not realize for quite some time that Owen was addressing him.

'I'm sorry, what did you say?'

'I can't believe you didn't hear me. I've just poured out my soul.'

'Pour again.'

The women giggled.

'I said', said Owen, 'at some length, and at considerable expense to my pride, how grateful I am to you, Lloyd. An uncharacteristic burst of sentimentality. I say it here, in front of your sister, in front of Nina, in front of . . . *her*, that as best friends go, you are the best. We all think you are terrific, Lloyd.'

The women blushed, but nodded their agreement.

'I know you've all been worried. "Chad" told me. Not that I particularly liked hearing it from him. But all is well. Doctor Porris says I'm cured, of something called Tourraine's Syndrome,' said Lloyd, for the benefit of the women. 'Owen knew a bit about it, but I swore him to secrecy. All gone now.'

'I'm so glad to hear it,' said Little Vic. 'That sounds most peculiar.'

'It's been for the best,' said Lloyd. 'Character building, as you would put it.'

'We came here to intervene,' said Owen, 'thinking you might need help. And here you were, drafting eminently sensible contracts and' – he glanced at Jane's friend – 'and entertaining. Our worries were misplaced.'

'Of course they were.' Lloyd drank again.

'You are *definitely* cured, then?' interjected Jane's friend, as if she suspected that Tourraine's Syndrome might be a sexually transmitted disease.

'No doubt about it.'

'Wonderful,' said Jane's friend.

'There's more,' said Owen, ominously. Four heads turned to hear him out. 'I have to say something, Lloyd, something I hope won't end our friendship or, far more important, jeopardize the agreement we've just signed. You might want to sit down.'

Lloyd sat.

'This couldn't have come at a better time,' said Owen, gesturing at the freshly signed contract. 'I've turned over a new leaf.'

Jane's friend snorted.

'A new Owen is born. A responsible, hard-working Owen. An Owen who has enviable priorities.'

'You're about to tell me something horrible,' said Lloyd.

'Not necessarily. I feel like a . . . I don't feel like your mate when I say this. I feel like a teenager. It's just that it's a good thing you've provided for my solvency at this particular moment, because – you're going to hate this.'

'Enough suspense, Owen,' said Lloyd, who was glad to be sitting down. The cruellest double-cross, just when Lloyd had made what he considered another in a long series of grand gestures. 'Sounds like you're going to get married,' he said, sipping again at his vodka.

'How astute,' said Owen.

Lloyd saw Nina's hand fly to her mouth.

'What is it?' Lloyd said. 'Just get it over with.'

'Sorry, Lloyd,' said Owen. 'Unavoidable. Carrying on in

secret. Ten years of avoiding the subject.'

This sounded vaguely familiar to Lloyd. He knew that he had only moments to prepare his face and posture for a reaction of unmitigated joy at the news of Owen and Nina's engagement. 'This is wonderful news!' he would exclaim, bounding across the room to kiss a cheek that was rightfully his, striding over to Owen for a firm handshake and important eye contact. He would drink the rest of his vodka and listen, with a glazed look, to their wedding plans. Of *course* he would act as best man – what an honour it would be. A honeymoon in Sicily – if I might be so bold – as a wedding present? – seriously, my friend, it's on me. Godparenting would not be long in coming. Good old Uncle Lloyd – a strangely reclusive figure, since his bout with Tourraine's. Odd that he never married – always one of the more eligible fellows, but that was so long ago. Who would have predicted that it would be *Owen* who would build the business empire – all started with that peculiar Sex Balm nonsense, years ago? What was his partner's name? And married to so fine a woman? Really landed on his feet, old Owen. Clubbable chap, these days, surprising, really. Jolly well *applied* himself, one supposes . . .

'God *damn* it, Lloyd. Are you *listening* to me?'

'Yes, of course,' said Lloyd. He stood up and started on his way towards Nina's cheek. He stopped halfway, as some of what Owen had said seeped through. 'Sorry, Owen, did you say Vic?'

It did appear, now that Lloyd concentrated on the people in his sitting room, that Owen was *holding hands* with Little Vic.

'I knew he was going to be angry,' said Little Vic, watching Lloyd's face twist itself into quasi-comprehension.

'Angry? Don't be so silly. Let me get this straight. You've been sneaking around behind my back as if I were . . . as if I were *married* to one of you?'

237

'I know it sounds bizarre,' said Little Vic, 'but we were just the faintest bit embarrassed.' She reached out and touched Owen's cheek, and smiled cutely at him. For Lloyd this sight was positively surreal. 'It seemed almost incestuous. We thought you ought to be told.'

'And now – marriage?'

'Almost definitely,' said Owen. 'If you don't mind.'

'Mind? *Mind?*'

Lloyd knew that there had always been a high probability that he would some day have a brother-in-law. He imagined that man as a virtual clone of himself, only wealthier and far more fun to be with; a solid, healthy, fertile, culturally mature, tastefully attired, land-owning, clear-headed, soft-spoken Englishman with a saint-like devotion to Little Vic and the concept of family in general.

'Mind? *Mind?*'

The brother-in-law Lloyd had imagined would have been the type to talk shares with Lloyd over brandy; to eschew the vulgar culture of the young or American; to belie Lloyd's theory that gentlemen had gone the way of empire; to place the providing of security and intellectual stimulation for his family at the top of his list of priorities; to be in almost every way as unlike Owen as possible.

'Mind, *Mind?*'

Several thoughts occurred to Lloyd as he sat down again and reached for his drink, aware that the eyes of all were upon him. First, that for years now he had tried to coach himself to trust his sister's instincts; he had endeavoured, not always successfully, and in the manner of a parent, to separate *love* from *control*. Second, that Owen was his best friend, someone he had always counted on not being anything like his imagined ideal brother-in-law. Third, that this news meant that Nina, sitting right over there, was unattached to Owen.

'Mind?' he said. 'I am *overjoyed*.'

Jane's friend clapped her hands and squealed.

238

'What a relief,' said Nina. 'I have been an accomplice, I'm afraid.'

'I understand completely,' said Lloyd, marching across the room to hug his little sister, then embracing Owen for the first time in his life.

Jane's friend clapped some more, as if wedding fever might be in the air and she might be next. 'I can't believe I'm seeing this.'

'Neither can I,' said Lloyd. 'Champagne?'

Lloyd felt winded as he fetched two bottles from his spare fridge.

'Wet, wet, wet,' he said to himself. He decided, grasping the bottles' cold necks, that all along he should have tried to be more like Owen, more happy-go-lucky – roughly half-way between the way he was and his worst nightmare of the way a man could be.

'Wet, wet, wet,' he said, returning with the champagne bottles cradled under his arms like fuel tanks, allowing the implications of Little Vic's decision to sink in. Love wasn't a *decision*, he had to remind himself. That was why they called it 'falling in love', rather than 'carefully analysing the situation and ever so gradually deeming love to be the most desirable of possible alternatives.' Lloyd had been guilty of the latter process; Little Vic had apparently allowed herself to plummet. Which of them was happier? Lloyd felt *boneless*.

'I feel like a village elder being asked for his blessing,' he said, pouring champagne into glasses he had not used in half a year. 'Sort of a tribal thing. And speaking of primitive societies, I wonder if I shouldn't start planning your honeymoon.'

'You aren't being sarcastic, are you?' Little Vic asked. 'I still can't tell.'

'Not at all. Someone has to plan the wedding – I don't think Mother will be prepared to go to the necessary trouble . . . By the way, Owen, my mother, your putative mother-in-law, if you can stand the idea, is under the impression that you are the editor of the *Daily Telegraph*.'

'No kidding? That *is* good news. We mustn't disabuse her. It will explain why I'm always too busy to visit her.'

'Not even properly *engaged* yet,' said Nina, who had marvellous parents, 'and already mother-in-law jibes.'

'We're not rushing anything,' said Little Vic. 'These are modern times. We're required to cohabit for several years first, aren't we, or we'll be the laughing-stock of our friends. That's really what we're saying, Lloyd. I'm moving in with Owen.'

'I see.' Lloyd made a few calculations and came up with the startling fact – actually not so unusual, the way London property had boiled over – that Little Vic could sell the mews house he had given her and use the proceeds to support herself, oh, for the rest of her life if necessary. That nest egg, combined with the emoluments he had just signed over to Owen, would see the couple living in some style. This made Lloyd happy.

'I know what you're thinking,' said Owen. 'And don't worry, I've given up gambling for good. Strictly nose to the grindstone. I'm going to rebuild the Middle East market, just you watch me. Make those potentates so potent we'll hear their cries of ecstasy all the way to Dover.'

'I'm not going to miss the travel,' said Lloyd. 'I'm not going to miss any of it. Except your company, of course.'

'Dare we ask', said Little Vic, 'what you *are* going to do?'

'Gather my resources,' said Lloyd, 'and see what the world has to offer. The whole idea of unemployment makes me feel young again. Refreshed. I feel very fortunate to be able to give life a quick rethink, at this stage.' Lloyd and Owen knew too many men their age who had raised their eyes from their desks to discover a canyon of routine surrounding them, unscalable walls of permanence on all sides.

'Lucky man,' said Owen.

'Oh, yes. Very lucky indeed.'

An uncomfortable silence ensued. Everyone took a sip of

champagne. Lloyd was still aware that Nina wouldn't look at him; this was either a very good, or a very bad sign. Lloyd knew that he had to seize this opportunity as if it were his last. To continue chatting with these people, to celebrate the two momentous announcements of the evening, would not be enough for Lloyd. He had promised himself. He could feel *action* rising in his chest.

'This must be awfully boring for you,' he began, his mouth dry, addressing Jane's friend. 'It's terribly late, and as you can see this is business, and family. Family business. Owen will ring for a taxi. Owen,' Lloyd commanded, 'please ring for a taxi. Put it on the company account.' A path was clearing before Lloyd. He had taken the first step. 'I'm sure you understand,' he said to Jane's friend.

Owen dialled the nearest telephone, gave Lloyd's address and Jane's friend's approximate destination. 'Five minutes,' he said.

The five minutes elapsed under strained conversation, brilliantly dominated by Little Vic. 'I'll never forget my return flight from Thailand last year,' she said, out of nowhere. 'Or was it two years ago? Never mind. Anyway, the *humiliation* of air travel, sometimes. My God. I tried to take advantage of an overbooking out of Bangkok, was flown to Manila, to Los Angeles, to Houston, to New York. *Days* had gone by. Out of New York at last, bumped to first class for my troubles, that was wonderful. Arrived at Heathrow thinking the authorities might *just* have redeemed themselves, *raced* through Customs, ready to forgive everything. I waited at the conveyor belt for my bags, just *tasting* the comfort of my own bed. The bags came along the belt, people swarmed around. And strewn amongst their bags were my *personal possessions*, one by one. Shoes, knickers, shirts, hair dryer, camera, more knickers, and I had to *pluck them one by one* from between the sturdy luggage of my fellow travellers. I assembled a tragic pile of my things next to the belt, almost in tears. The crowd thinned. The last bags circulated on the belt. I retrieved my bent tennis racket. The last item to appear was my tattered bag itself, torn and battered—'

The doorbell rang.

'Taxi,' said Lloyd, rising to his feet. 'Come.'

Jane's friend said her goodbyes, gave Lloyd a peck on the cheek as he held the front door for her. Lloyd closed the door and returned to his sitting room.

'I do apologize,' he said.

'Our fault,' said Little Vic. Nina did not look up, just sat sadly and beautifully with her fingers still crossed on her knees.

'Sorry, Lloyd, our fault,' Owen said.

Lloyd shivered.

'Very brave of you, mate. You handled it well. Such a large number of surprises.'

Another difficult silence.

'Was I mentioning travel?' asked Little Vic. 'There was another time when a deranged man on a flight to Milan insisted on forcing his way into the—'

'Vic,' Lloyd interrupted. 'I want to talk to Nina. Alone.'

'I find it quite amazing,' said Lloyd, when his sister and future brother-in-law had departed. 'Don't you?'

'Actually, no,' said Nina, severely. 'They were made for each other.'

'You aren't in a good mood, are you? Sorry.'

These silences were distressing.

'What did you want to say to me?' Nina sat very still, her feet and knees clamped together, her head bowed.

A single sentence would have done the trick, a subjective pronoun, a verb, an objective pronoun. Instead, Lloyd embarked upon a complicated and inconsistent analysis of his state of mind during the past six months, highlighting his previous inability to lie, his disappointing confrontation with the sum of his knowledge, his recent decisions regarding forthright behaviour. Nina listened closely, but her eyelids said, 'Get on with it.'

'You don't find this interesting.'

'I'm not sure how much of it I believe. Just because you knew a few Darius McLeod atrocities – sorry, *poems* . . .'

Lloyd said he had been concealing the full extent of his powerful recall in a concerted effort not to be thought a fool.

'Oh,' said Nina, suggesting with a tilt of one eyebrow that he might not have succeeded.

'What I want to tell you has less to do with Tourraine's Syndrome than it has with memory in general, general memories.'

'Yes?'

'Sorry. I've remembered one thing of importance. Forget Darius McLeod.'

'A pleasure.'

'Forget Plethicus, and Hobbes and Hardy.'

'I already have.'

'Forget all that. What I'm trying to say is that I was an intellectual for a while, and it was not at all helpful. Of all the things I remembered – and I cannot describe the hugeness of my memory – only the more . . . *emotional* memories survive.'

'People are like that,' said Nina, meeting Lloyd's eyes for the first time.

'I want a simple life. I have been through a period of deep, almost pure thought, and I think I know what the simple life is.'

Nina looked like someone who was being harangued by an evangelist and wanted to leave the room.

'I'm so sorry to bore you. I don't want to bore you. It's the only way I can explain. It's so . . . delicate. The mind, you see, contains more than a sort of matrix of letters and numbers and wiring, like an address book or a computer. The mind contains a sort of *mood memory* of emotional—'

243

'Lloyd?'

'Sorry, yes?'

'Do you want to go out for a walk? It's stopped raining.'

'What a lovely idea.'

Midnight in bourgeois London. The pub crowds had dispersed. Lloyd and Nina walked slowly, inches apart. Nina clasped her navy-blue jacket across her chest. Lloyd's head swam with normal, but no less bothersome memories. Some of his memories of Nina were like snatches of music that wouldn't stop singing in the mind. There was the day at someone's house in Spain, eight years ago, when Nina had rushed to the pool from yet another victory on the court, and dived into the water still wearing her tennis togs. She had surfaced at the edge where Lloyd sat, raised herself out of the water with her hands on his knees, and spat a mouthful of water on to his chest. Or seven years ago, at a party in London, when she and Lloyd had shared looks of derision at the expense of a loathsome accountant who blathered self-servingly on the subject of money, and how much of it he planned to amass. Or six years ago, when Nina had very long hair, and she had danced with a tall boyfriend while everyone else felt ill with envy. Or five years ago, when Nina came to London to live, and experimented with metropolitan clothing. Or four years ago, when Nina left her job complaining of harassment, and managed to ruin the career of her appalling swine of a boss. Or three years ago, when Nina had very short hair, and no job, and no money, and an unbelievable cheerfulness and optimism. Or two years ago, when she began to receive obscene phone calls and actually convinced the contemptible pervert to *tell her his name*. Or one year ago, embarking upon the year of the Special Relationship, saying yes, it was a good job, she would enjoy it, she would use her languages, she would travel, she would plug away and do her best, she would keep the special envoy in his place, she would do her country

244

proud. Or Nina now, wrapping her jacket around herself against the chill, putting up with Lloyd and his inanities, prepared to hear him out.

Lloyd looked at Nina's face as they walked, and felt such a wrenching pity that he thought death might be preferable to love. He loved her so much. She had a forehead and eyebrows, she had a nose and cheeks, she had a mouth and chin, she had a neck and shoulders. He wanted so badly to kiss her. He wanted to draw a sword and eviscerate himself. He wanted to hear her voice. He wanted to make her happy, which was impossible. Her expression, her courage, her body – all of these were amazing to Lloyd, and he wanted to tell her so.

'Look,' he said. 'A goose.'

There was a goose in the street.

'It must have come from the park,' said Nina.

'I've never seen a goose in the street before.'

'Neither have I.'

They skirted the goose, which both knew could be a violent animal, a vicious killer. They walked down a narrow street that led to a garden square. Lloyd wanted to stop, turn, grasp Nina by the shoulders and say, 'I love you *so much*.'

'I used to own that flat, there,' he said instead. 'Did you ever see that one? Fourth floor. Two bedrooms. Quite a decent eat-in kitchen. Managed to sell on a fifty-two-year lease, but, mind you, in those days . . .'

They walked on. Lloyd had not walked with a woman in precisely this way for thirteen years. Katie, that had been her name. Brown hair, dark eyebrows, interested in – no, he had walked with a woman in precisely this way just three years ago. With Nina. This very same Nina. They had walked away from a party together. Lloyd had talked the whole time about the role of the entrepreneur. Nina had been interested and beautiful, but mostly she had been polite.

'Uhng,' said Lloyd.

'What's the matter?'

'Just an unpleasant memory.'

'What memory?'

'Of what a . . . No, it's no use. I am against regret, these days.'

'How very wise.'

'Can you believe that building there? A carbuncle if I ever saw one.'

Lloyd looked down at his shoes as he walked. They were good, masculine, English shoes. He felt good in his shoes. He looked to his right at Nina's shoes. Nina had good feet; of course, there had never been anything obviously wrong with Nina. She wore navy blue shoes, an inch of heel, a pointy toe. She had to walk one-third faster than Lloyd. She wore stockings, because it had not been a sunny spring. He loved her so much. She wore a beige skirt, and her knees reminded Lloyd of tennis and sex.

Lloyd felt, and probably looked, like an adolescent. He had to shrug off a mountain of accumulated reserve. In a spasm of mad insight, he saw himself for the coward that he was. Mentally he reared up, felt a scream coming on. He picked out the third streetlight ahead, and vowed that in that cone of light he would stop walking and declare himself.

How did other people do it? Lloyd wondered, as he and Nina passed under the first light. Did they simply drink themselves to the brink of coma and slur endearments at one another until their clothes were shed and the altar beckoned? Did they write love poems, trudge out to the letter box, extend the envelope into the slot with trembling fingers, close their eyes and let go? Did they fall in love like delighted savages, unquestioningly, naturally, without the encumbrance of thought?

Lloyd had recently seen a young woman in a posh dress shop being fitted for her wedding gown. The woman was pitiably plain, with rings of hostile acne surrounding her mouth. The woman shop assistant stood behind her, holding the veil aloft, as the soon-to-be bride appraised herself in a triptych mirror. The young woman was terribly over-weight, flat chested and freckly. The gown clung to her bulges and sagged at her bosom. Lloyd saw all of this in one second as he walked past the shop. What broke Lloyd's heart, and what he would never forget, was the look of sheer *joy* on the young woman's face – a happiness reflected in the shop assistant's equally exalted expression. They were having such fun. Someone loved that young woman *so much*.

Lloyd and Nina passed under the second light. An empty taxi rattled hopefully by. Lloyd glimpsed Nina's face out of the corner of one eye. She wore a look of concentration, as if trying to add a column of sums in her head, or wondering if the Goodwill Parade would go ahead as planned. She wore tiny gold hoops in her delicate ears. Her heels ticked along the pavement as the third light neared.

Lloyd hoped he wouldn't faint again, hoped his voice would be audible if he dared speak. Twenty yards to go, like a duellist preparing to turn and fire. With every step his heart beat faster. He felt his brain relinquishing control at last. He stepped into the light, slowed his pace, blindly reached out for Nina's elbow. She stopped and turned to face him. He blinked. She blinked. The millions of evasive things he could say scrolled through his mind, and he shunted them aside. He opened his mouth to speak.

CHAPTER TEN

The first problem was that it was not the Fourth of July; then again, nothing during the Year of the Special Relationship had gone according to plan. The second problem was that the Americans wanted cliffs. 'Where are the cliffs?' they asked, juddering to the ground as they disembarked from the coaches that had brought them to Plymouth from London. They were told that cliffs were to be found in abundance not far off, but not the kind of cliffs they probably meant, which were hundreds of miles away. They photographed each other anyway.

There were several kinds of American who had come to act as crowd for the Hands Across the Water Fourth of July Goodwill Parade. There were London-based expatriates – bankers, mostly – in their stiff suits and regulation hair. There were package tourists, duped into paying their own way from all over the United States, porcine and nasal. There were soldiers, hundreds of them, ordered to attend, big men with surprisingly good manners, wearing desert camouflage. There was an academic contingent, one-upping each other on their profound knowledge of Devon's history and topography, and of the British psyche as revealed through centuries-old poetry. There were residents of Plymouth, USA, wearing pilgrim hats and buckled shoes and black plus-fours. Many people wore '1620' logos on their shirts or sun-visors. An argument broke out between the pilgrims and the academics when the latter group insisted that the Plymouth Colony was not the first to be established on the shores of what was now the United States of America. This disappointment aside, it was a generally enthusiastic group that assembled to observe or participate in the Goodwill Parade.

Lloyd watched their gathering with sarcastic detachment, feeling sporty in his retired person's dark glasses and blazer. He had been issued a special CYSR identity card, a *passepartout* that hung from his neck by a chain. He was free to move about the area, and even to enter the VIP pavilion, where human and canine bomb checks had now been completed. The Foreign Secretary and his wife had arrived early, and passed the time chatting to policemen.

The parade was composed for the most part of actors in period dress. The pilgrims led the way, followed by successive waves of historical caricature: seafarers, shipwrights, redcoats, minutemen, founding fathers, gouty kings, confederate troops, union troops, doughboys, Spitfire pilots, Second World War GIs, and futuristic representatives of the most recent joint war. A conspicuous shortage of funds had forced Chad to use local talent, so that most of the American characters were played by unemployed inhabitants of the West Country. There were plenty of weapons available to be trundled past the viewing stand, and the symbolic showpiece directly in front of the VIP section, Sean Davidson's tank sculpture. The fly-past had not yet been cancelled, and fireworks were said to have been laid on for after sunset. The royals had kept everyone guessing until the last minute.

Little Vic had arrived the previous day to handle last-minute crises. Lloyd had enjoyed lunch with her after his long morning drive, then watched her rush off to argue with a regional CYSR functionary who insisted his family of six had the right to sit in the royal enclosure. Lloyd had strolled about taking in the sights of goodwill, shaking hands meaningfully with American visitors and dignitaries. Nina had not yet arrived. She and Chad had left London headquarters two hours late, and were taking care of remaining business inside Chad's hurtling Jaguar. They were due any time now.

One visiting dignitary who had not arrived unnoticed was Governor Peele himself, who swept up to the VIP pavilion with such a self-important display of limousines and squint-eyed security men that many onlookers mistook him for the President. Lloyd happened to be nearby, and got a good look at the Governor. He asked himself a profound cause-and-effect question: Did perfectly grey temples, proud bearing and gun-metal eyes *cause* the election of such men, or were they elected on other merits and transformed afterwards through advanced surgery and the flush of power-wielding? Governor Peele had quite sensibly scheduled a two-month international fact-finding mission to coincide with the birth of Claudia Brown's child, which doctors had cheekily predicted would be delivered inside the maximum-security prison on Independence Day.

Governor Peele strode into the VIP pavilion, found it nearly empty of VIPs (save for the Foreign Secretary) and strode directly back outside to deliver an impromptu statement to the media; he would not be taking questions today, he said. This was a personal visit, a family thing. His son was the special envoy. A distant relative had been English. His statement concentrated on the fabulousness of his own country, its virtual perfection, its divinely inspiredness. There was a nod to Britain somewhere in his speech, as if she were a sad old chimpanzee that had given birth to Adam and Eve (the Governor did not believe in, much less understand biological evolution). There was mention of a dawning of a new world order. The Foreign Secretary was seen poking his head out of the VIP pavilion at this point, and Lloyd could have sworn the man cringed. Governor Peele had points to make about far-flung bursts of democratic and market-economy enthusiasm, which he said were good things; and points to make about last bastions of centrally planned economies and totalitarianism, which he said were bad things. He spoke of the pilgrims, as if he had known them personally: pilgrims were good things.

Lloyd had wandered through the security cordon, fanning his *passe-partout* before him, so that he was within garlic-breath distance of the Governor when the subject of pilgrims was pronounced upon. Lloyd *hated* pilgrims. He thought of pilgrims as filthy, narrow-minded little gnomes with absolutely no sense of reality. The pilgrims being singled out today – the quibbling zealots of *Mayflower* fame – were perhaps the worst examples of the breed. They stamped their little brass-buckled feet until they got what they wanted, didn't they. Creepy separatists willing to risk scurvy and capsizing in the middle of the Atlantic – whingeing and bickering about the civil body politic the whole way – just to roll up on the doorstep of a fabulous new continent and ingratiate themselves with the savages before slaughtering them. Lloyd didn't know much about history any longer, but he knew pilgrims would not have been his sort, would not have been welcome at his dinner table.

The Governor seemed to *love* pilgrims. He told the media that his first drawing as a schoolboy had depicted a pilgrim falling to his knees in Massachusetts, USA, calling out his thanks to God for having delivered him safely to a place where taxes were reasonable and the military could kick posterior whenever and wherever it wanted to. Perhaps he had distorted this anecdote through his prejudices, or at the very least telescoped several of the Governor's points, but that is the way the remarks had sounded to Lloyd at the time.

'Claudia Brown!' shouted a television journalist, an American wearing a toupee.

The Governor ignored what was not, after all, a question. He talked more of pilgrims, of the genius of his country's form of government, and finally of the warm feelings all Americans felt when they thought of frail old Auntie England across the waves.

The military band had struck up a tune. VIPs were asked to take their places. It worried Lloyd that Nina and Chad had not yet arrived. He recalled the American's reckless driving, his failure to grasp the divinely ordained law of driving on the left-hand side of the road. He scanned the crowd for Little Vic, who would be able to telephone them in Chad's car; she was nowhere to be seen.

A helicopter's rotors drowned out the band. The craft passed low over the pavilion, headed for a grassy landing area on the other side of the parade route. A carpet was swiftly unrolled. A receiving line was arranged, with Sir Ian at its head and the Foreign Secretary not far behind. There was a surge in the crowd, as salivating subjects and envious Americans pressed their way closer to the potential royal arrival. The helicopter hovered, turned, wobbled, touched down. The crowd's collective neck craned. Who would it be? Photographers jockeyed for position. Pilgrims were asked to remove their hats, which obscured the view of those to the rear. The VIPs practised their greetings, flipped through etiquette crib-notes. 'Your Royal Highness,' practised the Britons, bowing and curtsying to themselves. 'Good afternoon, your Majesty,' said the Americans, bowing, curtsying, clicking their heels, 'your Royal Highness, your Grace, your Worship, your Excellency,' curtsy, bow, scrape. Governor Peele had muscled his way into the CYSR line-up, where he had no business; his security guards outnumbered the committee members.

'Hello, Lloyd,' came a voice behind Lloyd's right ear.

'Oh, hello, Owen. Just in time for the royal entrance, we

hope and pray. When did you get here?'

'Last night. Didn't Vic tell you?'

'No.'

'I suppose she still thinks you might be uncomfortable with the' – Owen made a gesture that caused Lloyd to wince – 'aspect of our . . . acquaintance.'

'Please.'

'She's right, I can tell that.'

'Nonsense. Do you know where she is? I'm worried about Nina driving with that maniac. They should have been here an hour ago, easily.'

'No idea. And aren't you adorable in your concern. You're looking very well, Lloyd, I must say.'

'Thank you.'

'Last time I saw Vic she was trying to explain to the artist chappie that he was not allowed to spend the afternoon inside his tank thingy.'

'Shouldn't you be *working*, Owen?'

'Everything is under control. I've yet to break the news of your retirement to any of our clients. I thought I'd let them down gently. Tell them you're too busy consulting with Porris on the Baldness Cure to make the usual rounds.'

'You'll have to tell them sooner or later.'

'But you were the backbone, the bad cop, the visionary. It won't be the same.' Owen was distracted by the opening of the helicopter door. 'Here we go,' he said. 'The Royal. Oh, no, look who it is.'

It was a disappointing Royal, but people swooned and yelped and applauded anyway. The Royal waved a royal hand to the crowd, descended the short flight of steps with practised, gingerly placed royal feet. Before approaching the receiving line, the Royal was led to the open, grassy area where a plaque next to Sean Davidson's tank sculpture was hurriedly unveiled. The Royal trotted back to the receiving line before the photographers had a chance to capture Royal and Memorial in one frame.

253

'That's Chad's father,' said Lloyd, as Governor Peele bowed and nearly head–butted the short, flinching Royal.

'The monster?'

'Yes.'

'Filling in for his feckless son?'

'Keeping a low profile, by his standards. Oh, no, we're in line. We have to greet the bloody Royal.'

'No spitting, now,' said Owen.

'I'll try. God, look at the . . . the sheer *boredom* on that person's face.'

'Valium, do you think?'

'*I* would.'

'Which reminds me,' said Owen, 'we haven't had any royal clients since—'

'*Don't*. We were so close to a royal warrant . . .'

'Shame. I'll work on that.'

The Royal had something to say to each of the CYSR higher-ups, and a royal gift for each of the Americans. Lloyd had met royals before, and had always felt on the verge of anarchic gesture: throttling, kicking, theft of tiaras.

When his turn arrived, Lloyd delivered the proper greeting, with a perfect bow and smile. 'Thank you, thank you, thank you,' he added, despite himself.

'Your Royal Highness,' said Owen, bowing in a way that suggested he might have been on the verge of a newsworthy kiss, too low and too close, a vampire look in his eyes.

The Royal was swept into the VIP pavilion amid the din of a thousand single-reflex shutters. Lloyd and Owen followed loyally behind, nudging each other and holding down their guilty laughter: they really had absolutely no business here.

There were speeches and presentations to be made. These duties fell to Sir Ian, who performed them between sucks from an oxygen mask. A message from the American President, containing unintentional sexual innuendo, was read out by an excitable American functionary named Bart Forrest.

254

'Wouldn't have missed this,' Owen whispered. 'The emotion. The portent.'

'I can't believe Nina isn't here. After all the work she's done.'

'Look, it's Vic, over there.'

Little Vic, adorable in her skinny blue suit, prowled officiously behind the row of her betters, clutching a two-way radio. Lloyd had come to grips with her affair with Owen, and had quickly realized that such an alliance had been all but inevitable. There was the Dearth of Men to be kept in mind. Better the devil you know, was Lloyd's conclusion: men were beasts, and at least Owen was considerably in Lloyd's debt.

The Foreign Secretary had a few words to say, and he said them with feeling. There were two generals, a fat one and a thin one, who rhapsodized about one another. Sean Davidson was introduced, and was applauded as if he had broken new ground in the field of visual art. A royal lip was seen to be bitten as Sean mumbled his incoherent thanks and announced that he had still not gone to London, every day of his conscious life. He bowed, clutching his royal and presidential gifts, then fled. There was an uncomfortable moment when two portraits were unveiled, one of George Washington and the other of Queen Victoria; even Lloyd knew the pair had not quite lived contemporaneously, despite a superficial physical resemblance.

There was little left to say. The Special Relationship was . . . *special*. Governor Peele filled a silence with a ham-fisted toast to the absent Queen, which he managed to make sound like a manifesto calling for her head. Trays bearing juice and wine were circulated. Toasts were drunk. Chad's absence was remarked upon, then toasted. Hands were shaken sideways for the photographers. The Foreign Secretary asked if it wasn't a terrifically good idea for everyone to file on up the steps to the reviewing stand.

'Clockwork,' said Owen, who had spilled wine down his

shirt trying to suppress a laugh at what one of the generals had said. 'Hail Caesar!'

Lloyd and Owen sat in the reviewing stand wearing their dark glasses, feeling vulnerable. People tended to get shot or blown up in reviewing stands. Death could envelop them at any moment. They checked under their folding chairs and grimaced at each other. To live this way all the time would be intolerable. Little Vic, on Owen's other side, shushed them when they uttered their concerns aloud.

The military band played both national anthems; Governor Peele placed his hand on his heart and mouthed the convoluted lyrics. Lloyd thought about punctuation: 'Oh, say, can you see by the dawn's early light – what so proudly we hailed (at the twilight's last gleaming); whose broad stripes and bright stars were so gallantly streaming? And the rockets' red glare? The bombs' bursting in air gave proof, through the night, that our flag was still there.'

'An' the *'ome* . . . of the . . . *brave*', sang Owen far too loudly, in his *faux*-Cockney accent. The Royal stood in front of him. 'Sorry,' he said, to the half-turned face. 'I was inspired.'

Snare drums pounded out a cadence, and the Hands Across the Water Fourth of July Goodwill Parade was under way. An American announcer narrated a history of the Special Relationship over a Second-World-War-vintage Tannoy. He seemed to skip over the ugly, duplicitous parts, and concentrate on hand-holding during times of ghastly modern warfare. The war of 1812 was mentioned only in the context of unnamed 'differences' having been periodically overcome to the distinct benefit of both parties and that of mankind in general. The weather remained fair, and rows of marching history passed by under slanting sunlight.

Two hundred years of slave-owning Indian-killers processed symbolically before the stand. Mark Twain and Rudyard Kipling limped by. A wheelchair-bound Roosevelt lookalike rolled along next to a cigar-chomping Churchill. More recent presidents and prime ministers likewise paraded, usually arm in arm. One real former prime minister paraded in the flesh, casting a dirty look in the direction of the reviewing stand, unaccompanied by an American counterpart.

'Dire,' Owen whispered.

'Look,' said Lloyd. 'Those are thermonuclear weapons, unless I'm entirely mistaken.'

'Oh, good. I feel so much safer now.'

With a heart-stopping bang that had every secret service agent reaching inside his jacket, a tight formation of fighter jets ejaculated prematurely over the bay. The Royal was distinctly heard to mutter an expletive.

'Holy Christ,' said Owen, or perhaps it was the archbishop.

It was sunset, and time for strong drink in the VIP pavilion. There were still plenty of hands to be shaken and, before the fireworks, time for an absolute orgy of self-congratulation. The Royal tossed back the first royal beverage as if fearing that it might at any moment be snatched from the royal fist. Lloyd and Owen agreed that they ought to get drunk and drive back to London in the morning. Owen suggested that the VIP pavilion was rife with potential Sex Balm customers. Lloyd indicated that he was still worried about Nina.

When Little Vic had a spare moment, Lloyd asked her for Chad's mobile telephone number. She knew it by heart. Claiming an emergency, Lloyd borrowed a hand-held phone from the socially agile film producer who had been commissioned to document the Year of the Special Relationship for television. Lloyd dialled – or rather he inputted – the number his sister had given him. It rang. There was no answer. He tried the number again, with the same result.

'Busy, busy,' said Owen, sidling up to Lloyd with fresh

drinks. 'I thought you were supposed to be retired. Already scheming, are you?'

Lloyd returned the telephone to the producer and thanked her.

'I tried to ring Nina. She is almost certainly dead.'

'These things happen. Drink up, is what I say.'

They drank. Owen smacked his lips.

'What with all the excitement,' he said, 'it's all I can do to get a minute and a half alone with my woman.'

'*Please*, Owen.'

'She spoke to your mum. I *am* the editor of the *Daily Telegraph*.'

'Oh, Christ.'

'Mum has been informed of her only biological daughter's change of address. Thrilled, from what I gather.'

'Dotty.'

'That, too.'

'My mother is a hateful person. She only pretends to be mad, just to annoy. Be warned.'

'I've known your mother for fifteen years, Lloyd. She ain't pretending.'

Lloyd's palms were moist. He looked at his watch every thirty seconds. He kept one eye on each of the pavilion's entrances. He visualized the scene of the crash. A round-about, entered too quickly, wrong lane, wrong *direction*, head-on collision. Blood matted in Nina's hair. Dead in the arms of a policeman. Chad, uninjured, containing political damage on the telephone.

That was the way life was: it piled insult upon injury, made the man jump through hoops before applying the fatal chop.

'Sorry, what did you say?' asked Lloyd.

'I said', replied Owen, 'that the general seems to have pissed himself.'

It was true. One of the generals had wet his uniform. Everyone had noticed except for the fighting-man himself, who was in the middle of an anecdote of such hilarity that he had decided it would interest the Foreign Secretary.

'I have to get out of here,' said Lloyd. 'Fresh air. Peddle some Balm, Owen. I'll be back in a minute.'

Outside, the members of the Goodwill Parade were at ease. They ate ice cream, drank beer, goggled at the front flaps of the VIP pavilion. When they saw Lloyd appear, they photographed him. He put his dark glasses back on and pretended to himself that he was the King of Spain. He walked into the road and inspected the tank-tread damage. He found a group of journalists who were trying to interview a ninety-nine-year-old recipient of the Victoria Cross who could neither stand nor speak. He searched the car park for maroon Jaguars.

He remembered something he had not thought of even under the influence of Tourraine's Syndrome: his father's Great Love. This had come out in minuscule clues over a period of two decades. Like most things having to do with parental pasts, it was the vaguest of biographical facts, and not something children were inclined to dwell upon. With the new perspective of his current circumstances, Lloyd was able to imagine his father, ages ago, living in post-war London, in love. Under relentless and sometimes impolite interrogation, Lloyd's father had divulged to his son that the girl's name was Cynthia (or Susan, or Sarah – Lloyd could remember nothing any more) of a finishing-school type more common then than today. Lloyd's meek and introverted father had once – was this possible? – awakened in the arms of a young woman whom he loved, who loved him.

They would have strolled around the Inns of Court together, worried a great deal about contraception, pinched post-war pennies. Lloyd could tell by the look in his father's eyes when the occasional snippet of history squeaked between his pursed English lips: this girl had been his Great Love, his Only Love. They had made plans to marry, but there were real-life impediments to be overcome beforehand, such as pulling together a gentlemanly amount of cash. They went to formal parties together, to the cinema, to each other's parents' house for Sunday lamb. Little Vic, in an act of reckless but efficacious espionage, had discovered a picture of the girl in their father's atrophied stamp collection. Lloyd had only seen the picture once, fleetingly, whispering with Little Vic in the upstairs study that was supposed to be strictly off-limits to them. They wiped their fingerprints from the jaundiced photograph, and never saw it again. Lloyd had remembered to rebuke his little sister for her prying, but had later returned to search for the picture himself. It had been removed. Peter James always knew when his possessions had been tampered with; in this case, he had not mentioned his children's trespassing.

It was not the girl Lloyd remembered, but his father standing next to her, leaning against a wall, the picture of relaxed optimism. He really must have supposed that, having survived the war without displaying cowardice – quite the reverse – and having climbed the emotional mountain that led to love, he might be able to relax and enjoy his conventionally unfolding life. He was going to get married, become a barrister, think about judging and knighthood and many, many children. He would be prosperous, secure, and loved.

The woman with the sibilant name had died.

Lloyd learned of this when he was twenty-two years old. It had taken him three or four more years to screw up the courage to ask his father *how* the woman had died – not an easy question to formulate. In the end, spending a few days at his parents' house, he said, 'Dad, I have to know. Tell me how she, how the woman, how she—' That did the trick. Lloyd's father declined to tell him – angrily, by Peter James's standards. Two hours later, as Lloyd lay on his bed reading, a knock came on the door. Lloyd's father entered and apologized for having been short with him. He said he was happy to tell him what had happened, and that Lloyd was to keep in mind that it wasn't important, not really. Lloyd never knew if this meant her death wasn't important, or the *manner* of her death.

It was some sort of cable. There was a lot of tearing down and building up again going on in those days. Some sort of heavy, unmoored cable had decided to swing down from the heavens, whisk though the sulphurous fog, and kill the girlfriend. Lloyd's father did not say – but implied with a twitch at the corners of his mouth – that his girlfriend had been decapitated by the whipping, singing cable, which may have had a heavy object attached to its end. 'All very sad,' Lloyd's father concluded, and left Lloyd alone.

All very sad. All very sad, to have one's *happiness* dashed across the pavement. Lloyd could not imagine a shock so profound – not until now, when he imagined it with sick-making acuteness. If this was what love felt like, he wasn't sure he wanted any part of it. His dithering over the past few months was brought into sudden, pathetic relief. He felt that he was being punished for his cowardly indecision. His father had taken the emotional leap early on, but been slapped cruelly down. Lloyd hadn't even bothered, until just too late, to take the simple step that would have started him on a trajectory towards happiness. He felt *boneless* again.

The crowds had gathered for the fireworks. Governor Peele had emerged to press the flesh, including Lloyd's. Lloyd wanted to tell the man that his son had just managed to kill the woman Lloyd loved, then thought that to do so might be excessive. After shaking the Governor's hand Lloyd had to chuckle. My God, how childish he was. How self-pitying. To imagine a roundabout crash just for the sake of wallowing in gloom and despair. What would his father have said? This was not manly behaviour. He laughed out loud. 'Look at yourself, Lloyd,' he said, causing a clutch of pilgrims to look at him. 'Pathetic.'

He crossed the road towards the pavilion, laughing. He brushed past the Royal, who had decided to flee. He nodded hello to his friend the Foreign Secretary, who was telling people that it would be jolly nice if everybody could regain their places in the reviewing stand to watch the fireworks – then they could all go home. He spotted Owen in the centre of the tent, surrounded by VIPs, making suggestive gestures and getting laughs: peddling the Balm.

'Of course I'm serious,' he was saying, as Lloyd joined the group. 'Like a bloody cannon – sorry, Archbishop.'

It pleased Lloyd that Owen did not immediately introduce him to the gang of VIPs as the founder of the Sex Balm empire. Owen was his own businessman now.

'My card, gentlemen?' Owen passed around his brand-new business card. 'No need to be shy. Confidentiality ensured. Deliveries made in person – even buy you a drink wherever your local might be. General?'

Every one of the VIPs took Owen's card, including one woman VIP. They dispersed, laughing dismissively, but looking every bit like hooked customers.

'Pigeons,' said Owen. 'With *so* much money.'

'You're doing well, my boy,' said Lloyd.

'Did you enjoy your stroll?'

'Oh, it was pitiful. You should have seen me. Out there looking at the sea, feeling sorry for myself, thinking Nina actually *had* been killed in a car crash with Chad. Can you imagine it? Obviously there's a way to go yet until full recovery. Think of it. Mooning and pining and regretting . . . Owen?'

'Behind you,' said Owen. 'It's Vic. Not looking well.'

Lloyd turned to see his grey-faced sister squeezing through the departing crowd. She still had her two-way radio in her hand.

'Why the long face?' said Lloyd, now the most cheerful man in England. 'Dud fireworks? Pilgrims rioting? Come now, what's the matter?'

'There's been a car crash,' said Little Vic.

They sat in the glassed-in restaurant of a tourists' hotel,

overlooking the bay. Weather had moved in, and drizzle speckled the window panes. The fireworks display had been aborted after a single red rocket had been experimentally launched into the low clouds, only to burst mutely and almost invisibly, high in the gloom. Little Vic had left the table to check on the latest news from the hospital. Lloyd didn't know how to feel. Owen tried to put the situation in its best possible light, which was getting offensive. He had advised everyone not to panic. Doctors could do wonders these days, he said – and besides, how bad could it be?

Little Vic came back to the table and sat down.

'Well?' the two men demanded.

'It isn't good,' she replied, prolonging the suspense by taking a sip of her white wine. 'In fact it's quite bad.'

'Oh,' said the men.

'No safety belt. Facial lacerations, broken collar bone, one wrist broken, the other sprained, broken nose, black eyes, that sort of thing.'

'H'm,' said the men.

'The people in the other car were uninjured, apparently. Just shocked to see a Jaguar speeding around a corner in their lane. Lucky. There was a little girl in their car.'

'Jesus,' said the men.

'I hate to say this,' said Nina, who still wore the wide-eyed expression of someone who had recently cheated death, 'but Chad *deserved* those injuries. Maybe this will teach him a lesson. He's the worst driver I've ever seen. Imagine if he'd killed the little girl.'

'Or you,' said Lloyd, making a whistling noise.

'No presidency for Chad if he had,' said Owen. 'He got off easy.'

'Do you think we ought to visit him at the hospital?' asked Little Vic.

'That would be nice of us,' said Nina. 'And no, I don't. Look, my hands are still shaking.'

'Champagne,' cried Owen, gesturing at the waiter. He

263

ordered two good bottles, then looked back at his companions. 'It's my shout,' he said.

Lloyd was stunned. Nina was stunned. Little Vic was stunned. No one had ever, *ever* heard Owen say those words before.

'And dinner too,' he added, 'if you will do me the honour.'

No one knew what to say. It really was the dawn of a new world order, when Owen Hearn started to pick up tabs. Lloyd could feel his investment paying off already. Owen looked proud of himself, and five years younger; the curse of debt had been rescinded.

'Look at you, Lloyd,' said Owen. 'All glum. Cheer up, mate. It wasn't *you* in the car.'

'I'm just so . . . *relieved*,' said Lloyd, exhaling the word. 'I really, *really*,' he looked at Nina, 'didn't want you to be dead.'

Little Vic clapped. 'What a *nice* thing to say, Lloyd.'

Lloyd looked down at the table, embarrassed. He closed his eyes. It would be the worst possible thing if he were to weep.

With his eyes closed, he felt Nina's fingertips on the back of his neck, just above his collar, just beneath his hair. It was a delicious, heartbreaking sensation. She stroked his hackles and laughed softly, close to his ear. 'How awful for you,' she said. 'Worrying.'

'Now look, all of you, look,' said Lloyd, his eyes clamped shut. 'I really am about to cry.'

'Let it out, mate. Champagne's almost here.'

'There are tears in my eyes,' said Lloyd. 'I really am not kidding.'

'Weep away, Lloyd,' said his little sister. 'We're right behind you on this.'

'They're teasing,' whispered Nina, close to Lloyd's ear.

'I'm very . . . *relieved*,' said Lloyd, and a great tear popped through his clenched eyelids. The tear rolled over the edge of his cheekbone and made an audible splash on the table.

'Aw,' said Owen.

'There,' said Nina, and she kissed Lloyd's ear.

With a shuddering intake of breath, Lloyd opened his eyes and leaned back, allowing further tears to spread out over his cheeks, and seeing a worried-looking waiter manning the champagne.

'Sorry,' Lloyd said to the waiter. 'Having myself a little cry, if that's all right with you.'

Pop, went the champagne. Lloyd felt himself being hugged.

'We have a number of toasts to make,' said Owen, as the champagne was poured. 'We're going to get awfully pissed, if we aren't already. Have you a room in the hotel?'

Lloyd nodded, was hugged again. He thought back to his Italian Alp, the last time he had been carefree. Never again, he thought, not now that he was in love. He made a private mental toast to his father, who had lived thirty years or more with such a fundamental disappointment that everything that happened during that time must have seemed unreal. Maybe he *had* killed himself, after all, and the deer had merely been trying to intervene. Lloyd, who had never suffered any real disappointments at all, but who knew that many awaited him, resolved, despite the danger, to give himself over to love.

'To the Special Relationship,' said Little Vic. 'May it rest in peace.'

'Hear, hear.'

'To Chad,' said Owen. 'May he rest in one piece.'

'Ho, ho.'

'To Vic and Owen,' said Nina.

'Cheers.'

'To . . . all of . . . you,' said Lloyd, who was half laughing now.

'To all of us.'

'Oh my, oh my,' said Owen. 'What a lot of excitement.

Down here in the tail of England, here in the depths of recession. My goodness me, I'm drunk. We won the war – can we take the piss? My, my. A funny old world, do you not all agree that I am right in saying that? What a time to be youngish and in love. Here, let me pour. Rotten times, eh Lloyd? These are rotten times.'

'Ghastly,' said Lloyd, turning sideways to kiss Nina full on her English mouth.

The Death of David Debrizzi
by Paul Micou

Pierre Marie La Valoise is incensed. He has just read with
disbelief what he considers to be a criminally unfair
biography of David Debrizzi, the renowned French
concert pianist. He sees the book as yet another
self-serving attempt by its author, Sir Geoffrey Flynch, to
take credit for David Debrizzi's successes, and to glorify
himself by his association with his genius subject. Why
else, wonders La Valoise, would Sir Geoffrey's
recollections be so at variance with the facts?

Resting comfortably on the terrace of a Swiss sanatorium,
La Valoise takes pen in hand to rebut Sir Geoffrey's *Life*.
He weeds through its distortions and omissions, its
exaggerations and personal attacks, and supplies the
version of the truth that he had intended to incorporate
into his own biography, *The Death of David Debrizzi*.
'Never have I begrudged you your *Life*,' writes La
Valoise, 'any more than you would deny me my *Death* . . .
Given the state of my health, and the treachery of my
bastard of a British publisher – who loathes me merely
because I am French – I feel it is safe to say that your *Life*
will stand alone on the shelves for posterity, while my
Death will remain untold.'

With abundant wit and verve, Paul Micou's third novel at
last gives La Valoise his say.

0 552 99461 8

BLACK SWAN

The Cover Artist
by Paul Micou

'Outrageous farce is tempered by a gentle whimsy and the characterization and plot constantly surprise and delight'
SUNDAY TELEGRAPH

'Micou manages to hit many targets without losing the gentle freshness of the satire'
SUNDAY TIMES

'Micou's gift is for fusing outrageous elements into refined farce . . . His mix of Nice Nice and Nasty New York is a glamorous exposure of both'
DAVID HUGHES, MAIL ON SUNDAY

Oscar Lemoine's artistic medium is the celebrity nude caricature; his ageing black labrador, Elizabeth, is a late-blooming exponent of Canine Expressionism. The minor notoriety of Oscar's covers for the New York-based *Lowdown* magazine sends master and dog into exile in the South of France, where Oscar hopes to improve his primitive social skills – and to do what he can to develop Elizabeth's budding artistic talent. Oscar finds romance in Val d'Argent; Elizabeth paints a series of masterpieces.

Paul Micou's critically acclaimed novel, *The Music Programme* (also available in Black Swan), introduced an exciting new writer; *The Cover Artist*, the story of a man's social myopia and his dog's artistic triumph, emphatically confirms that remarkable debut.

'It's quick, bright, consistent, and probably has some secret ingredient to keep you coming back for more'
SAUL FRAMPTON, TIME OUT

'*The Cover Artist* is an effortless read, of the sort that is far from easy to write'
DAVID HONIGMANN, THE LISTENER

0 552 99408 1

BLACK SWAN

The Music Programme
by Paul Micou

'Evelyn Waugh is not dead; his spirit lives vividly on in the dark and measured hilarity of Paul Micou's first novel'
JAN DALLEY, OBSERVER

All is not well at the Timbali headquarters of the Music Programme. The imminent arrival of U.S. Congressional envoy *Charles 'Crack' McCray* threatens the Programme's funding. The panicking employees try to pull themselves together to form a united and competent front: Englishman *Dr Humphrey Lord*, Assistant to the Supreme Director, Late Baroque, finds himself in the front line of the Programme's defence. *Dan O'Connor*, putative Irishman and prized speechwriter, hopes not to be too distracted from his passionate pursuit of the French Ambassador's teenage daughter. *Wendell 'Skip' Skinner*, American jazz trombonist, nearly sinks the ship with a characteristic drunken gaffe. *Ludvik Kastostis*, the MAXIMALIST composer-in-residence, dashes recklessly to the end of his latest, loudest work, *Flamedance of Euphorion,* hoping to have something – anything – to show for himself. And somewhere, above it all, looms the mysterious, reclusive figure known only as the *'Supreme Director'* . . .

'The last writer to enter so funnily into the spirit of Africa was – best of all compliments – Evelyn Waugh'
DAVID HUGHES, MAIL ON SUNDAY

'A swirling, mellow brew of comic fantasy'
KEIRAN FOGARTY, LITERARY REVIEW

'Micou's dazzling, hilarious début is good news for those of us who have been waiting for someone to come along and show that humour and emotional chaos go together like good splinters and fingers'
JONH WILDE, BLITZ

0 552 99381 6

BLACK SWAN

A SELECTION OF FINE NOVELS
AVAILABLE FROM BLACK SWAN

☐	99421 9	COMING UP ROSES	Michael Carson	£4.99
☐	99380 8	FRIENDS AND INFIDELS	Michael Carson	£3.99
☐	99348 4	SUCKING SHERBET LEMONS	Michael Carson	£5.99
☐	99465 0	STRIPPING PENGUINS BARE	Michael Carson	£5.99
☐	99524 X	YANKING UP THE YOYO	Michael Carson	£5.99
☐	99208 9	THE 158LB MARRIAGE	John Irving	£5.99
☐	99204 6	THE CIDER HOUSE RULES	John Irving	£6.99
☐	99209 7	THE HOTEL NEW HAMPSHIRE	John Irving	£5.99
☐	99369 7	A PRAYER FOR OWEN MEANY	John Irving	£6.99
☐	99206 2	SETTING FREE THE BEARS	John Irving	£5.99
☐	99207 0	THE WATER-METHOD MAN	John Irving	£5.99
☐	99205 4	THE WORLD ACCORDING TO GARP	John Irving	£6.99
☐	99141 4	PEEPING TOM	Howard Jacobson	£5.99
☐	99063 9	COMING FROM BEHIND	Howard Jacobson	£5.99
☐	99252 6	REDBACK	Howard Jacobson	£5.99
☐	99384 0	TALES OF THE CITY	Armistead Maupin	£4.99
☐	99086 8	MORE TALES OF THE CITY	Armistead Maupin	£5.99
☐	99106 6	FURTHER TALES OF THE CITY	Armistead Maupin	£5.99
☐	99383 2	SIGNIFICANT OTHERS	Armistead Maupin	£5.99
☐	99239 9	BABYCAKES	Armistead Maupin	£5.99
☐	99374 3	SURE OF YOU	Armistead Maupin	£4.99
☐	99408 1	THE COVER ARTIST	Paul Micou	£4.99
☐	99381 6	THE MUSIC PROGRAMME	Paul Micou	£4.99
☐	99461 8	THE DEATH OF DAVID DEBRIZZI	Paul Micou	£5.99
☐	99122 8	THE HOUSE OF GOD	Samuel Shem	£5.99
☐	99366 2	THE ELECTRIC KOOL-AID ACID TEST	Tom Wolfe	£6.99
☐	99370 0	THE PAINTED WORD	Tom Wolfe	£4.99
☐	99371 9	THE PUMP HOUSE GANG	Tom Wolfe	£5.99